Praise for *The Joy of Funerals*

"A curiously engaging series of sho_____ women's alienation, rage, and lonelines_____ characters are lonely, but we are not _____ who like *Six Feet Under*."

—Rona Jaffe, author of *The Room-Mating Season*

"Alix Strauss's wonderful, subversive collection of stories . . . pays eloquent tribute to a particular kind of modern-day ingenuity: If you find yourself alone on a Saturday night, put on some makeup and pay a Shiva call. . . . This honest, dark, sly book does reading the Obits one better. It dares us to admit to ourselves that there is a peculiar kind of comfort born in the wake of a death, a universal communion that serves to remind us that we, in fact, are still alive."

—Cynthia Kaplan, author of *Why I'm Like This*

"[D]ark and spirited."

—*Vanity Fair*

"A collection of short stories that will both captivate and disturb you."

—*Marie Claire*

"This is a story collection by someone who 'gets' the ritual of funerals. . . . It's the perfect book for those of us who live for the stink of funeral lilies."

—*Jane*

"If there ever were a *Six Feet Under* of books, this is it."

—*Daily Candy*

"Each successive story builds momentum . . . leading up to the climactic title novella."

—*Los Angeles Times Book Review*

"Best Debut Novel"

—*New York Resident*

"Don't miss this darkly comic novel about funerals, sex, and loss. Throughout these cleverly interwoven stories, Alix Strauss navigates a taboo subject with wit and style. *The Joy of Funerals* is original and moving."

—Libby Schmais, author of *The Perfect Elizabeth* and *The Essential Charlotte*

THE JOY OF FUNERALS

A NOVEL IN STORIES

ALIX STRAUSS

ST. MARTIN'S GRIFFIN
NEW YORK

Some of these stories first appeared in slightly different form in the following:
  "Recovering Larry": *The Hampton Shorts Literary Journal*
  "Addressing the Dead": *The Idaho Review*
  "Swimming Without Annette": *Quality Women's Fiction*
  "Shrinking Away": *The Jen Journal*

www.stmartins.com

Book design by Nick Wunder

Library of Congress Cataloging-in-Publication Data

Strauss, Alix.
    The joy of funerals : a novel in stories / Alix Strauss.—1st ed.
      p. cm.
    Contents: Recovering Larry—The way you left—Shrinking away—Addressing the dead—Post dated—Versions of you—Swimming without Annette—Still life—The joy of funerals.
    ISBN 0-312-30917-1 (hc)
    ISBN 0-312-30918-X (pbk)
      I. Title.

PS3619.T743J695 2003
813'.6—dc21
                                                                2003041357

First St. Martin's Griffin Edition: April 2004

10 9 8 7 6 5 4 3 2 1

For my grandmothers:

Pearl Wolfson Sugarman
1908–1981

Elizabeth Lyons Strauss
1904–1994

Women ahead of their time, taken too soon

CONTENTS

Acknowledgments

I'd like to thank the following people for their involvement and input in making this project possible.

My dear friends: Melissa, who let me commandeer the dining room table with stacks of paper; Cohen, for car rides, late-night impulses, Red Truck Productions, and press trips; Lisa and Michael, whose excitement for this project was contagious; Tina and Greg, who have the best printer and printed out countless versions of my manuscript without ever charging me for paper; Ron and Aurli, who are "fantastic"; Cory and Richard, who gave me space to write and a home in Long Island; Paul, for parties and goodie-bags; Tori, whose computer skills were amazing; Tracy, who read everything I ever asked her to; Susan, Victoria, and Charles, who helped shape these stories from the beginning; and my parents, who allowed me to find my own place and never insisted I get a nine-to-five job.

Eric Copage, a terrific editor, who helped make the *Lives* article possible, and *The New York Times* for helping to inspire this work; my magazine and newspaper editors, who, each in their own way, helped make me a better writer; and the Sarah Lawrence Summer Writing Program, for their generosity and deep belief in my writing.

Kathy Green and the folks at Carlisle & Company, for their constant help and advice; Jennifer Weis, for her terrific notes and careful eye, who made publishing an exciting process; and the entire gang at St. Martin's, for producing a tangible entity I could be proud of.

Every Starbucks, Barnes & Noble, and Borders that allowed me to make their space my temporary office.

Denise, who never missed a beat and always shared her thoughts. Libby, Rona, Pamela, Cynthia, and Molly, for their kind words.

The Lonely One offers his hand too quickly to whomever he encounters.

—Friedrich Nietzsche

RECOVERING LARRY

The scraping sound of the match, the crackling and toxic smell of plastic comfort me as I light the photo. Candles scent the air in the kitchen with lavender as I watch Larry's beautiful face decompose and burn into tar, then turn to dark, powdery ash. Pictures of him are scattered on the Formica counter: Larry snorkeling on our honeymoon in Hawaii, Larry accepting an award, Larry in his college dorm. I breathe on the flame, encouraging it to seep through the glossy paper. Hot, red specks dance through gray sand, melting everything. I'm careful not to let any part of Larry fly away.

I collect the ashes from the fifteen photos with the precision of a surgeon, and scrape the thick, chalky powder into a pile. I then sprinkle my husband onto my bowl of cereal. It looks like charcoal confectioner's sugar is smothering my Rice Krispies. I add milk, stir, and eat. I start slowly, gathering wet clumps of Larry onto the spoon, bring it to my lips, open my mouth, and swallow. It tastes flaky and acidic. I don't mind. I shove spoonful after spoonful into my mouth, metal clicking against teeth, unchewed food scraping against the back of my throat. I ingest him, feel him travel through my cells, nourishing them. I breathe for both of us. I lick the bowl clean and wash the remaining dishes, set them neatly in the holder by the sink.

Twenty minutes later, a retching nausea comes over me. I sit on the cold tile in my bathroom, my head against the ceramic bowl, refusing to spit him back out. I will not lose him twice. Saliva builds in my throat, bile in my stomach. My hands shake. I'm drenched with sweat. I try not to cry. I almost call out for him, half expecting to hear the clomping of his loafers against our wood floors, feel his hand around my forehead, another on my back.

Even though I've got to pee, I hold it in. I will not let one drop of him escape.

The nausea stops. All is calm. The buzzing in my head finally subsides. I dress in silence.

I met Samuel on Tuesday, Larry's favorite day of the week.

We were both at the cemetery and I caught him out of the corner of my eye, watched his body rock back and forth as he performed the Kaddish, then placed a rock by the freshly dug grave. Like Larry's, there was no headstone yet. No identifying marks.

Before making a gesture of acknowledgment, I waited patiently for him to finish praying. I met his gaze, he gave me a small nod.

"Are you visiting your mother?" I asked, moving closer.

"My wife."

We both looked in her direction, then to each other.

"You?"

"My husband," I said.

"Oh." His eyes avoided mine. "I'm sorry for your loss." He kicked a stone with the tip of his black shoe. We watched it roll into the grass and stood there, silently waiting.

2

"Would you say a few words for me?" I asked, pointing to Larry's grave, the soil still wet. "I don't know any Hebrew prayers." Jewish tradition states you must wait one year before the unveiling of a headstone. Larry was gone only three weeks. "I know my husband would appreciate it. He was more religious than I was."

Samuel nodded and wiped a tear with the back of his hand. His face was kind. Lonely. I followed his rocking motion as he recited the prayer. Afterward, I reached for his hand, felt his skin, and thanked him. I had hoped to touch his prayer book, to run my fingers over the bumpy texture, even if just for a second. Maybe then I could forget.

Later, we sat on a stone bench next to someone's family plot. The Levines. I wondered how they had died, and if they were watching as Samuel and I held hands.

He told me about his wife, how she had hemorrhaged while giving birth to their daughter.

It was mid-October. I was coatless and shivering. Samuel took off his jacket and draped it over my shoulders. As he did, I leaned in and kissed him. His lips were unfamiliar and smooth. Like soft butter, left out for baking. A wave of nausea crashed up against my throat. It passed as I replaced Samuel's face with Larry's. Frightened, he pulled back. I placed my hand on his face, felt the coolness of his skin. He closed his eyes, I watched them flutter, tears pooling in my palm. Then I placed his hand on my breast. He buried his face in my shoulder. I held him there, cradled him in my arms. Then he kissed me. Hesitant at first, then hungrily, as if he were trying to feed himself.

Samuel mumbled something in Hebrew as he buttoned his shirt, fingers trembling as he tucked it into his pants. He took his coat back from me, shook off the dirt, and walked away, head bent low, body hunched over. I brushed off small clumps of soil, pieces of shrub, and removed bits of dirt from my nails. I walked behind him, listening to the sound of crunching pebbles beneath our feet.

I sat in my car, shaking, smelling of someone else, as Samuel's gray sedan pulled out of the cemetery.

At home I listened to messages from friends whose husbands were still alive. I sifted through the mail, sorting it neatly into two piles: mine and his. Condolence notes towered over his measly stack of preapproved credit cards, offerings for car insurance, and a college reunion announcement. Even Ed McMahon had not heard. How could he? I added them to the other unopened letters piled neatly in a box by the window.

I watched leaves drop. I traced the initials on his date book, looked through his calendar making notes of the engagements he wouldn't be attending. I put on his stethoscope, felt the coolness of the metal against my chest, and listened. I wrote notes from him to me on his prescription pad.

I found Jacob paying respects to a grandfather he said he'd never met. "Every Sunday we talk," he told me. He wore a navy blue yarmulke with his name stitched in white letters. He told me he was a junior stockbroker and that his grandfather died in a fire while trying to get across the German border when Hitler was in power. Jacob's father had the body transported to this cemetery thirty years ago. He showed me a photo of his grandparents: a black-and-white square with two smiling people seated on a horse. Then he added that neither he nor his father would ever buy German-made products.

It was easy with Jacob. All I needed to do was lick my lips, play with my hair a little, ask a few breathy questions in his ear.

I led him by the cuff of his monogrammed Oxford shirt to

the back section of the cemetery near the old gravestones. We passed by rows and rows of tombstones, a sea of fading grays and tans, breaking apart and chipping. The grass was brown, the trees thin and barren.

While he undid his pants, my eyes focused on the headstone with a red sticker slapped on it. It stood out like a tattooed number. The name was partially covered by dead vines, as if they were protecting the owner. All that was visible was . . . *ose . . . erished mother . . . ghter and wife*. No date. I tried to solve the puzzle as Jacob fiddled with the condom I'd brought.

Sex with Jacob was hurried and sloppy and I wondered if I was his first. He looked about twenty, and wore a grin the entire time as he shouted, "I can't believe this. I can't believe this," over and over. In the background I visualized him in a fraternity house, his brothers cheering him on to fuck the lovely lady. *Go, Jacob. Go, Jacob. Go, go*, their arms pounding the air, hands clenched into fists.

The sound of the train roared above our heads and collided with the chirping of birds and Jacob's panting. For a moment, I thought my head would explode from the noise.

When it was over, his face was flushed, his eyes glassy. His yarmulke had fallen off and I tucked it into my pocket before he could notice.

Afterward, Jacob thanked me profusely, extending his hand to help me up as I ran my fingers over the tight stitching. He wouldn't think to check until he got home, maybe before stepping into the shower or at bedtime as he routinely reached up to unclip it. He would panic for a moment, and then he'd remember and think it a small sacrifice for what I had given him. In return, I would become the story he'd tell at bars, to his friends on the floor, or to impress girls.

He walked me to my car and asked if he could see me again.

"I'm married," I told him. "Sorry," and slammed the door.

Jacob stood by my car, waiting for me to change my mind, roll down the window, and give him my number.

I started the car and when I looked up at him, his face had crumbled to disappointment, his eyes had lost their glow. From my rearview mirror he looked like Larry did in college. Boyish and eager, dark hair tousled, his once-crisp shirt disheveled.

We met during my sophomore year at Michigan State at a Halloween party. Larry was dressed as a Rorschach test, his head poking through a white sheet smattered with black paint. He was tall with thick, wavy hair. He wore brown wire-rimmed glasses, and had a smart look about him.

Entry was free if you came dressed in a costume in keeping with your major. I had been studying the role of women in TV as part of my communications degree, and had dressed up like a cop. An ode to *Cagney & Lacey*.

"Tell me what you see," Larry said, as he spread his arms out from his sides.

"Psychiatry major?" I asked, slightly tipsy from the punch.

Larry smiled. "Premed. Cardiology."

"Shouldn't you be dressed as a heart?"

"I won't tell if you don't."

We smiled.

"You're taking criminal law?"

I shook my head. "'Women in TV' class."

"God, are we desperate to save ten bucks or what?" I watched him take a swig from his plastic cup as he surveyed the room of costumed students. "So, what do you see?" he repeated, still grinning.

"I see you asking for my number."

When Larry would pick me up for a date, I'd get so excited,

I'd run around my apartment, hands shaking, spewing nonsense to my roommates. Very often they'd have to put lipstick and mascara on for me while I sat on my hands and tried to calm down.

When the police came to my door last month I thought perhaps Larry was pulling a prank. Our fifth anniversary was at the end of September, just two days away. I expected the cops to break into song, even cuff me and bring me to a romantic restaurant. I mentioned how similar their outfits were to the one I'd worn years ago as they told me about the accident. Larry's car had collided with someone else's, skidded off the road, and turned upside down. He died instantly, along with the others.

I almost showed them the photo of Larry and me at the party. They stood there, expressionless, asking if there was someone I wanted to call.

Roman was tall and broad, an unshaven immigrant from Yugoslavia. His hands were coarse and cold. He carried party-pink roses and wore a large cross around his neck. It dug into my chest as jagged twigs dug into my back. We kissed behind the mausoleum belonging to the Kesslers as he lifted my right leg up over his shoulder and slid his fingers deep inside me. He laid me down kindly on the ground, spread his large body over mine. His hands and arms were covered with long, black hair. His body was heavier than Larry's. I hadn't calculated on the additional weight. He felt thick, like peanut butter stuck to the top of my mouth. Every now and then my head bumped up against the smooth granite of the polished wall. I looked into his eyes, searching for recognition. Looked for traces of Larry. All I saw was a stranger in his forties, face pained, eyes glassy. He had deep lines between his brows as if he spent his whole day thinking. He smelled of day-old fish.

This was the second time I had seen him here. The first time was a week after Larry's funeral. We had talked for a few minutes. His breathing was hurried, as if he had been running, and he swallowed the last words to each sentence, gulped them down as if someone else was listening.

We lay quietly in the grass. I rested my head on his stomach and watched the tips of houses appear and disappear behind the gate. I thought about how the color of the trees had changed from a bright plaid of yellow, red, and green to muted brown. As I copied Roman's breathing, I wondered who would choose to live so close to a cemetery—and if there were any vacancies.

I told him about Larry. He told me about his dead daughter. That his wife, a Jew, insisted she be buried here. "A baby born with a tumor on her brain stem," he said. His English was poor so that *tumor* sounded like *to more*. "How does God let this happen?" he asked me as we stared at clouds that moved past us as hurriedly as Roman spoke.

There were times I wanted to dig up the graves, rip open the coffins, and see who these men visit, who they paid homage to, who they've lost. At night I'd fantasize about parading around the cemetery, decaying bodies in my arms, families trailing behind me, picking up fallen jewelry, clothing, and body parts.

"I would place them back in their homes and kiss them all good-bye," I tell him.

Roman smiled when I said this. "You are an angel who watch over my Melissa," he said, his voice smooth as the Kesslers' walls. "With you, my angel, I know she is safe." Then he kissed the mark his cross had made on my chest. It was raw and blotchy, and it stung when he rolled his tongue over it.

At home I showered, modeled my earned scar in the mirror, and checked the answering machine. I hadn't changed the outgoing message yet, so Larry's voice still said, "Hi, Leslie and Larry can't come to the phone . . ." No one commented anymore except my mother, who insisted I see a therapist. "Perhaps one that deals specifically with loss," she said, as if that could have helped. I liked hearing his voice when I checked my messages from outside. A serenity would move through me, like being immersed in a bath filled with warm water. And for a second, I would think it was him calling from the hospital, saying he was on his way, or that a patient had to have emergency heart surgery. Would I wait for him to eat? Could I pick him up at the hospital and go out for dinner instead?

Whenever Larry was late, he'd bring me goodies from work: tongue depressors with little notes scribbled on them in felt-tip marker: *You're my life-line*, a red ribbon wrapped around them; a box of cotton swabs filled with potpourri; a magazine stolen from the waiting room, *Property of St. Mercy's* stamped across the cover in red ink.

I ran my hand over the top of our phone machine, felt the coolness of the plastic against my fingers. I played the outgoing message over and over. The message kept looping in my mind, and eventually I couldn't tell where Larry's voice was coming from.

It was an unusually cool day for November.

I took out my bottle of Shalimar, unscrewed the top, and poured the contents over Larry's grave. It was absorbed immediately.

Off to my left, a funeral was in progress.

I watched the mass of bodies huddle together for warmth, saw the rabbi's mouth move, but was too far away to hear. I closed my eyes and conjured up each person who attended Larry's funeral. I visualized the way we stood in silence, how I was sand-wiched between Larry's mother and mine, how close friends and relatives stood haphazardly around the coffin. I remembered how Larry's mother heaved a shovel full of dirt onto her son's coffin, her face pale beneath her makeup.

I looked for the most grief-stricken person in the group. It was a woman in her late thirties, like myself. She was easy to pick out. Like the secret club I had been initiated into, we were all able to detect each other.

I had thought about joining the mourners, ached to be with strangers whose pain I could share, and for a moment, I was jeal-ous. I wanted to be the woman who donned the dark veil. I wanted my hand gripped tightly by sympathetic friends, my body held by caring relatives. Instead, I made eye contact with a tall man.

I followed him to the men's room and waited for him to come out, knowing he was perfect. From the back he looked just like my husband. I almost expected Larry to emerge from the restroom, hands damp, fingers fiddling with his belt.

He was surprised to see me waiting for him, even asked if I was feeling ill. I held out my hand, appearing as though I needed assistance.

He said his name was George, and I repeated it as we fucked. "George, George, George."

The stone felt cold and bumpy. George constantly looked up, making sure the mourners had not left without him. "I only have a few minutes," he said.

George was my favorite. His body was clean and fresh and fit with mine like Larry's used to. Same build, same features. His feet dangled over my toes, as his hands held my left arm over my head and pinned it down. My right hand ran instinctively through his thick, black hair, crept like a claw under his jacket and shirt, and down his smooth, silky back. I resurrected the fresh Clorox smell of Larry's clothes, heard the way he'd say my name, like the way he said hello on our answering machine. George uttered my name, too. Rhythmically, over and over, just as I directed.

"I love you," I whispered.

George came quickly. I winced in pain as he pulled out.

"Sorry," he offered, pulling up his pants. Then, looking like a soldier in battle, the tombstones his protective shield, he checked his post. When he was sure all was safe, he jumped up and walked briskly toward the moving group.

Minutes later, I brushed dead leaves off my clothing, picked out the ones that collected in my hair, and fixed my skirt. I only wore skirts now—they made life easier for both the men and me. I buttoned my coat and searched for another body.

It didn't take long. The cemetery was busy that day.

I walked up to a man who was standing with a newspaper, briefcase, and a computer-printed map the cemetery had provided of the newly converted section.

I placed my gloved hand over his, laid another on his arm, and leaned in close enough for him to smell Larry's cologne. "You look lost. Would you like me to show you the way?" I smiled and pressed my body into his. I felt his newspaper brush across my thigh. He stared at me, and said he was looking for the Gur-shen plot, section 330, row AD.

His hat covered his head, sunglasses hid his eyes. I saw my reflection, a distorted image, my brown hair askew, lipstick smeared.

"I can find it myself," he said.

His face was so close to mine that I felt his breath up against my skin. It tingled, filled me. I wanted to suck him in.

He cleared his throat. "Thank you anyway."

He turned and took a few steps. I had been staring at his back, unable to move, caught mesmerized by the brown leaves that had attached themselves to the cuffs of his trousers. Watched as they dragged along with him. He looked suddenly over his shoulder and I thought he had changed his mind. Saw the error he had made, the opportunity he might miss.

He just stood there, glaring at me. Then turned and quickly walked away.

I tried calling friends. I wanted to reach out, but I couldn't listen to the background voices of babies and spouses. When Larry's partner in his practice, Boyd, called, insisting we have dinner, I forced myself to go. At first it felt good to be out in a normal setting. People chatting, intoxicating smells wafting through me.

We sat in a booth, waiting. It was as if Larry were running late and had called, telling us to go ahead and order, that he'd get to the restaurant when he could. It was a familiar scene. The three of us out to dinner, me in the middle, Larry on my right, Boyd on my left.

"So, how are you doing?"

I shrugged, kept my eye on the door. Anything was possible.

"It gets easier." Boyd cradled his face in his right hand, his left inching its way to mine. He ran his index finger back and forth over my thumb, pressed the pads of our fingers together, my wedding band catching the light off the chandelier.

The food felt heavy in my mouth, the restaurant loud, Italian music reverberating in my head.

An hour later we sat in his car, listening to light FM. My street dark and quiet.

"This just feels right, Leslie," Boyd said, his hand on my

thigh. "Don't you think he'd want you to be happy . . ." His voice trailed off. "Could I come in?"

I thought of Jacob, of Roman, lives I'd touched, offered something to men who really understood grief.

When I finally answered him, my voice came out like a scratching sound. "Thanks for a lovely time," I said, car door open, foot already on the pavement. I went inside, called for Larry, and defrosted a Lean Cuisine.

At night I sat in our den, smelling Larry. Sometimes I slept in his leather chair, other nights I slept on the couch in his sweater. His robe, a blanket. I couldn't eat. Food tasted like metal. I stood looking in the bathroom mirror, counting my bones, resembling the bodies I visited. People at work kept asking if I was all right. When I met with clients to show them new homes, they looked at me strangely, as if I were diseased.

My boss suggested I take a vacation. Why? So I could spend more time at home listening to my own breathing, arranging and rearranging Larry's ties? I'd fold and refold his socks, put them in order of color. Then I'd organize them according to seasons— thin, crepe ones for summer in the back, thick, heavy wool ones for winter in the front.

I had dressed Larry in his navy blue suit, the one he wore when making speeches or accepting awards. I'd even remembered his favorite socks, his "lucky pair," he'd call them. Once black with white piping, they were now a faded brown and barely stitched together. He would wear them to his weekly poker game, and to operations he feared were risky. He had worn these on our first date, and during the first time we made love, insisting he keep them on. I kept trying to take them off with my toes, finally pushing the right one down to his ankle and inching it off his heel. I was still working on the left one when his roommate walked in on us. Larry jumped up, leaping for the door, naked except for the one sock.

I spent most of December sifting through department stores, looking for the perfect gift for Larry. What do you buy the man who needs nothing? I walked aimlessly, listening to Christmas Muzak sung by dead crooners while people stared at me. Bing Crosby, Judy Garland, Elvis all assured me this was a wonderful life. Well-intended salespeople, overweight schoolgirls who smacked gum in my ear, fast-talking women with high-pitched voices, and middle-aged men dressed in last year's suits all offered advice and made comments regarding my purchases. I decided on a black cashmere sweater, 40 M. "I love a man in a black turtleneck," the saleswoman said, winking, as if in on a secret. "And cashmere feels so good on the skin, don't you think?" She took my credit card, rang it through, and handed it back to me.

Harold was old. I wasn't sure how old, but he had an odor that elderly people carry with them, known only to passersby, a silent understanding that soon his time will be up. Even his name sounded old. His lips were cracked and his smell almost made me sick. When we kissed, he kept his mouth closed. His head was bald with brown age spots. I kissed it. It tasted salty and reminded me of the ocean air. Most of Harold's body was wrinkled and hairless except for small bits in his ears and some darker patches on his genitals. He seemed so fragile that all I did was hold his penis in my hand. He told me about his wife, Elsa. About their sixty-year marriage, how he was supposed to die first, how he wasn't there when she tripped and fell and that he came home just in time to see the body being carried away. At night he prays that God will take him, too. He cannot go on without her. He claims to hear her weep at night. That she calls to him. I held him in my arms for a long time, and let him cry. I was afraid to tell him that it was Larry's voice that woke me in the morning rather than the deafening sound of my alarm. That it was his voice I fell asleep to even though the news anchor's perfectly pronounced words came out clearly through the TV speaker.

Heavy, wet flakes of snow clumped together, making the cemetery look like a huge quilt. It was quiet that last day and you could hear the snow falling, blanketing the graves. It was so cold the air seemed to freeze in my lungs. It hurt to breathe.

Because of the terrible weather, the cemetery was empty. As always, I said hello to Larry first before searching for another human being. I walked aimlessly, the burial ground taking on a dizzying effect. Each path looked the same, each tombstone similar. Bodies after bodies, so many decaying, lonely souls.

In my frantic search for someone, I practically fell over Kelsey. Dressed in a light gray trench coat and matching umbrella, it was almost impossible to differentiate between him and the snow.

I led him back to Larry's grave, telling him the ground was softer there, that under the snow were patches of thick grass. Our bodies collided and sank into the dense, wet flakes. Water seeped into my clothes. The snow was cold but padded my thin frame. Larry was so close, only several feet away, encased in the mahogany coffin I had picked out.

Sex with Kelsey was hard and sharp, as if he were punishing me for something. I wanted to cry out but he put a callused hand over my mouth and whispered for me to be still.

He smelled like bug spray and reminded me of my days at

sleepaway camp. His body felt terribly heavy on top of mine, like the dead weight of an animal. Not like Larry at all. And I thought perhaps he was trying to squeeze the life out of me.

When he was ready to leave, I grabbed his body, forced him down, and squeezed my arms around him as powerfully as possible. He struggled for a second, his face panicked and angry.

"Hey, what are you doing?" He reached behind himself with his arms, trying to pull mine apart. He rolled me over, and like a slug, tried to shake me off. Even in my weakened condition, my bone-like skeleton, I was strong and fought as if this were the most important thing in my life, as if I were offering up a soul, trading one man in for another. "Take this one and give me back what's mine."

Kelsey rammed his head into my nose. I heard a crack and released my grip. He jumped up.

"Jesus Christ, lady." He popped open his umbrella. "Get some fucking help."

I heard his feet crunching in the snow until the sound faded. Then nothing.

I didn't know how many hours it had been since Kelsey left but there was a terrible throbbing in my nose. A dog barked in the distance; the sky got darker. I couldn't feel my fingers or toes.

Snow started to fall, blanketing me. They would probably find my body once it melted. Another mourner would stumble upon me. A small piece of my coat, or my shoe, would catch their eye. They'd come closer, crouch down, brush the remaining slush off my frozen face. My eyes would stare back, hollow and dead; my lips blue, my skin pale and thin.

I drifted, woke, and drifted off again.

THE WAY YOU LEFT

"Men are like the crap dental floss removes from your teeth," I remind myself aloud, and hence the lady standing next to me, as we both wait on a ridiculously long line at the Food Emporium. "Men change their minds, leave the best women they know, and ruin their lives, not to mention ours." I look at my shopping colleague, who nods empathetically as she takes a small step backward.

For the past six days I've thrown myself a pity party and, needless to say, I was the only attendee. But last night at 4:00 A.M. I had a breakthrough. Or breakdown. Somewhere between Oprah, Springer, and Ricki reruns I had a revelation. Some people do a spring cleaning of clothing. My older sister, Gwen, does a cleaning of her friends. I did one of my fridge. I threw out all of Jed's must-have items: truffles from Balducci's, caviar from Zabar's, escargots in thick, sweet oil from Eli's. I poured out the decadent containers filled with mini-olives, capers, and onions into the sink. Then I turned on the water and watched the confluence swirl into a brown mess and slowly disappear down the drain.

I inch up to the cashier, laying the frozen waffles, skim milk, and M&M's on the conveyer belt. It's not real food but it's a start.

I open the bag of M&M's, dig around for some red ones, and pop them into my mouth.

"This all you buying?" the register lady snaps as I pull out my checkbook. "You can't use that for less than twenty dollars." She flashes a nasty smile: her teeth are outlined in gold.

I don't want to get into an argument but I'm not terribly excited to stare at a barren closet, blank dresser drawers, and sit in a half-empty apartment. I take a stab and sign the check. She stares at me, mumbles something in Spanish I can't understand, and slithers away, calling for the manager. In her absence, she's left an open register and a line of angry customers behind me. I eat the last red M&M and pick up a copy of *TV Guide*. The cover reads "Meet Today's Nelson Family," with four people, two mothers and their respective children, underneath the headline. Absorbed in the article, I don't realize how quiet the store has become until it's too late. People have stopped talking, cash registers have stopped ringing, and an uneasy hum is heard. I look up to find three men dressed in black, standing in the middle of the market. Each is holding a large, shiny gun. The one in the middle steps forward.

"This is a stick-up. If nobody wants to get hurt, shot, or disfigured, you better all shut up." His voice has a deep, booming quality which resonates down the aisles. A surreal whirl of words that make no sense hangs in the air. The robber on the right looks nervous. He's shaking and coughing and looking around as if he's forgotten something. Our eyes meet. They look scared yet sturdy, and are an incredible blue, a mix of sea and sky. They're the bluest eyes I've ever seen. In fact, he sort of takes my breath away.

I look around to see what the other shoppers are doing. Except for a few retired old men, most are panic-stricken women, trust fund babies, those on maternity leave, and bored bridge players. I smile at Blue-Eyes and it looks like he's about to smile back when his partner yells, "Everybody down on the ground with your heads to the floor." An edgy anger has filled his voice.

People start crying and gasping while awkwardly trying to follow the robber's command. Bodies drop to the floor, jewelry and belts clink on the hard linoleum as a food domino effect takes place on the conveyer belts. Water bottles, containers of milk and orange juice, cans of soda topple onto packages of sliced turkey and bologna which in turn fall on chips and pretzels, all of which make a crunching, gurgling noise.

I, too, get down on the ground but I can't help looking up, trying to sneak a peek at my newest beau. I close my eyes and see pools of blue as I wonder if he'd be good in bed.

"He's kind of cute, don't you think?" I ask my shopping pal, whose body is sprawled out on the floor like a dog, arms and legs extended in all directions.

"Are you crazy?" she whispers back. Then, craning her neck, "Which one?"

"The one on the right," I whisper, sticking an M&M in my mouth. "Can you see him?"

"The one with the blue eyes?"

I nod and offer her some candy. She declines.

"It's his fault. He should be wearing some kind of mask or stocking."

She nods, agreeing.

I hear a few sniffles and lots of heavy breathing. In another aisle someone has the hiccups. The sound of moving feet, of cash being stuffed in a bag, and a shadow or two reflecting off the window are the only evidence that the men are still here.

"Maybe this is just one of those things that happen in life-or-death situations," I suggest to my comrade. "Like those people who suddenly gain enormous strength and lift cars and other heavy machinery in order to save themselves and their loved ones."

Someone shushes me, someone else clears their throat. I lower my voice a little. "Of course, I'd have to get his number, maybe contact the police, see if—"

"Do you mind?" she snaps.

"Oh, sure. Sorry." I glance back and she's assumed a praying position, hands pressed together, forming a thin teepee, her lips touching the tips of her fingers and her knees tucked into her body. She's probably thinking of a relative or her cat who's waiting for her to come home with cans of Fancy Feast in lemon salmon, or liver with onions.

I hear the sound of heavy footsteps. Then all goes quiet.

I look up and find Blue-Eyes leaning over my lane, staring at me. I wonder how long he's been standing there. Our eyes meet. I stop breathing.

His dark hair, parted in the middle, falls gracefully to the sides. His two-day-old beard growth, perhaps a small attempt at covering himself, outlines his angular jaw. I give him my best flirtatious grin as a loud bang comes from the left. Not a gunshot, the sound of something falling. I jerk my head involuntarily but see nothing. When I look back up, Blue-Eyes is gone. Confused, I turn to see what my shopping friend is doing. She's still in prayer formation.

The next thing I know, he's huddled over me. Chills race up my spine as he bends down.

"What you got there, little lady?"

His breath is hot on my hand, his hair smells of almond.

I open my fist and reveal the crushed package of half-eaten M&M's and my sweaty check.

"I'll take that," he says, squatting down next to me. His hand touches mine as he removes the contents from my fingers. His black ribbed turtleneck lies just over his waist. It's tight enough to tell he has a washboard stomach. His jeans, a perfect length, hit the front of his black boots just so.

I think about writing my number down on a dirty napkin I spot on the floor, but before I have a chance to look for a pen, the front man yells, breaking our moment.

"You people did good. Today, everyone lives." His anger is gone. In its place is a sadistic kind of joy.

As if hearing a dog whistle, Blue-Eyes stands up, grabs a canvas bag stuffed with cash, and follows his friends out the door without firing a shot.

"Are you in the book?" I scream, pulling myself up off the floor.

By now, everyone in the store has turned their attention to me, staring in bewilderment. "Sorry, aftershock flow of emotion," I say, trying to defend myself, still high on adrenaline, heart pounding, lungs gulping for air.

Minutes later, four police officers arrive. Two get statements, speak with eyewitnesses, while the other pair calms people down, assuring them they're safe. Excitement hovers in the air, mixing with the smell of shoppers' perfumed sweat and freshly baked bread. I pass hysterical customers, women clutching their handbags and jewelry, holding onto them for dear life; others are trying to collect themselves. I see one woman reapply her lipstick, fingers still shaking so that she looks like she's been struck by lightning.

I saunter up to one of the policemen, a heavyset, boyish-looking man. "Officer McDermott," I say in my most professional voice, hand extended, looking up from his nametag and into his face, "I'm with *The Grocery Store Tribune*. We're a small newspaper catering to the major supermarkets and the mom-and-pop stores. I was wondering if you knew anything about the men who did this. A local? Maybe their crib? Any leads would be helpful."

He half smiles at me, then breaks into a hearty laugh, revealing a space between his front teeth. Without further discussion, he walks away.

That night I turn on the news, anxious to hear an updated report on my new man. To my disappointment, there's no mention at all. The whole world, except for a handful of hungry mid-morning shoppers, has no idea the holdup ever took place. Some of the glow dissipates and all I'm left with is the memory of an event I can't actually prove happened, a dream I'm not sure I had.

I look out my window, cigarette in hand, favorite flannel shirt on, and stare into the cool darkness, wishing there was someone to call. Gwen is at a lawyers' convention in Chicago and if I called Jed, he'd just say I was looking for a reason to phone, a poor attempt to get back together, and dismiss the robbery story as fiction. I'm tempted to dial up my mother. I picture her sitting in her plush living room, engrossed in one of her magazines, *Today's Quilts*, calculating what thread she needs to buy at the store, half listening to me as I relay today's incident. The one person I want to talk to is my father. I resurrect his face, his bushy eyebrows and kind smile; then I think about Blue-Eyes. I picture him counting his loot at some dirty hole-in-the-wall bar, sitting in the back, toasting today's successful score with his partners. Maybe he's sitting in a rocking chair, feeling waves of guilt as he waits in a paranoid funk, gun already cocked in shooting position, thinking that someone is watching. Or perhaps he's standing by a window, staring out into the city, cigarette in hand, flannel shirt on, anticipating his next heist.

The phone rings. Startled, I answer it, thinking maybe it's the news after all. Maybe they just got a late start. You can't cover all of New York at once.

"Hello?" I say, trying to sound upbeat.

"Hello." The voice is raspy, full, and somehow familiar. There's a long pause and a buzzing.

"Yes, can I help you?"

"You ate all the red ones," he says.

My heart stops as I search for my voice. I practically drop the phone in my excitement. "Yes, well, I didn't know I'd be sharing."

"I'd like to return them to you. I felt a little bad for taking the whole bag."

He suggested we meet at Café Fiorello's in Soho. I dress in all black. Black turtleneck, black corduroys, black belt. My hope is to make Blue-Eyes feel at ease. I was going to wear a little-girlie dress but he seemed like the type to be attracted to a tomboy, and not some squeamish tart who's afraid of a little blood. I'm not sure he'll actually show—a man with a schedule as busy as his can change in a second. Especially when you're wanted by the law.

A tingly, nervous sensation fills my body as I wait for him. I haven't been this excited since I met Jed, a thirty-eight-year-old bartender, on a skydiving excursion. We sat together during orientation. He had the unshaven masculinity thing going on that I found terribly attractive. Every time he'd help me on with my pack and click the safety clips together, I'd get weak in the knees and my throat would go dry. We shared our first kiss before he dove. I tasted his saliva as I watched him twirling down, a white petal, free-falling through the air.

Jed was always testing the boundaries of his mortality. He drove racing cars without a helmet, went on experimental carnival rides that were still being tested for kinks, drank and ate dairy products way past their expiration date. That was until two weeks ago, when I came home and found him packing his belongings. This wasn't the kind of life he wanted anymore, and I wasn't the type of person he wanted to be around. He'd lost his flair for adventure once he joined AA. Those damn steps and all that coffee quelled his invincible inner child. Jed was like a prom date who never showed, leaving me to stand outside in the rain, my cream dress turning brown and wet.

Before Jed, I dated Bruce, a deep-sea diver who moonlighted as a part-time hitman. I don't think he ever killed anyone. Mostly he spied on people, followed them around and took an abundance of notes. He used to let me tag along. We'd have special names. I was Quick Silver, he, Crude Dude. He earned the name because he was always cursing and yelling obscenities. The smallest inconveniences would set him off: dry cleaning that wasn't ready on time, coffee at Starbucks was too expensive, people who were too stupid. It was very exciting to watch his face turn red and his nostrils flare, as if at any minute he'd have a heart attack.

My sister Gwen and I met him while vacationing at Club Med in Cancun. He was our snorkeling instructor and he and I would kiss underwater amongst the coral reefs, exotic fish swimming past us. He had short, blond hair, wore navy blue shirts that always appeared as though he'd accidentally shrunk them in the dryer, and had the most muscular arms and beautifully built body I had ever seen. His best feature by far was his tattoo of a speared shark with blood spurting out. When he flexed his arm, it danced.

Suddenly, I feel someone standing behind me. I spin around to find Blue-Eyes staring at me. He smiles and his eyes seem to spin, like marbles swirling across a linoleum floor. He sits and reaches into the pocket of his leather bomber jacket. For a second I think he's going to take out his gun and place it on the table. Instead, he reveals a two-pound bag of M&M's.

"Just wanted to replace what I took," he says, sliding it to me.

We stare at each other. I'm intoxicated.

"So, is this how you meet all of your girlfriends?" I ask, fingering the edge of the candy bag.

"Sort of, since we don't take any hostages." His face is stone serious.

"I was kidding."

"Oh." His expression falls back into a mellow look, face open. "I'm afraid I'm a little nervous." I watch his hands play with the sugar packets on the table. They look soft, his nails clean and buffed. I even see some clear polish. There's a softness in his eyes, too. A relaxed feel about his body. Even the skin on his face looks smooth and freshly shaven. "I've never met anyone who wasn't scared of us."

A warmth runs through me and I feel as if I've won an award.

The waitress appears. I order a double espresso, Blue-Eyes asks for decaf.

"Coffee makes me jumpy," he says apologetically, once our drinks are set in front of us. I nod understandingly. Sure, maybe he wants to be fresh and alert for his big night. Too shaky and that gun will fall right out of his hand. Or worse, he could become trigger-happy.

"It's actually a relief. I have to lie about what I do to most girls, and when I finally tell the truth, they disapprove of my career path."

I bat my eyes. "I'm not most girls."

. . .

We stand outside the coffee shop. People going in, coming out, all look like a blur as I stare into his face, wondering if I will ever see him again.

"What's your name?" I ask. I tilt my head, and somewhere in the back of my brain I can hear the theme to *Mission Impossible*.

He's quiet for a second, probably not sure whether he can trust me with such personal information, information I might be forced to give in order to help incriminate him later on.

"It's Mark," he finally spits out.

"Mark?"

"Yeah."

"Your birth name is Mark?"

The tingling and music stop. I must look disappointed because he lifts up my chin with his thumb and index finger. Standing in the sunlight, he looks like a superhero.

"You were expecting me to say Three-Finger Lou?"

"No. Well," I look at the ground, then back into his eyes. "Yeah."

"It's not like my parents prepared ahead of time for my line of work."

I nod, knowing he's right. "Mind if I call you Blue-Eyes?"

He smiles, bends his head toward me, and kisses me on the lips. During the subway ride home I say his name over and over. Mark. Mark. Mark. I want to get comfortable with it, like someone's last name you try out while you're dating. Fisher, my first serious boyfriend before the deep-sea diver—his last name was Listenstein. Gail Listenstein. Gail Marshal Listenstein. I'd repeated it endlessly till it stopped sounding like a mouthwash.

My mother blames my flair for abnormal adventure on my father, a tall Danny DeVito type who'd truly mastered the art of living. I was hooked the minute he and I played spy versus spy. We'd roll around on the floor; he'd pin me down and dare me to fight back. I'd stare into his eyes and wish I were stronger.

This roughhousing irritated my mother greatly. She'd come out from the kitchen, hands wet, dishtowel attached to her apron, to see what all the screaming was about. "Stop it, Al," she'd say. "You're going to turn her into a boy." Or, "I had girls, Albert. I'm sorry, but that's what they are." Then she'd turn away, muttering under her breath, "I should have divorced him a long time ago."

He loved playing elaborate games of hide-and-seek which covered a one-mile radius and lasted for hours. Once he stayed hidden for almost two days. For thirty hours straight I combed the neighborhood, knocked on doors, and called out his name, begging him to come out of his hiding spot. I refused to go home, fearful that something terrible had happened—maybe he broke his leg running, perhaps he was stuck and passed out from lack of oxygen or blood circulation and when we would find him, he'd be brain-damaged and drooling. For a moment, I thought he'd left us, that he'd finally had enough of my mother and decided to have the adventure he'd always wanted but couldn't since he had children who only held him back.

Our neighbor finally found him when a Frisbee slid under their house. There he was, curled up in the leaves, reading *Lord of the Flies*. I tried not to cry when he emerged. "It's all right, Gail," he said, holding me tightly, "I was here the whole time." For the next two weeks, I followed him around the house, never letting him out of my sight.

My father would tell us ghost stories late at night, Gwen and me in our beds, his face illuminated by a single flashlight, the bulb painted red to give a bloody effect. Other times he'd read from the local paper, explaining the disaster of the day, or share biographies about people who'd committed heinous crimes like

Charles Manson, the Boston Strangler, Jack the Ripper. Very often he'd pass out on the floor in the space between our beds. My mother would find him in the morning, covered by our blankets I'd thrown over him.

For most men, my lust for action is a temporary turn-on, a kind of viral infection that lasts one to three months and eventually goes away. Fisher holds the endurance record—half a year. We met in my criminal justice class at NYU. He reminded me of my father—same love of gore, same mischievous smirk. He was studying forensics and we'd watch old *Quincy* reruns while we studied, kissing during commercials and when Jack Klugman would make a huge discovery: water was contaminated; baby died of a rare blood disorder; bacteria in food ate away at people's white cells. We'd go camping and fishing. At night, curled up in our sleeping bags we'd zipped together, tent illuminated by the dull light of the lantern, we'd tell ghost stories, just like my father and I had done. Fisher's father was a war hero, and he'd describe amazing tales about life in the trenches, men with body parts that got blown off, skin that hung off bloody limbs.

"What do you tell people you do for a living?" I ask Blue-Eyes during our second date, as we sip drinks in a crowded bar on the Upper West Side.

"I'm in customer relations."

We both smile. This is our first shared moment. It feels wonderful, like receiving a lavish box of Valentine's Day chocolates.

"How often do you and your co-workers—"

"I'm not allowed to say."

"Oh, of course. For my own protection, right?"

"No, that's not it." He plays with his pink umbrella, and swirls his daiquiri around with the straw before taking another sip. "That time in the Food Emporium was only my second job."

I look at the bar.

"But we're planning something really big," he adds quickly. "It's very dangerous."

I squeal with delight. "Tell me more," I beg.

"I'm afraid that's all I can say at the moment." He holds up his hands, making him look like a scale with floating blue eyes. "You don't trust me?"

"No, that's not it. That's just all I know."

We wait for our table, wait for something to say. When I see two women get up from their stools, I make a beeline for them. As I do, a guy practically knocks me over and slides onto the leather seat with his date.

"Excuse me," I say, looking him in the eyes. He's a stubby man with a thick mustache, dressed in a jean jacket and matching pants. His shirt is unbuttoned to his navel and he has a gold chain which reads: *I'm still #1.* His date looks similar, except she's taller. "I think these were ours."

"Not anymore." He and his date laugh, their backs swiveling to my face.

"Boy, you have no class. What kind of guy is so desperate that he has to take a seat from a woman?" I say in a loud voice, looking for Blue-Eyes, knowing he'll handle this. "Honey?"

Blue-Eyes walks over to us. "That's okay, no problem," he says, squeezing my arm and leading me off to the side. "Sorry for the bother."

"Those were our seats," I point out, martini glass in my extended hand. "You didn't have to take that from him. You're a man of power, a don't-fuck-with-me kind of guy."

"I'm not big on confrontation." He shrugs and sips his banana daiquiri.

A moment or two pass in silence. Then, in a valiant attempt

to raise my spirits, he whispers, "We shall talk only in code." He looks around the room. "The package is missing."

"The doorbell is broken," I say. We break out in fits of laughter, getting disapproving looks from patrons. I'd like to reach for Blue-Eyes's gun and threaten to shoot anyone who feels inclined to stare nastily at us again—the power of a firearm is a large one, but he doesn't carry it around. It makes him anxious.

It isn't long before Blue-Eyes and I fall into a comfortable routine like most couples. We read the Sunday *Times*, shop for lobster at the fish market, watch foreign films at the art houses. We go to Shakespeare in the Park, we hold hands, he explains the plot to me over decaf espresso at quaint, out-of-the-way coffee shops. He's perfect except he pays for everything in cash, we have no phone conversations that don't require the use of a quarter, he's paranoid about cell phones, and I don't know his last name or where he lives. He never brings me home. I never meet his friends, nor his mom, and he never wants to meet mine. I don't know what he does when we're not together. I listen to the radio, watch the news, hold my breath, and live with uncertainty. I don't mind—it keeps everything mysterious. The sad thing is, it's the best relationship I've had this decade.

Sex, however, is fabulous. Blue-Eyes comes alive with the lights off, the room illuminated only by scented candles. Sometimes we make believe I'm his hostage. He ties me up, uses old belts from my closet for my wrists, and some blue tape that comes off walls easily for my legs. One time we used the red-and-white string that came with the box of cookies from the bakery. He pretended to get angry, threatened to kill me if I didn't behave. He slid a toy gun from my chest to my navel, got a kick out of seeing it move up and down on my stomach. As punishment he shot vodka into my mouth from it. Another time, he poured sugar over my belly and we acted out a scene from *Scarface*, making believe it was coke. Blue-Eyes quoted Al Pacino while licking my body till the stickiness was gone, till I begged him to let me go, till I came. I've asked him to wear a black ski mask, but Blue-Eyes doesn't like his head being covered. He claims it makes him claustrophobic and disoriented.

I like him best when he describes his holdups. Unfortunately, he's a lousy storyteller. I have to ask the questions like an acting coach. "Describe the room. What do the customers' faces look like? How did you feel before you went in?" Blue-Eyes does okay, but with a little pressure, I'm afraid he'd confess to being involved with Watergate.

Sometimes he brings me a souvenir from his jobs. These are my favorite, most cherished objects. Tangible evidence of a life worth living. Blue-Eyes's loving baubles—a gold ring with small diamonds, and mini Scotch and gin bottles from liquor store holdups—mix with other trinkets from my men: a swatch of fabric from Jed's parachute, Bruce's mini-flashlight, the newspaper clipping of how my father died. I twist open the Scotch, clasp the opening between my teeth, snap my head back, and let the golden liquid side down my throat. My body starts to feel warm and tingly. I reach for another and make a silent toast to my father. I sip the vodka and finger the yellowed newspaper article. I kiss the uncomplimentary picture of my father, open another bottle, and find comfort as the contents burn my insides, filling up the loneliness.

My parents met when my mother applied for the job of putting makeup on dead people. She had gone to school for cosmetology but never developed an artistic flair. My father was her last hope. He owned a mortuary and connecting cemetery, given to him by his great grandfather, who had inherited the property in a card game. I'm not sure why they dated, or for how long, except they decided to marry when my mother announced she was pregnant with Gwen. A cemetery was no place for her, she told him, let alone children. They moved to a little white house, the kind my mother had read about in magazines. She had been secretly clipping pictures out for years. Big, beautiful houses with picket fences and maple trees that hung just so. My father sold the property and we moved to Connecticut before Gwen was born. He took a job in the hospital, working with dead bodies. My mother would never let us tell people what my father did, just that he had a big position at the hospital. People assumed he was a doctor.

On Sundays he would bring Gwen and me to see the bodies. The smell was terrible. We'd wear white powder under our noses and plastic gloves on our hands. He'd wheel out their bodies, bloated and white, arms and legs disfigured, wounds that hadn't healed, operations that went askew. Then we'd go for ice cream and make up stories about who they were and how they died: a Mafia man who made billions until someone bumped him off, a black-widow woman who married men for money and was murdered by an avenging relative, a coked-up drug dealer eighty-sixed by pimps. On rainy days, we'd go to the movies. We'd sit in the front row, holding each other's hands. When scary parts came, we'd send quick squeezes to our partners like sparks in a campfire.

In the sixteen years my parents were married, my mother never had a thrilling moment, never lived life on the edge, barely laughed for fear of ruining her makeup. She was a beautiful, squeamish woman who wore bright colors that always seemed faded on her. The yellow, electric blue, bubble-gum pink all seemed dull, like her body was sucking in the color and holding it hostage somewhere inside.

When we moved, she fell in love with the rich folks. She wanted to be like them, live like they did, dress as they would. She'd have her hair and nails done every few days and walk around looking in the windows of the expensive stores. When we were school age, she took a job in the best private school in town, working as a librarian so we could get a free education. Very often she would waltz into the living room with books other mothers had returned for their children. *Mindy Grover said her daughter Kelly loved this book. It's about sisters who live in a magical garden and they have tea parties with the vegetables.* Gwen and I would look up from the TV and roll our eyes in our father's direction. *"Jesus, Lydia,"* he'd say, coming to our rescue, *these are girlie books. Where's the scary parts?*

One day, my father didn't come home.

My mother had labored away in a hot kitchen to make a gourmet meal she'd read about in *Ladies' Home Journal.* "Elegant food," she called it. The kind you could serve at dinner parties: glazed ham, baby carrots and brussels sprouts served in a white-wine-and-butter sauce, chicken cacciatore with cranberry gravy, pineapple upside-down cake. We hated this. We wanted franks and beans or the types of meals Dad made. He'd name each dish according to color. Red Jell-O with cherries in it was called human eye mold. Spaghetti in hearty tomato sauce became monster brains. String beans in pesto, mold. For dessert, he'd buy chocolate bars and hide them somewhere in the living room. Unable to deal with the banter and endless questions—*Are we near it? Is it hidden in something? Can we see it from eye level?*—my mother would retire to her room, to her world of magazines with pictures of kittens sitting in baskets or of beautiful gardens on the cover and how-to articles inside: "18 Ways to Become More Mate Compatible," "48 Holiday-Saving Secrets," and "How Safe Is Your Food?" But this time, my mother's cooking efforts really went uneaten rather than unappreciated. The brisket turned dry and dark brown, the vegetables cold and hard.

At 8:30 Sunday night, a postman rang our bell and handed us a package. Inside were clues to where my father was. The note read *Find me if you can*, with cut-out words from newspapers and a tarnished key. My mother thought the whole thing a joke and went to bed. I read the note over and over, tried to fit the words together to form sentences, but the puzzle was too hard for a twelve-year-old. Around midnight, and still seated at the kitchen table, Gwen passed out, her long, brown hair spilling over the pieces of paper. I worked through the night, chest tight, eyes bloodshot, trying to solve the caper. By day two, still no Dad and severely sleep-deprived, we called the police. They found him at the zoo. He was in the insect hall and had been bitten to death by infected flies. It was accidental and was in all the papers. Supposedly, he had climbed on a ladder to get a better look at the cockroach exhibit. The floor, slippery from a recent cleaning, caused the ladder to slide out from under him where he was thrown against the encased glass window, shattering it on impact.

My mother had the mortician dress my father in a black suit, a suit he hated and only wore to other people's funerals, and his white dress shirt which he claimed itched. The day of his funeral, I woke up Gwen and explained my plan to her, insisting she get dressed and help me change our father out of the "funeral" outfit and into something he'd be more comfortable in. I'd bribed our neighbor, Buddy Conell, with twenty dollars to help, and the three of us rode our bikes at 6:00 in the morning to the chapel, crawled in through the window, and found my father waiting for us in the main viewing room. We opened the coffin. The stale smell of a musty barn hit us instantly.

We dragged my father out of the coffin and stripped him down to his boxers. His body was cold and his lips were blue. His face was badly scarred from where the glass had cut him and much of his back was covered with large, blue-and-purple bruises from the fall. He seemed very small, lying on the floor of the chapel, and I held my hands in his, rubbing them back and forth, trying to warm his body. I stroked his head, stared at his face, all the time expecting him to open his eyes and scream, "Got ya!"

We changed him into jeans, a Star Trek T-shirt, and a safari jacket. We had trouble hoisting his body back into the coffin. He was so heavy. Gwen was standing off to the side, crying, and wouldn't say good-bye. Buddy had his arm around her and kept saying, "Shhh." I placed a flashlight and several true-crime novels inside the coffin, ran my hand over his face, as if trying to memorize it, and finally kissed him on his blue lips.

One evening, Blue-Eyes doesn't come home. I wait, pasta thick and overcooked, dessert melted, candles burned down to stubs. I watch the news. Nothing. No reports, no catastrophes, nothing unusual.

Perhaps my man's been shot during one of his heists. Maybe he's hiding out from the feds, wounded, cold, in some dank, deserted place. Maybe he can only send word via pigeon that I'll find pecking at my window, bloody note attached to its leg. Or maybe a boy will knock on my door, hand me a letter written on a paper towel or McDonald's napkin: *I'm fine. Won't surface for months. Carry on without me.*

I'm actually worried. Perhaps in their feeble attempt to get in and out, B.E. (Blue-Eyes) and his band of merry men have been seriously hurt. A tightness returns in my chest and I suddenly feel very helpless. I pace the apartment, gather first aid supplies, and boil water. I collect Neosporin, large gauze pads, rubbing alcohol, even scan the Web for information on how to remove a bullet, should that be necessary. I think about calling missing persons, but what would I say?

As I wait for news from Blue-Eyes, I pull out my box of treasures and line up all of the tokens he's brought me: rings, earrings, a fake nail, beaded bracelets. I wonder who wore the jewelry he returns with. As if I'm back playing the morgue game with my father, I create tales from what little information I have about how the objects look, their condition and smell. I imagine the earrings belonged to an old lady with no family, the retrieved nail from the pinkie of a recovering coke addict, the insubstantial diamond ring a measly offering from a bitter divorced woman who cheated on her husband. Sometimes I wear the jewels. Other times, like a gambler's lucky charms, I carry them in my pocket, fingering them every so often. My favorite of the stash is a Gatsby pocket watch. It reminds me of the one my father had. He won it in an essay contest the *American Journal* was sponsoring for Halloween: "The scariest thing I ever saw . . ." He was twenty-five and working at his grandfather's cemetery. He framed the article right above his desk and often used it as a selling tool when perspective plot buyers came by.

He hardly ever let Gwen and me hold the watch. Sometimes, he would press it against our ears and let us hear its ticking. "This is the sound a time bomb makes," he'd say. And if we were very careful, he'd let us wind it before he went to work. He carried the watch everywhere, insisting the ticking comforted him. When the police found his body at the zoo, they knew what time my father died, 10:09, because the watch cracked when he hit the floor. Like my father, it was permanently broken.

I think about Fisher. About my father, his not coming home, and wonder if I've ever mentioned his death to Blue-Eyes. Maybe it's all one big surprise. Perhaps he's planning a similar stunt.

Blue-Eyes calls two days later.

"Sorry," he offers. "One of my friends was driving to Philadelphia and I thought I'd visit my father."

"You could have called," I yell into the receiver. "Let me know you weren't bleeding to death. I had no idea where you were. What? Your dad doesn't own a phone?"

"Sorry. I wasn't thinking."

Blue-Eyes and I have fallen into the life of Floridians in their eighties. We eat early at the same restaurants, watch the same TV shows—I opt for *Law and Order*, he claims it makes him hyperventilate. *It's like being at the office. Couldn't we watch a soap or game show?*—and go to Barnes & Noble. I skim through books on serial profiling, Blue-Eyes salivates in the theater section.

Tonight finds us at the Food Emporium, the place where it all began. Blue-Eyes and I stand on line alongside well-dressed men in three-piece suits, daddies doing last-minute errands, and dowdy, tired-looking women. Surprisingly, there are no children, except for Blue-Eyes.

"We should have gotten here earlier," he whines, "then there'd have been no wait." He looks at his watch nervously, fingers the black plastic band of his Timex. "Mother can't stand it if I'm tardy."

"Fine. Why don't you just leave me here. I'll carry the heavy bags home, stuff that you want—purified water, HoHos, Tab, veggie burgers—all so you can meet Mommy."

"No, you're right. I'm sorry." He sighs. "It's just that . . ."

Blue-Eyes is in the middle of apologizing when a familiar hush falls over the store.

As if someone's called our names, we both look up in sync. The doors fly open and four people dressed in furry costumes barrel into the Emporium. Things are moving in slow motion and at top speed at the same time. Each figure is dressed as a well-known character: Donald, Mickey, Dumbo, and Snoopy. Masks hang down over their noses, stopping at the top of their lips, covering most of their faces. Dark Ray-Ban glasses protect their eyes, making them look like Disney gone hip.

"Jesus, what's with this place?" I say. "Is robbing it a prerequisite or something?" I smile. Blue-Eyes doesn't.

Snoopy steps forward and clears his throat.

"Snoopy? Snoopy isn't part of the Disney group. Can't they get sued for that?" I joke with Blue-Eyes, but all the color has drained out of his face.

"Shut up, Gail. These guys are serious."

"You know them?"

"They're legendary."

People are still moving about when Snoopy fires a shot into the air. Plaster ceiling bits fall to the floor. The smell of burnt bagel hangs in the atmosphere, mixing with smoke residue. Some customers start screaming and crying. Everyone freezes. Panic and thrill rise in my chest. I can barely contain my excitement.

Unlike Blue-Eyes's mangy bunch of boys, these fellas have it down. They come armed with tape, a stopwatch, black sacks, massive sheets of bulky wood, the works. Within seconds, the doors are nailed shut and sheets of wood are placed up against the windows and screwed into the metal beams.

"If they should ask for a hostage, I'm going to volunteer," I inform Blue-Eyes, my attention directed toward the four men racing around the store.

I try to raise my hand to ask a question, but Blue-Eyes wrestles me down. "Are you out of your mind?" he asks, his voice cracking. His hands are like ice, his face wet.

"Calm down, honey, we're safe. They can't hurt us. You're in the 'biz,' and I'm a friend of yours. It's like dating someone and having to be nice to their kid sister."

Blue-Eyes just stares at me. "You're sick, you know that?"

"I'm sick? I'm sick? I'm not the one holding up supermarkets and liquor stores for a living."

"Gail, keep your voice down."

I look at Blue-Eyes standing limp, face pale, and I fantasize about one of the holdup men slipping on the shiny linoleum, thanks to his padded feet, smacking his head on the floor in the process. Oops, lights out. Perhaps the one dressed as Donald. He looks the most unbalanced. His mask is on crooked and his glasses seem loose. He keeps pushing them up with his gloved index finger. Now a felon short, they'll need to call upon some outside help. Even out the odds. "Is there another experienced robber in the house?" Snoopy will ask. And out of nowhere, Blue-Eyes can leap from the scared pool of people, stand tall among the big boys, and win one for the gipper. I turn to share this with Blue-Eyes and find him crouched down in the corner, shaking. For a moment I think he's kidding. When I realize he's not, it all ends. Like a drug has worn off and everything I liked about the person is over, as if it never existed. All I see is Blue-Eyes—rather, Mark—metamorphosed into someone I don't recognize. Even his eyes seem less blue.

"I can't believe this is happening twice," I whisper to Less-Boy. "The chance of this occurring to the same person must be one in a . . ."

"For Christ's sake, Gail," Mark's lips are pressed together tightly, "shut up."

We're shushed by others and the thrill kicks in.

Dumbo runs through the store checking for additional people while Donald trails behind covering him from the back. I watch Snoopy, who, I assume, is the ringleader. He has a charming walk, confident and bold, even with his furry feet.

A minute later, the deli and fish guys appear, their hands held over their heads, aprons stained with blood and smelling of meat and cheese. A few straggly, dazed customers are collected as well.

"Phone lines cut, floor's swept, back of the store's empty," Dumbo informs his fellow men. "Storeroom's been cleared out, truck's waiting."

The four nod in silence.

"Okay, we're going to do this clean and easy," Snoopy barks. He has a British, James Bond–like accent. It's silky and smooth, like velvet. "When I say move, men go on one side," he points to the wall that houses the chips, dips, and candy. "Women over there," he points to the frozen food section. Both are far away from the automatic doors and windows. "Okay, move."

No one stirs. I start to collect my belongings and walk to our designated spot, but find I'm the only one following directions. Mark pulls me back.

"Didn't you hear him? He asked us to move."

Everyone is looking at me.

"He asked us to move," I repeat to a woman standing next to Mark, who in turn looks to her right. People look to each other for directions. One woman grabs a plastic bag and begins to fill it with her groceries. A man in a three-piece suit opens a beer. The sound of the can seems unusually jarring.

"What is this, a fucking cocktail party?" I say, loud enough for Snoopy to hear. I try not to look in his direction, but I'm praying he's staring. I can almost feel his shaded eyes on my face.

Irritated, Mickey fires another shot. More plaster falls. The air becomes thick with powder. "Are you all waiting for personal invitations?" he shouts. Like an earthquake, the movement is sudden and careless. Customers are coughing and choking as they bump into one another, each trying to get to their appointed spot like school children. Women cry as disgruntled men curse under their breath. I'm the first to reach my target, nabbing a spot toward the front.

As frantic women push their way in, I get nestled in between a woman with bad breath and a big hat and another who smells like she's been dipped in perfume and smoke. I look for Less-Boy and see him pinned between two men in tan trench coats. I eye the line and notice that Mark is whiter than everyone. One man lights a cigarette, another bums one off him. The clicking of the lighter is loud and sounds out of place. I see the small stream of fire, watch the smoke leave their mouths, watch them inhale, then exhale together, like twins breathing. Some men try to act macho, looking flip and uncaring, older men seem withdrawn and frightened. I look at the women on line with me—they, too, are a mix of horror, agitation, and depression. We look like a school dance, boys on one side, girls on the other, with nothing but the floor to separate us.

Donald and Dumbo take to the registers; Mickey works the men, Snoopy collects from the women. "Here we go—Christmastime," Mickey says, a lyrical joy to his voice. "Drop it all in—wallets, watches, and jewelry into the bags. Do it clean and easy and we'll have no problems."

I see Snoopy walk past me and I think about having sex with him in the back of the Food Emporium in the cold cuts department. I visualize slabs of fresh meat, pounds of cole slaw, pasta salad, our naked bodies on crushed ice. I imagine his muscular body as he rips off the mask and sunglasses, unzips his costume, and stands in front of me in a white T-shirt and boxers with green dollar signs printed on them.

During collection time, someone's cell phone rings. Like a climactic point in a tennis match, we all shoot looks in the shrill's direction.

"It's my husband," a woman says apologetically, as she digs through her oversized black handbag. "Should I answer it?"

The thugs form a small huddle in the middle of the floor and confer for a moment. "Toss it in the bag," bellows Snoopy. His voice is intoxicating. Even angry, he sounds sexy. "That goes for everyone. Beepers, too."

A slew of small, colorful objects make momentary appearances as the noise from the snapping of plastic makes a cacophony of sounds.

The closer Snoopy gets, the more the familiar tingling inside me increases. It spreads like ants crawling over my body, irrigating my blood stream, making me feel a prickly heat in my fingers and toes.

There's some discussion coming from the men's side. I take my eyes off Snoopy and scan the line to see what the problem is.

"Hand it over, man, all of it," Mickey snarls at one customer. I can't see who because Mickey is covering him. Next to him, though, is Mark, who is hovering like a frightened cat recoiling from a predator.

"Hey, man," I recognize Mark's whimpery voice, "just give them what they want." Then to Mickey, "Here you go," and hands him his Velcro wallet and beeper, his Timex watch and keys to his apartment. He offers them up to Mickey like Oliver Twist, hoping for exemption, or a second helping. "Just don't hurt anyone," he adds.

I roll my eyes up at Snoopy, then grimace. I can see Snoopy

smirking, too. His lips curl up ever so slightly and just touch the edges of his plastic mask. He has perfect teeth. And they're real, too. Not the capped kind. He runs his tongue over them. I mimic him, then wink. I flash him my toothy, white smile and try to flirt as I remove my ring, the stolen one Mark brought me a few months ago. Coyly, I drop it into the black sack. I smile, feeling like a pro, and add my name and phone number, which I wrote on someone's register slip I found on the floor, to the lot. Then I wink again.

Snoopy pauses, probably assuming I have a nervous twitch. His gloved hand picks out my note. My body feels on fire as I watch him open it. He looks back at me, head tilted, and licks his top lip with the tip of his tongue.

"Call me," I mouth while I make the official phone signal, thumb and pinkie extended, other fingers curled in, and bring my hand to my mouth and ear. He smiles and shows his pearly whites. The light catches them, making him appear as though he's in a toothpaste commercial.

He takes a small step toward me and raises his gun in my direction, stopping only when it's aimed at my head. Snoopy is five, maybe six feet away from me. My heart stops. He cocks the metal, jerking the gun upward slightly, indicating that I'm to stand, I do as I'm told. My body feels frozen and heavy, my mind races.

There's dead silence.

Everyone's eyes are on us. I've never felt so alive in my entire life. I hear the humming of the fluorescent lights, then the ticking of the clock overhead, which sounds like my father's pocket watch. Snoopy and I stand still. My heart is pounding. I'm sure he hears it, too. *I can get out of this. Think. Think. Dodge a bullet, say something witty, smile, flirt . . .* The room fades and the light ringing in my ears becomes louder. I see myself standing there in the supermarket. See Snoopy and the pointed gun. Then I see my father. See the photo in the newspaper. See him lying on the cold floor of the zoo, insects crawling on him, pieces of glass surrounding his body, neck broken. I blink and Snoopy comes back into focus, like drops wearing off at the eye doctor's. I stare back at him.

"Take me with you," a voice says. I look around and realize it's mine. Not meek or soft, but strong. Confident.

A beeping starts. I look from Snoopy to Mickey, who's holding up his wrist. "That's it, boys. Show's over."

The two D's collect the black bags from Mickey. The three pull out their firearms and stride over to the cellar doors, heave them open and drop them loudly on the floor. It resonates with an awful, booming sound. Mickey scurries hurriedly in first, followed by Donald. Dumbo remains still and clears his throat.

"Sorry, love," Snoopy says, British accent in full swing. "Not this time. Perhaps next go-round." He nods, taps his forehead with his gun, and salutes good-bye. I watch his body disappear into the dim stairs until there's nothing in the spot but darkness. Dumbo follows. As furry paws reach out to close the metal doors, Snoopy pops back up and tosses something at me. I flinch, but catch it after it hits my chest. It's my piece of paper. My hands are shaking as I open the crumpled-up ball. I look down, thinking I'll see my own number, but it's been crossed out. The name *Hunter Clark* is scribbled in its place.

The cellar doors bang shut; I can feel the heavy metal closing in my chest. The sound of thick chains and a lock comes from inside the storeroom.

Then silence.

No one moves at first. It seems like everyone is either holding their breath or expecting someone to shout "Cut!" Eventually people start to gather themselves. A few men come to the women's side and help them up. Some hold each other, some cry, some just remain frozen. Four men try to pry the automatic doors open, while others look for ways to remove the wood that's been affixed to the windows, or break the glass.

The store manager climbs onto the middle conveyer belt, his foot slipping every so often. "Please calm down. First, is everyone all right?" When no one answers, he continues. "Okay, there's an alarm in the back of the store. Stan has pushed the button, so the police have been notified and, I assume, are on their way." He takes a deep breath, trying to suck in all the air in the room. "If you can stay and give statements, that would be wonderful. For those of you who need to get home, you're all on the honor system. Take your groceries and pay us tomorrow."

People cheer like they've just seen the New Year's Eve ball drop. Some men slap hands, women pile groceries into brown paper bags.

I watch everyone move past me. Through me.

I put the paper in my pocket and find Mark hurriedly packing up our groceries, shoving cans of Tab and the box of HoHos into his knapsack while asking someone what time it is.

I wait to see how long it will take him to look for me. How long it will take him to realize I'm already gone.

Shrinking Away

Helen is dreaming of snakes. Massive, slimy creatures that wind themselves around her body and throat. They are heavy and thick and make it impossible for her to move. In other dreams, sneering black birds latch onto her shoulders and fly off with her while bugs crawl into her mouth. She often wakes, gasping for air or leaping out of bed to jerk on the light and search for roaches or spiders that have crept under her sheets. Her therapist, Marty, says she's repressing guilt and this is how her body deals with it. Helen thinks he's wrong. Helen thinks it's Marty who interrupts her thoughts, attaching himself to her fantasies and controlling her subconscious.

The sound of the alarm is jarring and hauls her out of this reverie. Her shirt is wet and clings to her damp skin. The room feels dizzy. She feels dizzy, as if she's been treading water for too long. Boxes, newspaper, and brown tape litter her Upper West Side apartment. She hasn't packed the coffee machine yet and the fridge is still stocked. On the door is a list of meetings which is pinned down by magnets in the shape of handbags. Next to it is her gym schedule. If she can get organized, she can hit her 9:00 A.M. debtor's meeting followed by the 10:30 A.M. aerobics class.

Helen keeps a dress list, recording what she's worn to each meeting. Every week, in honor of the occasion, she purchases a new outfit. No one in the group has noticed that she's never worn the same thing twice. And if they did, no one has commented.

No matter what she buys, whenever possible she pays in cash. That way, her father won't find out. All of her credit card bills are sent to him and he must give his verbal approval before any purchase is rung through. Her father asks the salespeople a litany of questions ranging from "What is my daughter charging?" and "How much is the outfit?" to "Do you feel this is something she needs to have or is she being extravagant?" Every now and then she gets an eager seller who is desperate to make their commission. They disobey the annoying notice that pops up on the screen when the card's numbers are punched in. Sometimes, she bribes them or gives them head in the back room. Last week she swayed the manager with a hand job for twenty percent off of the earrings at Barney's. It was surprisingly easy. They were leaning up against the end of the glass case, he on one side, she on the other, their hips just touching at the corner. She slipped her hand into his unzipped fly and earned her discount. She never told that to Marty. She simply showed him her new purchase, leaned in close, invading the special space between patient and doctor, outlined by the two identical leather chairs. He liked them. She could tell. They dangled from her ears and she asked him to touch them. If Marty were her husband, she would dress him in T-shirts from The Gap and suits from Armani rather than the crewnecked sweaters and crisp Polo shirts his wife buys him. Helen thinks this makes Marty look too "Father knows best," and ages him by ten years. She bought him a pipe once, but he didn't get the joke.

Helen likes Marty. He's tall and charming. Though he won't tell his exact age, he did say he was in his early forties, which makes him six or eight years older than she. Sometimes she doesn't talk, she just watches him. Takes visual notes of his sympathetic eyes, his pressed-together lips, his open and accepting face as if trying to take a tiny piece of him with her. He has a small scar over his left eyebrow and sometimes during a session, when she is close to crying, Helen stares at it. Her friend, Tess, told her that at $110 an hour, twice a week, she should stare at Marty's dick. Tess is also in Debtors Anonymous. The two have been going for almost a year and a half. If the meeting is taking place in the late afternoon, they gather for lunch first with other women from the group and sometimes shop afterward, perusing the sales racks, browsing department stores. Helen doesn't mind the meetings—she rather likes them. A handful of gruff men talk about Home Depot. Or they spew stories about appliances and home fix-it jobs, shiny cars, and box seats at sporting events. Some bitch about their wives and the enormous bills they ring up. That they can't keep going to work and coming home to stuffed closets and empty bank accounts. The women discuss shopping trends, sample sales, outlet stores, and warehouses. Last week one woman explained how the tactile feeling of suede turned her on. That a velvet shirt gave her an orgasm in the stall at Neiman's. Other women talk about the void shopping fills, the supposed hole they are trying to cram with objects and clothing. The need to be loved. This might be true for most, but not for Helen. It's not about the void, it's about the taking in. The holding onto. Bags make her hands feel occupied. They hold her down, anchor her to the ground, make it impossible for her to take flight. If she were to drown, her many bags would keep her afloat. She can almost see herself coasting on a huge raft made out of protective bubble from Crate & Barrel.

She likes jewelry best. Small trinkets that fit comfortably, easily into pockets and handbags, slip off her fingers or wrists before dinners with her parents, sessions with Marty, meetings in church basements. Pockets allow her to caress them without anyone knowing. The safety of objects, she thinks. That's what it's all about.

She and Tess are shopping at Tiffany's. The necklace, a gold-link chain, is too constricting and reminds Helen of her snake dream. The air is cut off from her throat and her hands shake as she rushes to remove it. In her harried state, she almost cuts her finger on the safety clasp.

Earlier that day, she and Tess saw the perfect sweater for Marty. A navy blue cashmere V-necked sweater. She longs to dress him up, take him out for dinner, pretend he isn't married and he isn't her shrink. Her parents would approve of him, finally feel as though she had done something right with her life. Marty would be what her mother calls "a lucky snatch." She visualizes having a family dinner at Mr. Chow's. Her brother and his wife, her mother and her much older, wealthy acquaintance, her father and his secretary (or hatcheck girl or some woman he met on the subway), and her and Marty. Her mother would order steamed vegetables and several glasses of wine, her father would feed his lady friend, and her brother would haggle about the bill, commenting how the lo mein tasted pasty. Helen can see Marty clasping her hand under the table as he bites into an egg roll or chomps on a rib. In between the digs and vicious looks her father would throw her mother and the sneers and nervous coughs her mother would make, Marty would lean into Helen and say, "Your father's so clearly passive aggressive and I had no idea how truly dysfunctional your mother was." Then he'd kiss her right under her earlobe, smearing a hint of Peking sauce on her pricey earring. But instead, all she has are weekly fuck sessions with Marty that take place at the Four Seasons.

. . .

The urge to hit Bloomingdale's supersedes her morning meeting at work. Her boss won't miss her. He's an alcoholic and as long as she looks pretty, provides coffee and Advil, she could come in at 3:00 P.M. and he wouldn't care. He allows her the long lunches. He takes them, too. Her job often requires her to be out of the office most of the day, scouting for locations. She works on *Scavengers*, a reality show where real people are given a list of items that they must acquire. The first team to complete the list wins. Helen is in charge of securing the objects, finding the sites, and obtaining the rights to film in them. Department stores and malls love her. It's because she's a good customer, and they feel comfortable with someone who frequents their shops so often. The free publicity doesn't hurt, either.

People like Helen. She's friendly and effervescent, a brilliant negotiator, and knows the ins and outs of every mall and specialty store from Manhattan to Vermont. They are unaware she's afraid to sleep. That she takes pills and drinks pots of coffee before bed. That she often feels invisible. That the receipts and the useless objects she insists she have make her feel alive. Very often she leaves these stores with free stuff or coupons and discount cards given to her by well-meaning managers and zealous salespeople.

At 6:30, the realtor stops by with the new clients/soon-to-be-homeowners. Mr. Kramer wants to add molding to the ceiling and make the two closets into one large walk-in. Mrs. Kramer is adamant about turning Helen's small office into a baby's room. They are lovely people, and Helen almost offers to help them furnish the apartment with the perfect home decorations and fabrics.

All Helen can think about is the profit she's making, practically doubling her investment, and the things she'll buy. The gifts she can give friends and co-workers. Once a week she visits the children's ward at Sloan-Kettering. She brings stuffed animals or painting sets, coloring books, and packages of pretty pastel beads.

Selling her apartment is a smart move. She really needs the money, and her parents never visit. What they don't know won't hurt them. She's promised Marty she'll pay off all her debts and fix her credit rating. It's part of the deal. She's staying at her brother's for the next six months while he's away on business in Tokyo. His office is sending him there to head up a new banking system or something. Every time she asks him specifically what he does for a living, he gives her the same nonlinear answer so that Helen never really knows what he does, except that he works for a bank but isn't a banker. "Your brother is a very important man," her mother told her last week. "They're investing millions in him." Helen plans to spend the next four months looking for another apartment, maybe a walk-up. Something smaller. Something near Marty's office or even in his apartment building. She needs no doorman. She's hardly home. Besides, her apartment is more for storing her possessions then it is for storing Helen. She wonders if moving closer to Marty means she'll see him more. Catch him jogging or walking with his frumpy wife. A woman who, Helen envisions, has a bad sense of style, frosted hair, and sports last year's suits cut too big and hemmed too short.

Helen has always had a talent for fashion. Senior year she won best dressed and most likely to succeed. She learned quickly that people bonded over clothing and makeup. That the cool, popular kids were always the best dressed. And that complimenting someone on their watch or handbag was a great icebreaker. She worked as an accessories editor at *Seventeen*, and then *Glamour,* before working as a costumer on *One Life To Live*. Eventually she ended up at CBS and shopped her way through the food chain, becoming a locations director for TV shows. Before her shopping problem developed five years ago, she was the favored child. Now her father rarely speaks to her and her mother no longer asks how she's doing.

Her parents divorced when she was fourteen. Aside from a few holidays, they rarely saw each other. After Helen was arrested for shoplifting and given a court date, her parents formed some bizarre friendship. In reality, Helen's purchasing compulsion forced her parents to get along for the first time in their lives. If nothing else, she is responsible for that. Now, along with the mandatory sessions with Marty and 12-step meetings, her parents get together once a month with her and her brother as a sort of family therapy. They go over her bills, ask her for additional receipts, and look at her bank statements, checks, and pay stubs. All of this is kept in a large red accordion folder.

Her arms are laden with packages when she walks in and notices the machine blinking. The first call is from her mother. Her voice is slurred. Helen looks at the clock: 5:49 P.M. She must be on her third martini by now. She keeps meaning to introduce her mother to her boss. She envisions them having hazy lunches consisting of liquid. The next message belongs to a voice she doesn't recognize. "This is Doctor Pinter. I share space with Dr. Radkin, and was given your number through his service. I'm afraid Dr. Radkin will be unable to keep your 6:30 P.M. appointment tomorrow. I'd like to discuss the reason for the sudden cancellation. Please call back when you can. I can be reached at 212-445-9676. Thank you."

She calls Marty's machine first and gets his normal outgoing greeting: *Please leave a message and telephone number and your call will be returned within the hour.* His deep, soft-spoken voice—which reminds her of melted dark chocolate—sends instant comfort through her body. She tries Dr. Pinter.

"Hello?" The voice is crisp, almost irritated. Tired.

"Hi. This is Helen Shapiro returning your call."

"Could you hold for a second?" Helen hears the ruffling of papers. "Yes, Helen. Thank you for phoning back." He breathes deeply into the phone. "I don't quite know how to say this, but there's been an accident, and Dr. Radkin will be unable to continue treatment."

"What? Is Marty okay?"

"There was a freak incident and he passed away last night."

Helen drops the bags and hears something crack. The pitcher she bought at Tiffany's. A thank-you for her brother and his wife for the use of their home. "How? What happened?"

"He was leaving an appointment and pressed the elevator button. The doors opened, only the elevator wasn't there and he unknowingly stepped forward."

Helen visualizes Marty's lean body free-falling down the dark shaft. She sees him dressed in one of his crew-necked sweaters that makes him look like an old man, his gray trench coat still folded neatly over his arm.

"Are you all right?" Dr. Pinter continues. "I realize this is a shock, and if you'd like to talk with someone . . . I know you don't know me, but I'd be more than happy to see you. Or perhaps I can recommend someone else. A woman, maybe, if that would make you more comfortable."

Helen has moved on to another scene. A hotel room. The hotel room where she and Marty had sex. They would finish their session late Thursday night. Helen would walk out first, take a cab to the Four Seasons, check in, and wait for him in their room. Fifteen minutes later, a knock would come. "Who is it?" went the game. "Room service," he'd answer back. "But I didn't order anything." She'd open the door, swaddled in a plush terry-cloth robe. This last time, Helen inquired about purchasing it. She billed it to Marty. One more charge her father would never know about.

Their bodies fit so well together, tight and comfortable, like the robe, like the snakes in her dreams, that she had trouble relinquishing him to the other woman. Trouble understanding that there was someone else he went home to. Someone who met him at the door, welcomed him in with a gin and tonic in one hand and a hot meal, lamb chops with mint green jelly, in the other.

She loved Marty most in this room. Here there was no pen skipping across lined paper, no sympathetic nods, no white noise machine used to drown out patients' voices, or her own as she spewed stories about her parents, about the shopping, about the bubble raft. His breathing seemed faster in the hotel, too. His actions quicker, his body language more aggressive.

Marty would leave first. He'd kiss her on the lips, then move to her forehead, and say, *Good health is invaluable.* Or *Love has no price tag.* These were things Helen should strive for, steps they were working on in therapy. After he was gone she'd shower and lounge around in the robe or she'd invite Tess over and the two would order room service and watch QVC. They'd wait till the last second, until the product had been marked down to the lowest price possible, and call to purchase the items (rhinestone bracelets, silver bangles, rolling rings in faux white gold), all charged to Marty. Sometimes they ordered a bauble for his wife and had it delivered to his home. The note would read: *For my one and only.* Marty never seemed to mind and rarely handed her the bill.

"What did Faye say when you gave her my last gift?" Helen inquired one time.

"She thought it was sweet, I guess, and mentioned I had good taste." Marty shrugged. "Who knows what she thinks. She's a simple woman who's hard to please. But that's Faye, a walking contradiction." Then he scribbled something on his legal pad.

Sometimes she bought him little things, things she felt his wife wouldn't notice: a new pen, a money clip, a key ring. During her sessions, they would talk about the gifts, why she purchased them, why she felt he was worthy of them, how it made her feel to give them to him . . . "Less hollow? More secure?" he would suggest. Helen would look away and sometimes cry. On these rare occasions, Marty would reach for the box of Kleenex resting on the small, round table and lean forward, offering it to her as if it were an engagement ring. She always refused. Instead, she'd reach into her handbag and retrieve a silk handkerchief. "I'm not going to become a 'tissue patient,'" she'd say. These were the people who came out of the office, eyes glassy, noses red. The women's makeup would be smeared, the men's faces would be blotchy. This look screamed, *My life is riddled with issues*. Not Helen. Whenever she left the crowded waiting room Marty shared with three other shrinks, the patients would look up at her, the men from their *New York Times* or *Wall Street Journal*, the women sifting through *Vogue* or the *New Yorker*, and think, *Who is that well-put-together woman? She's too chic, too pretty, to be here for herself. She must come for someone else.*

Dr. Pinter is still talking to her. "At least let me give you my pager number. Please, call anytime."

She declines his offer but asks where the funeral is, and if the family is sitting shiva.

"Yes, of course, just a moment. I'll get the address."

She already knows Marty's address, but lets this Dr. Pinter share it with her so he can feel as though he's done something. So he can think he's a good shrink.

Before he hangs up, he tells her mourning is helpful, that wanting to say good-bye is a very healthy response.

. . .

Helen skips the funeral and decides to sit shiva with Marty's wife instead. She's wanted to see the apartment for a year and walks in with a two-pound box of Godiva. It looks so pretty in the untouched gold bag that Helen doesn't want to part with it. Almost can't relinquish her hold. She feels that way about makeup too. It all looks so clean and perfect that it pains her to dab the brush into the creamy blush or run the tiny black applicator over the eye shadows. She even has trouble removing the little piece of plastic that sits gracefully on top of the makeup, protecting the colors and the mirror.

Faye greets her at the door and almost takes Helen's breath away. Marty's wife is beautiful. She's a sophisticated, handsome woman with defined features. Her blond hair is real, unlike Helen's, and her skin is flawless. She's dressed smartly in what Helen bets is this year's Valentino suit and black Jimmy Choo shoes. Her face is sallow and she moves slowly, as if her clothing is too heavy.

They shake hands.

Helen mumbles something about how insightful Marty was, that she feels lucky to have been his patient, even if it was for such a short time.

The apartment is a little dark and cluttered with furniture. Folding chairs have been placed in every available spot in the living room and study. The walls are lined with shelves of books. And at first glance, Helen thought it was wallpaper. At closer range, she realizes they are authentic. The books are real. As real as Marty's death. The couch and loveseat are done in cracked brown leather, the exact opposite of the smooth surface of Marty's black leather office chairs. Helen wishes she were sitting in one of them now. She would give anything to stare at Marty's scar, look into his eyes, and smell his faint rustic cologne.

Helen can't tell who's a patient and who's family and friends.

As far as she can count, over forty-four people have come to pay their respects. She takes a slow, thoughtful lap around the apartment and ends up sitting on the couch next to a woman close to her own age. The woman seems a little lost, as if she wants to blend in but is having trouble doing so. Helen is in midsentence when her eyes settle on several vases filled with white roses. They stand erect on the floor in a ceremonious pose. She lifts her head up and notices another vase. Or maybe it's a bowl? Why would anyone put a bowl on the mantel? That's when it hits her. Helen wills herself to stand, to take a step closer. Like the shelves of books, the house feels deceiving. Her body feels light and airy.

"Isn't it the most bizarre story you've ever heard?" asks a woman standing behind her. "Seventy percent of his bones were broken in the fall. When they pulled him out, they said his body was like a rag doll. Lifeless and flimsy."

Helen stares at the talking person next to her.

"Can you imagine? His face was unrecognizable. That's why they chose cremation."

Helen's dog, a cocker spaniel named Wilma, was cremated. Her father wanted to stuff the dog, but her mother threatened to leave him if he did. As a compromise, her mother bought a light blue urn and kept Wilma on their windowsill in the kitchen. Eventually she was brought to the family mausoleum when Helen's grandmother died three years later. Both the dog and her grandmother sit side by side, kept company by relatives Helen never met.

"Are you a friend or part of the family?"

Helen wants to hit this woman with her handbag, whirl it at her head.

"Which is it, dear?"

Helen cannot speak. She cannot breathe. Her chest is tight, her throat swollen, mouth dry. She bites down on her tongue, trying to create some saliva. Her head feels unconnected to her body. "Do you think I could have a moment alone with him?" She looks from the pasty woman to Marty.

"Of course," she says. "Certainly."

Out of the corner of her eye, Helen sees the lost-looking woman from the couch approach. The rude woman takes her arm and glides her away. "She'd like a minute or two alone. I think it's one of Marty's patients. You know, Faye invited them all . . ." The woman's voice fades. The room darkens. All Helen can see is her reflection in the urn, small and faint. She puts her hand on it. Feels the solidness, the cold sensation of brass. She whispers a little prayer, something about starting over, about giving away everything she has ever owned. All she wants to do right now is strip herself clean. Stand in front of Marty in their hotel room naked. No plush robe, no bangle bracelets or shopping bags. A second hand comes to meet the first as she lifts Marty down. She wants to see what's inside. Needs to know what's left of the man she saw for two years and fucked once a week. It's filled with beige-and-brown sand, and small, granular pieces of bone. Suddenly, Helen needs to have it, have him, more than anything she has ever needed before. More than the pricey earrings, more than the untouched creamy blush or the QVC rolling ring.

A scream comes from the kitchen, a curdling cry of realization. It's the sound of acceptance. The understanding that Marty is never coming home. Helen turns to find that most of the guests have formed a ring around someone. She spots Faye on the floor. She hears "oohs," and "shushes." Someone says, "Get her to her feet." Another suggests giving her water. A third insists space and air is what is needed.

Helen finds herself standing by the front door, fighting with the heavy knob. Marty is in her arms, her handbag is swung over her right shoulder. Her hands are wet with sweat but are as steady as a gunman's. She pulls the door open, steps forward, and closes it quietly behind her. She rings for the elevator, then, not wanting to wait, takes the stairs. She rushes down the steps like Jack running from the Giant as pieces of Marty dance inside his container. She checks behind her, half expecting to find Faye towering over her, but no one is there.

Once outside, she walks briskly, innocently, then breaks into a full run. Marty knocks softly against the brass walls, as if he is trying to say something. "Love is priceless. Love is priceless," she hears.

She runs all the way home anyway.

ADDRESSING THE DEAD

The mortician digs into his breast pocket, removes a card from the small billfold, and thrusts it at me. "Georgia's really the best," he says. He looks like Gomez from the Addams Family: thick mustache, zoot suit, big, bulgy eyes. The card feels thick in my hand. I stare at it. A makeup brush and compact are printed in the middle, *Georgia Besser: Funereal Cosmetologist* is written underneath.

He sits down at his desk, motioning me with his fingers to fill the empty seat across from him. "It's an open casket, right?" I watch him make notes on a piece of paper. "That's rather unusual for Jews, isn't it?"

This morning, two men came to take the oxygen tank, Demerol drip, and hospital bed from my mother's home, leaving me and the super standing in awkward silence until all that was left was her furniture. My parents divorced when I was nine; my father died a few years ago from a heart attack. For the past seventeen hours, I've been an orphan.

"My mother left instructions insisting on a viewing. She wasn't very religious."

He nods, makes more notes. "Anyway, Georgia's wonderful,"

he continues, as if selling me a used car. He flips through a long brown agenda book on his desk, takes his bony index finger and runs up and down the lined pages. "If you'd like to see her work, there are services here tonight at 7:00, open casket." He looks up expectantly.

"Wouldn't that be improper?" I glance around the room for a pitcher of water. "I wouldn't want to . . ."

"Nonsense." He waves a large paw at me. "It's done all the time. Besides, it's not like you can wait. Your mother's service is scheduled for Wednesday, right?"

I nod, dazed.

My friend, Maggie, accompanies me to Mrs. Goldstein's service. We sit in the back row, quietly, her hand around my arm as if trying to hold me up. When it's time to view the body, the mourners form a line in the chapel, anxious to pay their last respects.

"What do you think?" I say, a foot away from the casket.

Mrs. Goldstein's hair is a perfect layer of curly red locks which appropriately cup her face. Her cheeks are rosy and healthy. Her eyelashes are long and elegant, lids dusted lightly with gray and gold shadow, which blends together in a subtle, soft way. Maggie and I lean in closer, trying to get a better look. She smells like lilacs, and her lips are full and glossy. In fact, she looks as if she's asleep, waiting for a prince's kiss to wake her from a trance.

"She's beautiful," Maggie whispers.

All I can do is nod.

"She *has* to do my mother," I announce, once Maggie and I are outside. I say this as if applying for a job I desperately want.

"She really did amazing work," Maggie agrees.

It's cold, but the sky is light for April. We hover together, shivering, looking like twins in our conservative black skirts and jackets.

A woman is leaning up against a silver Mercedes convertible, smoking a cigarette. She looks like Elizabeth Taylor did in her forties, plump but still glamorous. "You should have seen Mrs. Goldstein when they brought her in," she calls to us, a raspy, southern twang to her voice. "She was all puffed-up and pale," she adds, making circles around her face with the hand holding the cigarette loosely between her fingers. "Poor dear, her lips were peeling and dry, her skin all cakey, and her hair was, like, brittle. I deep-conditioned it for over an hour."

She pushes her body away from the car and walks toward us. "I used an entire bottle of foundation." She's wearing a long, dark, V-necked dress and a brown velvet shawl with silver-and-gold-colored roses running through it. Her bright auburn hair is in a bun held together by gold-colored chopsticks. A few loose tresses frame her face. Sparkly diamond earrings dangle from her lobes, accentuating her neck. Her skin is smooth, like a porcelain doll with a tan, and her lips are painted a sexy blood-red. Her eyes are soft blue and seem to take you in while sizing you up all at once.

"Still, it all pays off in the end. She looked so pretty and peaceful, didn't you think?"

I look at her, watch cigarette smoke rise from her long fingers, coral and turquoise baubles on each hand. She smells like gardenia, summery and sweet.

"No one wants to look ugly, even the dead. You never know who they're going to meet in the afterlife, and if they look like shit, they'll be pissed." She laughs, then winks. "You have wonderful cheekbones," she adds, her thumb and index finger pressed gently against my chin. She twists my head from side to side.

"Truly gorgeous, but sweetheart, if you don't mind me saying, your makeup is all wrong." She flicks her cigarette; red flakes fall like specks of rain.

I look at Maggie, who arches her eyebrows.

"I could do wonders for you." She drops the remaining cigarette to the ground, stomps it out with her foot, and extends her hand. "I'm Georgia."

When I don't move, she reaches for mine and shakes it slowly. My throat goes dry. Her hand feels warm.

"This is Beth." Maggie steps in, nudging me with her elbow. "We work together in Manhattan. You did a lovely job on Mrs. Goldstein."

Georgia's blue eyes shift from Maggie back to me. She's still holding my hand, her grip more firm. "I'm so sorry, darlin'. Walter told me all about you. I lost my mama years ago from cancer, too."

I smile. Everything will be fine. This woman will make my mother look beautiful.

At night I sit in the living room in my mother's apartment, making list after list of things to do, people I need to call, arrangements I have to make. Little, purposeful check marks have been put next to deli platters, relatives' names, and the obituary section of *The Times*, who has promised to print the fifty-word blurb I've submitted. I've packed up most of her belongings. Her clothing will go to the Salvation Army. Her furniture has been tagged and is waiting, like a child, to be picked up by a parent after school. Her letters, jewelry, checkbook, passport, and photo albums are in expandable suitcases in the trunk of my car. I've flushed her bottles of medicine down the toilet, poured mouthwash, hair spray, and shampoo in the sink, tossed the empty containers in large plastic bags and hauled them to the curb for the garbage men. They sit next to shopping bags filed with her underwear, nightgowns, stained sheets and pillowcases which no one would want, not even the homeless. The refrigerator, too, has been emptied, scrubbed down, ready for the next occupant.

I found a deck of cards in the kitchen drawer; someone must have given them to my mother as a gift. They're open, but barely used, and have pictures of Impressionist paintings on them. Monet. Renoir. I fan out the stiff cards and consider playing solitaire. After I graduated from high school, my mother took me to Paris for a week. On our second night there, we couldn't sleep and played gin rummy till 3:00 A.M. The next day we found out European Pepsi had twice as much caffeine in it as ours did. When I visited, I'd always ask if she wanted to re-create our night in Paris, cards in one hand, six-pack of soda in the other. Too sick to leave her bed, gin seemed like a good a way to bond. She preferred crossword puzzles or TV, things she could do on her own.

My father was the true card player and had a poker game for over twenty years. Each Thursday night was devoted to a deck and the seven men he played with. Every two months they'd convene at our house. I adored having them over. I'd serve them soda and beer in tall glasses with hearts and spades printed on them. I'd run around handing out napkins and paper plates, happy to do the job my mother rejected. Uninterested in striking up conversation with our guests, she'd hibernate in her bedroom. The men would pat me on the head, tell my father what a wonderful helper he had. But once the game officially started, I was banned from the room. I loved hearing the laughter, the rhythmic plop of the chips being tossed into the middle of the table, which was covered in black felt so the glass top wouldn't get scratched. Loved hearing the cards being shuffled, the muffled sound of my father's friends—even the smell of cigars wafting under my bedroom door was comforting. On these evenings, I got to sleep in my parents' bed until the game ended. I'd creep into their room, find my mother reading the paper, half watching TV, and insist I couldn't sleep. "Too much noise, too many strange voices," I'd whine. "Okay, five minutes," she'd say. I'd climb into bed with her, be the first to insert myself into the cool sheets. I'd position my body at the very edge of my father's side, as far away from my mother as possible, and hold my breath, play dead. The only noises came from the turning of the paper, her breathing, and the low hum of the TV. If I lay still enough, she'd think I was sleeping. The luxury of lying next to her was worth the anxiety that at any moment she'd say my five minutes were up.

I enter the chapel and wave shyly to Gomez, who signals back. "Straight ahead. To your right there's a flight of stairs," he says. "She's just down there, working away."

The stairwell is clean and well lit. I grab the railing and listen to my shoes scuff against the cement steps.

I find Georgia sitting in a black padded chair, hunched over a coffin, humming and talking to whoever she's working on. In the background, Anne Murray is playing on a scratchy record. Georgia's fresh gardenia smell swoops over me like a quiet hush. I want to melt into the floor, curl up in the corner, and watch her work all day. I knock on the frame.

She spins around. "Welcome, sweetheart. I was just wondering where you were." She tilts her head down and peers up over the specs perched on her nose. "Come on in, put your butt in a seat. This here is Mr. Molesworth. Can I get you some coffee or a glass of iced tea?"

I step inside, take her in, marveling at the fact that I'm allowed down here. It's warm. Musty, too. A large wooden desk with a folding top is against the wall. To the left is a rug, a velvet couch, and a Victorian coffee table. A metal lamp hangs down from the ceiling over the coffin. Two grand windows, one directly above the coffin and the other above the couch, add natural lighting. An antique record player, the kind from the forties, is next to a mini refrigerator. Stacks of weathered album covers lean up against it. Bottles of liquor sit on top.

"Beth, would you be a dear and hand me the foundation called Light Coffee? It's over there in my box."

I walk to a long table toward the back of the room. Her makeup box looks like a witch doctor's kit, filled with rows of frosted containers. I search for the correct color; bottles of Chanel clink like ice in a glass as my hand touches them.

"Little magic potions," she says, reading my mind. "Only the best for the dead. Nothing looks as smooth as Chanel." I want to bottle Georgia's soothing, gravelly voice and take it home with me, listen to it at night when I can't sleep.

Trays of eye shadows, blushes, and self-tanners are off to the side. Lip gloss is stacked one on top of the other in round containers. Eyeliners and lip pencils stand in silver cans next to a large Lucite tray spilling with lipsticks and nail polish. On a shelf above the table are eight wigs on Styrofoam heads. They stand alongside bottles of hair dye, shampoos, and conditioners. Several glass jars, the kind you'd find in a penny-candy store, house cotton balls, Q-Tips, and triangle sponges which resemble tofu. A black silk case with white velvet trim is laid out on the table. It holds ten or so brushes. My hand strokes them lightly.

"I know it's a sin to wear fur, but I make an amendment for brushes. That one's for smudging, that's for the brow, and that little angled baby is for eye contour. This one cost over a hundred dollars." She holds up a long, thick brush with a Lucite handle and silver neck. "Go ahead, put your hand on that one over there." She points to the largest brush in the set. "Don't they feel great? Makes me wish I could just lay my fat, naked body on a blanket of mink. But that would be wrong." She winks and turns back to the coffin.

On another shelf are bottles of perfume in pretty containers, gold rubber hoses attached to each. "The light-colored ones are for the women," she says, patting Mr. Molesworth's face with powder. "The darker, fatter bottles have cologne. Even the dead deserve to smell good."

I bring her the bottle of foundation. Her hand touches mine as she removes it from my fingers and sets it on the table next to her. "Mr. Molesworth was the unfortunate victim of a water ski-ing accident," she says. The ski swiped most of his ear off and the tip of his nose. I watch as she reconstructs his face with putty. His ear looks almost perfect, and unless you got on top of him and put your face up to his, you couldn't tell a thing. Even his nose looks well attached.

"If I'm doing facial reconstruction, I sometimes give 'em a little lift, a better mug than what they came in with." She looks up at me from her chair, putty still in her hand. She puts the tin down, then pushes away from the coffin and rolls over to her desk.

"Tell me about your mother," she says, taking out a large notebook like the one on the mortician's desk. She writes some-thing on the top of the page with an antique pen. "I tend to do a better job if I have a good feel for who they were, what they like, dislike . . ." Her voice trails off as she waits, expectantly, writing utensil in hand.

I take a few steps closer. Her handwriting is swoopy and el-egant.

"A person's makeup and choice of color say a lot about her personality."

I don't know what to say. How do you stay loyal to yourself and your mother at the same time? "She liked fine china, but hated to cook. She said it was too messy and made a perfectly clean kitchen dirty."

Georgia stares at me, blinking.

"She played bridge," I add, choking on my words, voice cracking. "She kept shopping bags from major department stores— Sak's, Bloomingdale's, Bergdorf's—in all shapes and sizes." I look down at my fingers. I'm supposed to give the eulogy and the best I can come up with is that she had a lot of bags? "She was very private," I try again. "She loved beauty products, and always wore makeup. Her wigs were made out of the best hair money could buy. They were shipped here from a salon in Italy. When she went in for her operations, she insisted on wearing her lipstick and fake eyelashes. She drank Scotch and always wore slippers." I look around the room, shaking my head in disappointment. I take a deep breath and continue. "She loved brooches. She had drawers full. It was the most incredible collection." Two times a year, she'd clean them. There were turquoise or sapphire spiders with silver legs and tiny stones for feet, emerald frogs with onyx eyes, sets of gold beetles and diamond bumblebees, blue and orange butterflies, and birds in every color. My favorite was a silver snake with a ruby tongue. I'd sit in the next chair, observing. Pink cleaner was for gold or silver pins, solution for those with intricate design or gems. There were also two bowls of water, one warm, the other soapy. Specially treated polishing cloths sat in a folded pile. My job was to hand her the tarnished pins, one at a time. I longed to dip them into the solution, or dry them after they'd been cleaned, but my mother was afraid I'd get fingerprints on them.

"Did she work?" The fat silver fountain pen scrapes effortlessly across the page. Even the way she writes gives life to the dead.

"She was a travel agent, and stayed in the best hotels in Europe and Asia. She was always quality-testing hotels and restaurants.

Georgia perks up. "Did you ever go away with her?"

"Once." The graduation trip floods my memory for a moment.

"Is that what you do, too?"

"No. I'm a librarian at a high school."

"Oh, well, that must be lovely. There's something wonderful about books."

I nod and force a smile.

"Don't worry, sweetie. You've given me lots to go with. I feel as though I know exactly who your mother was."

Georgia rolls back over to Mr. Molesworth and picks up the putty.

"Bet you thought I'd forgotten about you, Bert."

She looks up at me. "There's beauty in the dead. Something wonderful about giving them a last gift. Something they can take with them." She beams. Rays from the sun stream in, illuminating the cave of the underworld, illuminating Georgia. "The dead who are brought here from the hospital are hardest to figure out. Poor folks have been stripped of all their character and material possessions." She sighs. "Some people have no respect," she mutters, staring off. "They toss you in and carry you out, not caring what happens to you in the interim."

She shakes her body, as if trying to lose a memory, then looks back at me. "Don't worry. She's going to look marvelous. I promise."

I move toward the door. "I was wondering if I could come back after lunch. Maybe bring you a picture of her before she got sick. She was a perfectionist, and I just want . . ."

"That'd be just fine. She'd love to know you were here."

I turn to leave.

"You never told me her name. What can I call her?"

"Marion, I guess. Calling her Mrs. Resnick sounds too proper, don't you think?"

Georgia nods. "Marion it is." Then adds, "Beth, if you'd like, after we work on your mother, I'd be happy to do you, too."

I bring a photo of my mother in her wedding gown, another of her in Italy, and a more recent shot of her wearing a wig. I bring Georgia lunch, too—a corned-beef sandwich and pickle, cream soda, and an iced tea, in case she's not a fan of soft drinks. She's already working on my mother when I get there, talking softly to her.

I knock and walk in. Georgia doesn't look up.

"Your daughter's here. A sweet thing, she is."

I watch her stroke my mother's nearly bald head, brush loose strands of hair away from her face. She's so gentle with her, as if she's known my mother for years, as if she were the most important person in Georgia's life.

"She's very pretty," she says, shaking the Chanel bottle back and forth, the color blurring from her fast movement. The bottle clinks against her rings and bangle bracelets. "I think Warm Bisque is good. It's one of my favorites. Makes me think of hot soup nourishing the soul." Georgia lifts my mother's rich, brown wig off the dummy and sprays gloss on it. I watch it disappear inside the coffin.

I take a few steps closer, see my mother lying in the red birch casket, dressed in the outfit I'd picked. She looks good in her navy suit, her favorite pin, a frog sitting on a lily pad, clipped to her lapel. I went with the deluxe model—extra padding and special ventilation system. The funeral is tomorrow. I've found a rabbi, and Gomez has taken care of the flowers, car service, and reception. I lean in, crane my neck, feeling slightly dizzy. Georgia has done a lovely job. She's put the glow back in her cheeks, and given a smooth, even finish to her skin.

"You all right, darling? Maybe watching wasn't the best idea."

Minutes later, I find myself seated in a chair, head beneath my knees, in full plane-crash position. There's a damp cloth around my neck. Georgia presents me with a cup of tea, then rests a hand on my back. The cup clanks in my grasp, hot chamomile spilling over the edges, drowning the saucer. "That was close," she says, removing the cup from my grip. She places it on the wooden stand next to me, her hand still positioned on my back. It feels warm, solid. "I haven't had anyone faint in here since Mr. Wellington died six years ago. His 100-year-old mother passed out the minute she saw the body. She's still living on Fortworth Street. Has a party every Fourth of July. It's quite a hoot."

A few days pass. Unable to return to work, I take the train to Rockville Centre and walk the ten blocks to the chapel.

Ready for my makeup lesson, I stand in her door frame, waiting to get noticed. A record is playing, though I can't make out who the singer is. Her voice is low and husky, the song, sad. Georgia is by the sink, cleaning brushes, soaking makeup sponges, and washing out glasses. I watch her rinse a bowl and flash to my mother cleaning her jewelry, her collection of pins spread along the table, a top cloth protecting the glass. I can almost smell the cleaning polish. I put my hand into my pocket and finger one of my mother's pins. A thank-you for Georgia. It's a butterfly made out of topaz.

Georgia jumps when she sees me. "Jesus." She puts a hand to

her chest. "Honey, you scared me. How long you been standing there?"

The word *forever* forms on my lips. "A few seconds—I didn't want to disturb you."

"Ready to look gorgeous?" She draws out the word *gor-rrrgeousss* and dries her hands on the cloth.

Her palm sweeps over my forehead as she pins back my hair with brown tortoiseshell barrettes. I tell her about the funeral, how lovely my mother looked, how many people came, how thankful I am to be here. I watch her run her fingers over the bottles of foundation. Like a psychic waiting for a signal from beyond the grave, she stops at one, then moves her hands two bottles over, settling on Matte Buff.

"Here we go." She shakes the bottle, twists off the top. I'm nervous, like sitting in the dentist's chair for a cleaning. I know it's not going to hurt, but it still makes me feel queasy. I look into her face, try to keep myself together. Her black lashes are long and thick, her eyes hypnotizing. She's wearing brown and purple eye shadows, Egyptian style.

She grins at me, then bends at the waist. "Ready?"

I smell her perfume, mixed with stale smoke. I flash to a summer night, visualize Georgia in her car, top down, hair down, too, smoking a cigarette and listening to Ella Fitzgerald.

She cups my chin in her hands. "I'm going to make you look beautiful," she whispers, then kisses my forehead. I want to cry. I swallow hard, half smile, and look away. I can feel my eyes water.

"You have contacts?" she asks, dipping the sponge into the foundation.

I shake my head no, too scared to open my mouth, afraid a moan will escape.

The sponge is cold against my face. It feels thick and wet. My eyes flutter and I count to twenty in order to calm down. Then I feel nothing. When I open my eyes, Georgia is frowning. The brown sponge sits in her hand, lifeless. Panic rises in my chest. I've done something wrong. Maybe I wasn't still enough.

"This is going to sound crazy . . ."

Please don't stop. Please don't say you just remembered something and that I have to go.

". . . I'm a little embarrassed to admit this. I've gotten so used to working on people lying down that I don't think this will do. Besides, it's killin' my back." She looks around the room. "Let's try the couch." She clasps her hands together, then reaches for her rolling chair. Scraping past me, she arrives at the couch before I do. She pats the worn, brown-colored cushion. "Come on."

The velvet is soft, the fabric warm from the sun. I lie down, feeling foolish.

"All right, here we go." I want to rub the side of my face against her nubby wool shawl and tell her the story of my life. Tell her not to leave me. Ask her to just hold me for just a few minutes, long enough to pretend I'm not alone.

"This isn't working. I'm sorry, darlin'. You're just too low."

My chest tightens, heart pounds.

She turns her head toward the coffin. "Would you mind? Old habits die hard."

I walk hazily to the casket, the sound of Georgia's squeaking chair trailing behind me. The room looks wrong, fuzzy and out of focus.

"Go ahead, crank her open."

I place a hand on the top, feel the cool, glossy lacquered wood as I raise the frame open. I step out of my shoes, move them with my foot off to the side, making sure they're neatly aligned. Georgia holds my arm and helps me in as I hoist one foot off the ground and swing it into the padded cream lining. Another hand is placed firmly on the lower frame and I hop on my right foot a few times before lifting myself into the large box. I slide my legs in, think of a magician sawing the assistant in half. The coffin smells of cedar and is surprisingly cozy with its padded silk interior, cushioned bottom. The small, confined space feels comforting somehow.

"This is for Mrs. Donavan. She's coming in a few hours." Georgia shakes her head from side to side, bites down on her lower lip. "Terrible, terrible tragedy." She reaches for her glass of iced tea. She sips daintily through a straw, leaving an imprint of bright red lipstick behind. "Only forty-one. This is one of the more expensive coffins. You're lying in an $11,000 mobile home."

My eyes feel heavy. Another record drops down from the holder and onto the player. Patsy Cline's low, aching voice drifts through me. "*Crazy, I'm crazy for feeling so lonely . . .* "

"Sometimes I take a nap in them if I don't have another client coming for a few hours." She reaches for her pack of Parliaments. "You don't mind, do you? I never smoke when I'm working, but I *so* need one." She slips one out from the case and puts it in her mouth. I hear the click of her lighter, see the red tip of the cigarette glow. "Once I fell asleep here over the weekend. I had a wretched cold and took too much Nyquil. I got dizzy, and next thing I know, it's Monday morning and crotchety old Walter is shaking me awake. When I looked up at him, he was really pale. For a moment, I thought, shit, one of my clients is coming back for touch-ups." She laughs, blowing smoke rings away from my face.

Crazy floats in the background. I feel sleepy. A brush sweeps lightly across my right cheek, soft as chick fur. In the sixth grade we hatched a chicken in an incubator. Each of us got to hold it for a few minutes. I lay motionless, as I did years ago in my father's bed, afraid to breathe, afraid Georgia will stop working on me. I think about my father in the hospital, the way he looked before he died. I think of my mother lying in the ground, her body cold, her soul lonely.

Georgia runs a thumb back and forth over my forehead. "Ssshhhh," I hear her saying, "it's okay. It's okay." Her voice is like a lullaby, soft and soothing, like the blush brush skimming over my face. I'm not sure why she's calming me. "Try not to cry, honey. The makeup will stain the lining." Her voice has a caring, teasing quality.

I do what I'm told.

I lie as quietly as possible and pretend that I'm dead.

Post-dated

Go with the optimistic outlook of a woman awaiting execution.

Practice your best flirtatious smile in the bathroom mirror of the restaurant as you talk yourself into believing that this could be the one—the ambitious, caring, honest, funny, wonderful guy you've been looking for. Smile to yourself as you think you will have the best marriage of all your friends. That waiting has its own rewards. When all your girlfriends are getting a divorce, they will be the ones calling you at midnight, crying to your husband as they apologize for phoning so late. Your groggy spouse will whisper supporting words to your women friends before handing you the receiver: "You're better off," "He's doing you a favor," "You deserve to be happy . . ." When you get on the phone, it will be your friends who say, "What a great guy he is." "Gee, who would have thought." You will smile at the irony as you listen to them sob.

Check your watch and mentally kick yourself for having gotten here so early. Perhaps you should have let him pick you up. Wonder if this makes you look anxious and easy. Why *did* you agree to meet this person who, you are told, is everything you could possibly want in a man? If he's so great, why then, at thirty-six, is he still single? Ask the same question of yourself.

Despite your reluctance, you really do want to share your life with someone. You honestly love the idea of having both your voices on the machine, reading the *Times* in bed, brunching on Sundays with other couples, and becoming a Norman Rockwell painting—though at this point you'd settle for Andy Warhol.

Think about your sister, the married one, as your mother puts it when she describes both of you to other people. Her husband's a lawyer. A successful one who works at a big firm. Your sister doesn't know he made a pass at you last year at Thanksgiving. She is unaware that you were not the first. That he takes long business trips. That he cheats often. Several months ago, you saw him with another woman at a restaurant. He pretended to ignore you when you passed by, only to accost you in the restroom later, begging you not to tell.

Hate the way you always feel like a third wheel the moment friends say there's no room in the car for you. If you were with someone, that would never happen. Admit to yourself how your heart sinks a little when your girlfriends enter, hands clasped to their husbands, voices melding into each other. While applying mascara to your blue eyes, remember how terrible you felt last month while dining with your old college roommate and her spouse. When the check arrived, he asked you for one-third of the bill. Your girlfriend sipped coffee as you both watched him take your cash and replace it with his gold card. Wonder who you will go to parties with—if you are, for that matter, invited to any. Dread the holidays, all holidays, even ones you don't celebrate, like Kwanzaa. Perhaps tonight's date will end all this.

Start to have doubts as you stand under the fluorescent light, your makeup sprawled across the marble top. Ask yourself what the problem could be. You're a good conversationalist. You talk to both your parents, buy American-made products, and hold down a good job. Your teeth are relatively white and not crooked. Your hair, a rich brown, is clean and bouncy. Your skin is clear. Consider the fact that your friends might be right—perhaps your expectations are too high. Dismiss this thought by insisting you are worth more. Much more. You deserve the best. Talk yourself into believing this by claiming your married friends were just lucky. Hit the soap dispenser until the last drop of pink goo comes dripping out, just enough to wash your hands with while you contemplate whether everyone meets their husbands in college. Maybe you, too, should have majored in an "M-R-S Degree" instead of anthropology.

Do a final study in the mirror. Remember some hurtful remark your mother made years ago, *Guys hate women with stiff hair*, as you add more spray to your already coiffed do. Think about your parents' relationship and realize you'd rather spend an eternity living alone than living like them. Wonder if one really can break a cycle.

Move out from the bathroom into the bar area, wondering if this date will let you order an appetizer or if he will make you pay for half the bill or if he'll talk about his ex all night while picking his teeth with the edge of the Sweet 'n Low packet during coffee.

Once in the bar section, survey the crowd and search for your blind date. When no one else looks as if they, too, are trying to look like they're meeting someone, play the "I'd-go-out-with-you" game with the other patrons. Make eye contact with a handsome man sitting on the third stool, then make eye contact with his girlfriend. Take two steps away from the couple.

Order a drink. Take one long sip. Feel the coolness go down your throat. Feel hungry. Think of how many lonely people there are in the world. Compare yourself to your neighbor who lives on the fifteenth floor. The one who smokes in the elevator, shuffles around the lobby in her slippers and housecoat with holes made by cigarettes, looking like an older, uglier version of Bette Davis before she died. Insist that will never happen to you. You are better off. You are out, standing next to pretty people and men in expensive suits, drinking white wine, waiting for the man who will change your world. Your life is full. Yes, full indeed.

Glance at an open menu by the bar. First scan it to see what appeals to you. When you see nothing, read it more slowly. Cautiously. When your eyes rest on the lobster ravioli in a thick cream sauce, force yourself to jump down to "Fish." Brain food. Food that looks good on your plate. Decide to order the sole. Not the Dover sole, since it's the most expensive, but the Boston sole. He will be impressed. He will think, *You are a sensible orderer.* He will share this information with his mother when he recaps the evening. She in turn will tell yours, who will repeat it to her friends. Her friends will think your mother has done a swell job raising you. After all, you knew to order something expensive, but not too expensive. This will end up on the ten o'clock news. People will call and congratulate you. Others will e-mail or write little notes on cards that appear in the mail for free, each asking for advice on dining and dating. This could change your profession. You could stay home, raise the children, work part-time—all because you ordered sole and not something fatty and rich like you actually wanted.

Look at your watch again. Mr. Blind Date is 9.5 minutes late. Eye the door. Sigh.

Late-Man finally enters the restaurant, looking disheveled, in jeans and no tie. Observe that he is the only one dressed in casual wear. Try not to appear disappointed that he looks more like Mel Brooks than Mel Gibson. Shake hands. Overlook the fact that his handshake is like a dead fish, clammy and warm. Look to see if his fingernails are dirty. This will decide your future. Visualize yourself doing endless loads of laundry, beer cans strewn around the plush mint-green living room carpet bought on sale at Sears, while you make three different meals for your very picky children, Sally, Cindy, and Jared, who is allergic to peanuts, a genetic gift from your mother-in-law. His nails, thank God, are clean. Breathe a sigh of relief until you realize there is clear polish on them.

Richard looks nervously around the restaurant as he tells the hostess he'd prefer to sit away from the window. Stare at him oddly. Follow the hostess to the middle of the room. Watch her lay down the menus. You and Richard sit down at the same time. You both smile at this. Make a mental note that he has nice eyes, soft and blue.

Appear interested as he tells you the story of his life. Every now and then, frown or furrow your brow. When he asks if you hate blind dates as much as he, say something witty like, "Blind dates are a level of hell Dante forgot to include in the *Inferno*." He will laugh. When he does, he reminds you of a blue-eyed Pinocchio turning into a donkey.

The waiter finally appears. You used to order just an entree and a diet soda, thinking a man will appreciate a cheap date. But then you heard through a friend last year that your date interpreted your diet drink as a "person who wasn't interested in having a good time." Now you order an appetizer, entree, wine, and coffee. If your date is really irritating, you tack on dessert.

Tonight, order mixed greens, the good-girl sole, and another white wine. You have learned most dates look and sound better blurry. Besides, he's already told you he has a large portfolio. Wonder if that's the only thing of his that's large.

Look around the room at other couples, all of whom appear as though they are able to have relationships. Pick out the dates from the married ones. The table of four couples is having a wonderful time. There is laughter and bottles of wine, and hugging and slapping of hands, and girlfriends leaning over chairs, whispering into each other's ears. Feel a stab of longing. Disregard it as you look back at Richard, who smiles and lifts an eyebrow.

He orders the lobster pasta you wanted. "Wow," he says when the waiter walks away. "Fish is really sensible. Wish I could stick to that, but hey, you only live once."

The conversation is flat, dull, and tasteless, similar to your fish. He quotes stocks, not Dorothy Parker. He tells you about his last relationship, which ended eight months ago, that his brother had a nervous breakdown last year, but his family doesn't discuss it, and that he just bought a boat.

When he takes a massive forkful of his meal, he bites down on the silver. This sounds like a nail scraping against your bones. He downs his gin and tonic, holds his glass up to his ear and shakes it loudly for the waiter and the three couples at the surrounding tables to hear. You want to kill the man sitting across from you, the man with the large portfolio, the fattening food, the good job.

Then something happens. As he tells you a story about his golden retriever, Lox, his whole face changes. Love and affection spread across it like a rippling wave.

"He was born with one eye. I used to tell people he was winking at them."

Perhaps you were too quick to judge. Maybe he's apprehensive or insecure about being on a date. Perhaps there is a good man underneath all his pretentiousness. Catch something soft in his eyes as he removes a photo of Lox from his leather wallet.

"I had him since he was two months old. I put him down last summer." For a moment, you think you see a tear. Remember the clear polish. Wonder if he's gay. Practice Richard's last name until it flows easily from your mouth. Then insert your first name with his last. Realize that Loretta Stein sounds like an aging soap opera star rather than a museum curator. Say *That's my husband by the onion dip* quietly, as you watch Richard eat. Say *husband* over and over until the word no longer makes you anxious.

During dinner, his cell phone rings. Try not to act irritated or surprised when he answers it, his mouth full of creamy pasta. "Hello?" He looks around nervously, his eyes eventually settle back on you. "Can't, I'm on a date." He laughs. Then his face turns angry. "I said I'd fix it." Pause. "Well, they'll have to wait." Pause. "Not sure yet—think the jury's still out on that one." He laughs again, as if he's trying to look more important then he really is. "Six, six and a half. Got to go. Bye." He hangs up and explains, "That was a friend who wanted a stock price." Make a mental note he is a liar. Feel like a sucker for falling for the dog story.

Dishes are cleared, the tablecloth cleaned. You have a cappuccino with skim milk. Fat-Boy orders port and chocolate mud cake smothered in raspberry sauce, which matches the color of your lipstick. He invites you to sail with him. Decline politely, explaining that you get violently seasick, which is how you feel now.

He asks to walk you home. Then asks to use your bathroom. Figure he's already in your apartment, he might as well stay. Despite his boring conversation, his insipid comments, and pathetic demeanor, he is a good kisser. Gentle and breathy. You are surprised by this, by how nice it is to feel something.

Roll over and look at the stranger lying next to you. In the morning light he looks worse than you remember. In fact, he looks like your father—a younger, shorter version. Feel empty. Try not to cry. Do not offer to make him breakfast or coffee. Sigh heavily. See if this prompts some change. When he doesn't move, sigh again. If this fails, pretend you just remembered you have a 9:00 A.M. Pilates class and if you cancel, your gym will revoke your membership. Tell him it's imperative that you go. Tell him your girlfriend, Heather, is waiting for you. Continue your fabrication, explaining that she is holding your spot by the window and if you don't show she will stop speaking to you.

Eventually, he leaves.

Change the sheets.

Strip the bed.

Spray Lysol.

Shower.

Come out of the bathroom, notice your answering machine light is blinking. Instinctively know that it is your mother. Do not play the message.

When Fat-Boy-Bad-Blind-Date-Man calls the next day, say you are on the other line. Tell him you will call him back. Don't.

When your blind-date outfit returns from the cleaners, rayon black pants, matching black jacket, and lilac silk shirt, bury it in the back of your closet. Tell people you have met someone special so they'll stop offering to fix you up.

Another Saturday rolls around. Ask your friend what her plans are while you look through a pile of stained take-out menus. Refuse to feel left out when she replies that she and her boyfriend and two other couples are having dinner at Lotus. Think about asking if you can join. When she doesn't offer to change the reservation from six to seven, hang up. Repeat the story to your mother, who asks you, "Wouldn't you feel uncomfortable sitting there anyway?"

Proceed immediately to the kitchen. Eat something. Anything. Realize shopping for one sucks as your eyes rest on a large bar of Cadbury chocolate.

The next day you are on the subway, sitting too close to a man who keeps smelling you. His big head is tilted in your direction and it looks as if he's trying to place your scent. In order to avoid any further contact, try to look preoccupied by staring at other passengers. Opposite you, an old lady is reading *The New York Post*. Written in an overly simplistic black headline is, *Man Found Dead While Still On Cell Phone*. Fall out of your seat. Wasn't this the person you were just out with? The Good-Kisser-Stiff-Drinker-Late-Date-Man your mother fixed you up with?

Ask the owner of the paper, an unattractive woman who looks as if she's part of a traveling circus, if she would be kind enough to let you see the article. Offer to buy her paper at twice the newsstand price. When she looks at you as if you were demented, relay the whole story. She stares at you blankly, and taking pity, eventually tears out the page. Not the whole page because she is still reading the back of it—the *Styles* page, and whoever wore a see-through ball gown to the VH1 Awards is more important than seeing if you almost dated a felon, gambler, or drug dealer.

Look at the picture. Blind-Date-Boy's bloody face and body is smashed up against the cement steps of his town house. His cell phone rests near his cracked skull. The photo is not flattering—not that many people look better dead than alive—but he looks more bloated than you remembered. From the photo, it's hard to assess if he had a heart attack, which caused him to fall and thus hit his head on the steps, or if he was pushed. Regardless of how he died, you still expect to feel something, something for this man whom you saw two weeks ago, whom you watched eat poorly, drink too much, and whose extra, unused condom still resides in your nightstand.

Skim the article for details and to see if your name is mentioned—not that you think it would be. You haven't spoken to him since that morning in your bed. But you never know. He may have told a neighbor or best friend about your date.

Think now that you can no longer have him, that maybe he was the one. You did have that one moment in the restaurant . . . Maybe he's just not good on fix-ups? Now you'll never know. Now there'll be no second date, no second chance at a possible wonderful life with a possible Mr. Right.

Feel cheated. Perhaps you could have fallen in love on the second date, fallen for his family, his mother and father becoming surrogate parents—better, more supportive than your own. His brother, the one who had the nervous breakdown that no one talks about, could have become like a brother to you. You could have taken family vacations to Florida, Puerto Rico, the Bahamas.

Wonder if he really was that bad. Your vision at 4:00 A.M. that night was cloudy and the Xanax you took made you feel swirly and dizzy. Maybe you could have changed him into the man you wanted him to be. How crucial are manners? These things can be taught. Armani suits bought, hair fixed—he did say he loved his dog. He could be capable of the important things— love, comfort, kindness. Perhaps your list is too long, maybe you've seen one-too-many romance movies. That thing about refusing to settle, all the blah, blah, blah of wanting the perfect relationship, is overrated. You don't know anyone with a perfect marriage, or a good marriage, or even a decent marriage. And what good is a list on New Year's Eve or Valentine's Day, or on Saturday nights which spin into lonely Sundays with nothing but the overwhelming *Times* and reruns of *Austin Powers* on HBO to keep you company? What does one's ability to quote Dorothy Parker imply anyway? What does love really mean if your soul mate, your only Mr. Right, was found dead, facedown, covered in his own blood on the cement steps of his town house? You didn't even get a chance to see how his home was decorated.

Pretend Richard (now that he's dead, you've decided not to

call him Dick, out of respect) is still alive and allow yourself to fantasize. See yourself moving Mission furniture bought at Bloomingdale's into his home while the Salvation Army removes chipped Ikea and an old futon from his bedroom. See dinners with his friends and yours, lounging in your large living room, playing Celebrity. Visualize filling out the registry at Bloomingdale's, laughing as you both get confused with the computer. Think of all the exercise you could have gotten from walking up and down those steps, the great condition your thighs would have been in for the coming summer. Now it's all over. Done.

Envision the funeral. Think of how uncomfortable it would have been. To have to stand at the service saying, "Thanks for coming" to strangers, sandwiched in between his mother on your left, his father on your right, the nervous-breakdown brother off to the side somewhere muttering to himself, while you receive compassionate nods from drawn faces. "How sad." "How did you meet?" "Were you going to set a date?" Then you'd have had to recap the entire evening and your relationship to these well-meaning strangers whose only connection to you is a man you're not sure you even liked.

What if you had married him? Think of all the gifts needing to be returned, water pitchers and glassware from Tiffany's, cake platters and silver from the Pottery Barn. What about the cash you would have received from family and friends? Surely they'd expect you to give it back. And you and Richard would have already spent it on your honeymoon trip to Hawaii.

Realize you'd be a widow, a widow in your late thirties. A new box to check, a new way people would look at you, their gaze at your forehead or chin rather than at your eyes. You'd be the new whisper at all the clubs, your mother's friends would be overly supportive, their heads shaking sadly from side to side. *So young. What a shame.*

Picture yourself at 12-step meetings with other newly widowed women. Laugh at the irony. That after a lifetime of being single and trying so hard to find the perfect person, or at least settling for someone nearly perfect, you, once again, would be single.

At 5:23 A.M. the next day, have a revelation. What if he was in the Mafia? He didn't want to sit near the window—perhaps he was afraid of being shot. This could have been your life, looking for shooters in restaurants, married to a man whom you never really loved, with shifty business relationships and illegal transactions. Who knows what the hell he did once he was at sea on his boat, probably bought with laundered money from loan sharks or drug dealers or who knows what. The paper said *accident,* but isn't that a term tossed around merely to hide the truth? And who has a heart attack at thirty-six, then falls just so, cracking his head against the step? This all seems a little too fishy to you. Wasn't his father a cop or something? Now it's all becoming clear, forming in your mind like thick icicles dangling from the rooftop of a farmhouse.

Comprehend the fact that one good dog moment is not worth a lifetime of misery. You are worth more. You don't need to sell out. You have plenty of time to meet Mr. Right. Pace in your bedroom, excitedly making lists of places where you could meet men, singles parties you wouldn't be embarrassed to be seen at. There are book clubs to join. Exercise classes to take and charity functions to attend.

Hope returns. God has spared you. Not only is Stiff-Drinker-Good-Kisser-Illegal-Transaction-Blind-Date-Man out of your life, you never have to worry about running into him with his new fiancée, or having him pass you in the street with his co-workers only to hear him mutter as you pass by, still in earshot, *She was a great fuck but what a bitch.* Realize death has done you a favor. Yes, death has saved you from a life of anguish and woe.

VERSIONS OF YOU

At work, Shannon stared longingly at Lilly, the stick-thin, twenty-six-year-old Asian legal assistant. She observed Lilly's slick, almost rehearsed movements as she swiveled in the chair, cradled the receiver against her skinny neck, and fingered a paper clip.

Every day, Lilly donned the same outfit: V-necked sweaters which fell off her left shoulder, revealing skimpy, sleeveless Lycra dresses underneath. The only subtle changes were in tones and material, all of which came in shades of grays, tans, and blacks.

Shannon watched intensely, wondering how long it would take this woman—a girl, really—who sat across from her at work to have a nervous breakdown. The signs were clearly there. The all-night smoking sessions, the diet consisting of Marlboros and Coca-Cola, and the juggling of two jobs—the one she had here and the one her social calendar dictated.

She checked her messages at home while she watched six co-workers gather around the coffee machine, sharing stories of courtroom dramas, client tantrums, and lavish business lunches with celebrities in chic SoHo restaurants. As sugar got passed around hand to hand, like a game of telephone, the story changing slightly with each person, and laughter melded into one sound, she felt more and more alone.

There were no messages for her. Just her own voice telling her no one was there. She was tempted to say something so the light would be blinking when she walked in.

It was almost four when she logged off the Internet. The office was still a whirl of hectic interaction and she wished everyone would settle down.

At 4:00 P.M. exactly, the bells from St. Patrick's Cathedral began to chime, their booming gongs sounding like a mournful chorus. Though the office rarely did anything as a group, Shannon pictured everyone taking a moment of silence—the phones could be put on mute and a machine would record incoming messages, people would not be allowed to walk around, eat or drink, or be on the computer. Her co-workers, poised at their desks, would bow their heads, hands clasped in front of them, while others would stare out in a dreamy, meditative state, as if allowing the music to engulf them. But these were unrealistic wishes. If only she could blink them to freeze like Samantha did on *Bewitched*. Then she'd be able to enjoy her moment.

On most days she would get up a moment or two ahead of time and stand alone by the large windows and stare at the magnificent church across the street, their Fifth Avenue view completely unobstructed. She would hold her breath, close her eyes, and listen to the saintly, overpowering music. If she placed her hands on the glass, she could feel the vibration, the power.

Some days she remained in her seat and just watched the office function without her help. She'd sit and watch Lilly as she talked on the phone, voice yelling over the bells.

As far back as she could remember, her mother had never instilled any religious values in her. But Shannon took comfort in knowing, or at least hoping, there was a God. A large, omnipresent father figure watching over her. This was her gift back. Perhaps the better person she was, the better her life would get. She tried going to church, even attempted to join the choir, but she had a terrible voice and couldn't carry a tune. She was going to mouth her way through the musical numbers until she found out there were auditions.

At home, she switched on the radio, more for the background noise than the show, fed Mr. Chips, and opened a bottle of cheap wine. The living room was banal. The whole place was. No matter how many magazine articles she read, all promising a metamorphosis of sorts if only she did this, or adjusted that, added more yellow, opened up the room here and moved the sofa there, nothing had worked.

She was in the middle of eating a tuna sandwich and watching *Wheel of Fortune* when the knock came at her door. The word was *Oklahoma City*, and she'd solved the puzzle before any of the contestants.

"Evening, miss. Sorry to bother you." He tilted his hat, bent his out-of-shape body forward, and grimaced as he strained back up. The man looked tired and near faint. His disheveled hair, slumped shoulders, and fat tie smattered with coffee stains reminded her, somehow, of her father.

It was just past 7:45 when she offered him water, which he readily accepted. His hand shook as his callused fingers and nails, thick with dirt, clenched the old Bugs Bunny jelly jar. He looked at it and smiled, his yellowed teeth reflecting off the clear glass.

He had been out all day in the heat without making a single sale. "You're my last hope," he told her, still standing outside on her porch. She wasn't sure if this was a line or not. Salesmen would say anything to a potential customer; she knew this first hand. Her father had been a salesman, too. *Girls ain't cut out for selling*, he told her. *No daughter of mine is gonna sell nothing.*

She was five when he left. Two when he broke her heart. Three months when he last held her. She couldn't remember his first or last name. The only recollections she had were of her mother calling him *honey*, or *your father*. Later he became *that asshole* and Shannon was forbidden to bring him up. He was never mentioned. Her mother even changed her name from Sarah to Shannon, insisting it was important for her daughter to start life over, then insisted she take her mother's maiden name. The pictures were removed; the articles of clothing he had left behind—ratty suits and bowling shirts—were tossed outside to rot. Eventually they were picked up with the rest of the trash, vanishing like him. But unlike her father, she believed this man— this man with the matted hair, the worn shoes, the gray wool pants whose hem had been lengthened too many times.

Without thinking, she invited him in, eager for the company.

She watched him take out the book, the letters "KL" embossed in gold.

"A combination of two letters comes every week. You pay in installments. If you're not satisfied after you've received all twelve, you can send 'em back for a full refund." He smiled like a game show host, an older, uglier version of Pat Sajak trying to make the parting gifts look better than they really were. A bead of sweat formed at his brow. She watched as it gathered momentum and made its way down his face. He wiped at it with the back of his hand and continued his sell.

She wanted to help him, but what would she do with a new set of encyclopedias? She had no children, no one to give the leather-bound books to as a gift. The print was too small for her mother to read so donating them to the nursing home wouldn't do her mother any good. Those ladies prefer playing cards and score pads, *TV Guide*, and crossword puzzles.

He laid the large book down heavily on her wooden coffee table. "Well, what'd ya think, miss?" he asked.

"I'm sorry," Shannon said, searching for words, "I just don't have the need for them. But they're lovely. Really."

He put the book back in his bag, sighed loudly, locked the old case, and stared out into the room. When he showed no intention of leaving, she cleared her throat and stood. Moving slowly, he gathered the rest of his things and hoisted himself out of her peach-colored chair.

They walked to her door in silence; he thanked her for her kindness and hospitality. She watched as he climbed into his lime green 1974 Chevy, started the old car, and pulled away. She lingered for a moment, staring at the trail his suitcase had made in the dirt.

He had left his card on her table. The paper was thin. Cheap card stock. The words had faded and were cracked. The first name was easier to decipher. It started with a B and seemed rather long. Benjamin? Bartholomew? His last name was a challenge. Most of the word had been worn away. All that was left were bits and pieces of letters, none of which formed a single, readable consonant or vowel. The title, however, was mostly intact. *Books and Nooks, salesman, 516-997-6564.* She left the card on the table.

The answer came to her at 4:00 that morning. It was as if God himself had awakened her out of a deep sleep with the word "Lilly" running through her head. She would call this Benjamin/Bartholomew the Salesman first thing in the morning. This would be her good deed. A good deed for two people. She could barely contain her excitement. She did deep breathing exercises like the ones she'd seen on TV talk shows to calm herself down and fall back asleep.

The card was sitting exactly where she had left it: it looked worse in the morning light, as if an elf had come and removed more letters in the middle of the night. She dialed the number, expecting to get a machine, too early for the old man to be up.

"Hello?" The voice sounded tired, like a moan.

"Is this Mr . . . um, is this Ben? She guessed.

"Speaking."

"You visited my home the other day."

"I visit many homes, miss."

"I gave you some water?"

"A Bugs Bunny glass. Yes, I remember. What can I do you for?"

"I've decided to buy the encyclopedias. I have a friend at work who would love them."

"Well, this must be my lucky day." There was a trill in his voice, an excitement, and she could hear he was smiling. She hung up and hugged herself, her large arms squeezing her body as if to knock some enthusiasm out.

She heard Lilly's edgy voice before she actually saw her. Lilly was always in a crisis. She either lost her keys, had been taken advantage of by a man she met in a bar, or something wasn't working out the way she wanted.

Shannon ran up to Lilly the second her fatigued face appeared.

"Hi," she said, bouncing in front of her.

Lilly was still wearing yesterday's clothing, a black silk dress and sweater, which was draped over her bare shoulders. She reeked of smoke and liquor.

"I have a surprise for you." The words fell out of her mouth.

"You do?"

Shannon nodded. "Yes, but it won't be here until Friday—I ordered it for you."

Lilly crinkled up her nose in confusion, then smiled. "Whatever. Thanks, I guess." She moved past Shannon to her desk where she immediately picked up the phone, turning her back to the rest of the office.

This would work, Shannon thought. This would be her ticket in. She envisioned Lilly sitting at her desk, Shannon presenting the large book to her. Lilly would shout gleeful sounds of excitement and wrap her skinny arms around Shannon. Then tears would well up in her eyes as she thanked her profusely.

The transition from co-workers to friends would happen naturally, easily. She pictured the two or them eating lunch, Lilly waiting for her by the elevator or the main reception area.

"Thai?"

"Sure," Shannon would answer. And the two would nod, smile as if they had shared a secret, and off they'd go.

She visualized Lilly introducing her to her swanky friends, taking her to exclusive underground bars that played funky music and served drinks in frosted colored glasses. They would go shopping together, Lilly helping her find clothing that hugged her body in all the appropriate places. She saw herself in cable knits, sweater sets, silk shirts to help hide her fat body. She would even join a gym. Lilly's gym. The two would be inseparable.

She waited nervously in her car outside the diner. Ben had called her machine saying the book was in and could they meet for a quick second at the restaurant by the train, since it would be more convenient for him. His day was jam-packed and he would be going in the opposite direction to drop off two thousand napkins with witches, ghosts, and pumpkins for someone's Halloween party.

In preparation, she had put on her best dress. It fit snugly over her middle. She brought her stash of eye shadows and lipsticks: turquoise, purples, reds sold to her by saccharine salesladies who swore these were her perfect colors. She wanted to look her best, wanted him to see her at her premium.

She sat listening to oldies but goodies, applying mascara, looking as if she were going on a date. A date? What a joke. The only man to ask her out in the past five years was the cable guy who came to upgrade her system. He had offered her free *TV Guide*, a small attempt to sway her into having dinner. A perk, he said. "I'm a fella with connections." Then he had laughed. "Do you get it? Connections." She had smiled politely as he ran wire up her wall. "Something sure smells good," he said as he tested the set. But she was only boiling water for macaroni and cheese.

She studied her face in the rearview mirror. She looked like a fat china doll with too much blush and harsh lipstick. No matter what she did to improve her looks, she would always be the fat girl no one wanted to play with, the fat girl who had no father.

Ben had said 6:30. Shannon checked her watch: 7:05. She sipped Diet Coke and waited in the diner by the window, not knowing what else to do.

It didn't matter—she was used to waiting. As a child she would wait by the screen door, anxious for her father to return from his long day. Before he had a chance to get out of the car, she would run up to him, eager to carry his heavy suitcase filled with useless items everyone was supposed to need in their lives: corn on the cob skewers in the shape of crosses with Jesus glued on them, a toenail clipper/cigar cutter, flower-scented vacuum bags with pictures of Elvis's face on them. Too heavy for her, his old tan suitcase would scrape along the dirt road back to their house, leaving a path behind them.

Her father was often late for dinner. *Let's give him five more minutes, okay?* her mother would say. But five minutes turned into ten and ten turned into twenty. By then the food was overcooked, dry, and cold, salad wilted, mashed potatoes thick and turning yellow. Eventually hunger would prevail and she and her mother would eat.

Hours later, she would watch her father inhale his reheated dinner on an old metal tray while he watched Jack Benny and Milton Berle on their black-and-white TV. She would sit on the opposite side of the couch, her small body scrunched up against plastic pillows and cushions. Fearful of disturbing him, she'd hold her breath and make believe she was paralyzed, praying he would talk to her, tell her about his day, ask about hers. *What'd ya do in school?* Without answering, she would leap off of the couch and come running back with a picture she made and proudly stand before him, waiting for his approval. He'd turn off the TV, put down his fork, and take the picture from her hands. *My, ain't this here fine. You're a real art-iste.* This never happened.

She'd give Ben five more minutes. Besides, she had already told Lilly a surprise awaited.

Ben's car finally pulled up. She watched him get out, watched him open the car door, put his feet on the cement, and wipe his face with a dirty handkerchief. With one hand on the top of the door frame and the other on the seat, he raised himself out. Once standing, he reached into the car and retrieved a large brown package. Memories of her as a young child appeared like balloons popping fast and loud: him yelling at her for not being quiet during his TV time; her blowing out candles with only her mother and her aunt to wish her a happy birthday; her father's body underneath the covers as he slept, the sun shining brightly into his room. She sat staring out the diner window, looking at Ben, feeling as though she couldn't breathe.

She waved as he entered. When he caught sight of her, he smiled and nodded his head, unzipped his tan jacket, and took off his hat. He eased himself into the padded bench, his face wet with sweat. Shannon looked at their reflection in the window: they looked so similar in shape, two weebles wedged into a booth.

"Sorry I'm late. Car trouble. Then I had to drop off an order. Salesman's job is never done." He slid the package to her, as if he had smuggled drugs.

"Here ya go. A/B." He called for the waitress. "Cup of coffee, please," he said to her. Then added, "She's a real pretty one." At first, Shannon thought Ben was talking about her to the waitress, then realized he meant the book.

Shannon pushed it aside.

"Don't you want to see it?"

"It's for a friend."

"Oh," he said. His eyes were soft.

She had an urge to hold his hand, ask him who he was.

He reached for a fistful of Sweet 'n Low and shoved them in his pocket. He took a wad of napkins and added them to his stash. She thought he was going to take the salt and pepper shakers, too, if she hadn't been sitting there. Maybe sell them to would-be customers, pitching them as authentic diner items. *It's very fashionable and hip*, he'd tell bewildered housewives and frenzied men with crying children in their arms.

He glanced up. "Anything on the table is fair game. Besides, they expect it. That's why it's out here." He grinned as packets of sugar fell out from his hands.

She was comforted by his familiar looks, the smell of his hard effort, the kind of life he led. She had resurrected her father's face so many times—midnight when she couldn't sleep, on the train, at the supermarket standing on line—that she couldn't remember what was real and what was a feature she'd created so he'd look more handsome.

She should have brought her mother down from the nursing home. See if there was a spark of recognition. But her mother lived in two places, half this world, half another. She would never be sure if her mother truly thought this man was her father or if she was just answering "yes" through her medicated haze.

"How long have you been a salesman?" she asked.

"My whole life."

"Have you lived here long?"

"Moved around from town to town."

"Your wife must be proud that you're still . . ."

"Ain't married."

Did that mean ever or just no longer. "Do you have family here?"

He looked up at her, his pudgy hand in mid-reach for Equal packets. "You're full of questions."

"Sorry. I just wanted . . . I mean, I was hoping . . ." Not knowing what else to say, she sucked on her straw and made a sharp, hissing noise.

"No, I understand. You want to know who you're buying from. Lots of folks feel better buying from someone they know. But a pretty thing like you should have no trouble finding someone to talk to." While she watched him take another fistful of napkins and shove them in his coat, something inside her cracked open.

The waitress came by and slipped the bill on their table. The thin, green paper with the words *Thank you for your patronage*, printed lightly on the top, lay facedown. Shannon wanted to see if he'd reach for it first. *Pick up the check*, she tried to tell him mentally. Her father had never taken her out. Never showed her off to anyone, never bought her a soda or candy, never wiped a malted milk mustache off her lip.

"So, check or cash?"

"What?"

"The book," he said, pointing. "How do you want to pay?"

Shannon removed forty dollars from her bag, laid it out on the table as he took out a dollar.

"Thank you, miss. This should cover the coffee. Glad we could meet. This sure saved me a bunch of time." He gathered himself, slid out from the booth, and started to leave. "Oh," he said turning back, "your next one should be in on Tuesday. Could we meet here?"

She nodded.

"Alrighty, then. Same bat time, same bat station." He laughed and walked away.

Shannon fingered the faded dollar bill that lay faceup on the table. Felt its age, put her hand over the wrinkled top. She took his bill and replaced it with three of her own. That would cover her Coke and tip. She should have written a check. Perhaps he would have recognized her mother's last name. As far as Shannon knew, he didn't even know her name, had never asked her for it.

He was just pulling out when Shannon started her engine. If she hurried, she could follow him home.

Shannon got to the office early, the book heavy in her arms, her makeup smeared. This would all be worth it in the end, she told herself, as she dropped it noisily onto her desk.

There was no sign of Lilly.

At 10:52, Lilly finally made her appearance. Shannon was up and waiting at her desk before Lilly had a chance to take off her coat.

"This is for you." She had written a little note in black ink on the top. *To make your day a little easier.* Now she stood like Vanna White, pointing to the book.

Lilly looked at the package and stuck her cigarette in her mouth. Shannon watched as it dangled from her lips, collecting ashes.

Lilly read the note, smiled for a second, ripped open the brown paper, and stared. "What is this?"

Was she blind? "It's an encyclopedia. One comes every other week. I ordered you the whole set." Shannon beamed.

Lilly stood, blinking at her.

Shannon's eyes dropped to the desk as she searched for something else to say. "It's real leather." She looked back up at Lilly. "They're really quite wonderful. My cousin has a set and is always saying how terrific they are. She does similar work—she's a fact-checker," Shannon lied.

"Where does she work?"

"What?"

"Your cousin. Where does she work?" Lilly jabbed.

"Vogue."

"You have a cousin at *Vogue*? What's her name?"

"I just thought you'd like to have them, too." She ran her finger over the edge of Lilly's desk. She tried to get her body to move, wanted to tell her feet to go, but she couldn't.

"Well, thanks." She picked up the phone and waited for Shannon to leave.

After a moment, she slumped back to her desk and curled her heavy legs into herself.

At lunchtime, Shannon sat in a closed stall in the bathroom and unwrapped her sandwich, peanut butter and jelly, and a small container of cranberry juice. She heard the door open and instantly recognized Lilly's smell of cigarettes and Obsession.

"Can you believe that? I mean, how weird. She just handed me the thing and then claims she has a cousin or something working at *Vogue*."

"How do you know she doesn't?" The other voice belonged to Nina, her boss's daughter.

Shannon didn't move.

"Because, I know all the editors there. I'm going to call. What's her last name?

She looked through the small crack and watched them model for each other. They stood in front of the mirror, molding their hair with spray and applying lipstick.

"Dorren, I think."

Shannon saw Nina run her fingers through her hair, then check her teeth. Perhaps she should have sought Nina's friendship instead.

"She just kind of hovers over you, but then never says anything. And she's always knocking into things," Lilly added.

Shannon stuffed as much of the thick sandwich into her mouth as possible and tried to hold back her tears as peanut butter oozed out. She was sure they could smell her lunch wafting through the stall, mixing with Lilly's pungent scent.

"Christ, if I have to deal with this each month . . ." Lilly said, blotting her lips.

"Maybe you should give it back if you're not going to use it?"

"Yeah. I guess."

She watched them leave, heard the door slam shut.

Shannon choked for a bit before she was able to regain her composure, then stood in front of the bathroom mirror and saw her blotchy reflection.

. . .

The book was on Shannon's desk when she came into work the next day. It was just sitting there amongst the pile of bills. Lilly was nowhere in sight.

Not knowing what else to do, she called Ben, hoping he was home.

"Books and Nooks," he answered.

His flat voice brought her some relief. "Hi, this is Shannon."

"Who?"

"The woman from the diner?"

"Oh, yes. Hello right back to you. I hope there's no problem with the book?"

"Well, actually, I need to cancel my subscription."

"Why?" He was almost crying.

"I was wondering if I could get my money back, like you said."

"I'm afraid you can't do that. You need to wait till you receive all of them."

"But that makes no sense."

"A/B is really not that good, C/D is much better," he assured.

"It's not that, they're lovely books," she wrapped the telephone cord around her finger, watched the tip turn red. "It's just that the person I bought them for, the person I was giving them to . . . died." That was all she could come up with.

"Oh. I am sorry."

Then all went quiet. She waited for something to say, waited for Ben to add more to the conversation, and when he didn't, when the sound of static coming from the end of the receiver was too much to take, she said, "So . . ." and listened to her voice trail off.

"I guess under the circumstances I could make an exception.

You've only had it for two days. But I'll have to charge you half. I already ordered the other and there's a penalty for mid-cancellations."

A swell of grief and relief passed over her, like waves crashing against her temples. He would help her. Make an exception. Maybe he did know.

When Lilly came back from lunch, sipping iced coffee, dark glasses on, laughing loudly on her cell, something in Shannon snapped. A small cord had been cut, like the one the TV guy had replaced on her walls.

She waited for Lilly to sit. Waited for her to hang up the cell and pick up the phone on her desk. She waited half an hour more, her body trembling, nausea whooshing inside her. When Shannon could wait no longer, she walked over to Lilly's desk.

"Why didn't you want them?" Shannon's voice was low. Soft. But there.

"What?" Lilly said, covering the mouthpiece. "I'm on the phone, do you mind?" Then back to her call, "Sooooo sorry. Someone in accounting wanted to know . . ."

Then a little louder, "The book. Why didn't you want it?"

"Calm down." Lilly looked around nervously. "No one asked you to buy them in the first place. Jesus."

Without thinking, Shannon took the phone out of Lilly's slim hand and hung up.

"Who the hell do you think . . ."

But Shannon talked over her as if possessed. "You didn't even bother to look at it."

Lilly gawked, surprised. Co-workers were staring.

"I tried to do something nice for you . . ." Her voice broke.

"Why?" Lilly snapped back.

There were snickers from office mates, and suddenly Mr. Perlman was standing over them. "What seems to be the problem, ladies?"

"Nothing," Lilly was quick to say. "Shannon was just asking me a question about the Bellenger case and that she couldn't find the client's hour sheet . . ."

And then the bells.

Shannon had forgotten.

Lilly rolled her eyes, her face smug, and kept talking. Shannon knew they made fun of her. But at this moment she wished the bells would just drown out Lilly's voice.

She counted in her head along with the chimes, hoping that would speed up the process, first by twos, then by threes. She did this at the dentist and gynecologist, and during turbulent flights to Florida when visiting her aunt and uncle. Her feet would twitch left to right, her head would stay focused. But it was useless today. She felt beads of sweat drip down her back and bleed through her white silk shirt. Felt the dampness under her arms grow wetter.

She watched the large clock above the counter turn to 7:00. Ben was a half-hour late. Maybe saying he would meet her was just a line. Maybe he had no intention of showing up at all. What did he care? He already had her money.

On rare occasions, her father would let her pretend to be the customer and pitch her some of his items, ones he insisted would make them rich. She would be all kinds of people—the hard sell, the pushover, the indecisive buyer. Then, without warning, he was gone.

She had stood waiting for him all day. The next day, too. She lingered all week by the screen door, peering out into the summer heat and dust, expecting him to come home and announce that he had sold everything and from that moment on, he would never be away from her and his wife again. A month later they received a letter on lined white paper explaining how he needed to be on his own. That he was sorry.

Her soda was now a mix of melted ice and light brown water. Her napkin was shredded into tiny white bits that lay clumped in a small pile. Who the hell did this salesman think he was, telling her he'd meet her and then not show? How dare he. She had been taken advantage of all her life. Not now. Not anymore. She threw some money on the table, grabbed the book, and got into her car.

Traffic was light and it only took her twenty minutes to get to his house, an old, rundown shack with thick layers of caked paint peeling off one another.

The door was barely attached but she knocked on it lightly, her body shaking. When she received no answer, she banged her fist harder, even yelled for him a few times. Still nothing. She tried the knob. It was open, the lock broken and worn down.

The house was musty and wet. There was hardly any furniture, just a ratty-looking couch and an old TV, the kind she had as a child. She swore she could smell her father's cologne, Old Spice, waft through the apartment. Everywhere she looked were boxes, each filled with items, an endless path of useless stuff. *What's junk to some is treasure to another,* her father once said. She ran her hand over brass money clips, letter openers with Disney characters on them. They sparkled and shimmered. Her hand went to a pen with a girl on it. She held it upside down and watched the black dress disappear to reveal a naked body, legs curled up, breasts large and ripe. Her father had sold items like these, kept them in a large closet piled high. Occasionally he'd show her something from a catalogue. She'd run her hands over each item, all of which possessed magical powers.

She walked down a dim corridor, calling out for the old man, never receiving a reply.

She stopped once she got to his bedroom. The door was ajar and even though she was sure he wasn't home, knocked on the frame. She pushed the rickety door and rested her eyes on the man lying on the bed.

Her heart raced, filled with anger. He was asleep. He hadn't been hurt or injured or working.

She stood over him for a moment, thinking that would rouse him. Then she shook him. Softly at first. Then harder. She grabbed hold of his fat shoulders, bounced him on the bed. "Wake up, old man. Get up." She started to hit him, slap his face, tears rolling down her cheeks. "Wake the fuck up."

It was then that she saw the photo.

Next to his body was a picture, an old, fraying black-and-white Kodak square of a woman holding a baby standing next to a man. Both were smiling. She reached for it, her hands damp. The baby could have been her. The woman, her mother. She wasn't sure. She scanned the room, panicked, searching for other pictures, something to prove she was his, anything that confirmed she existed. The room was dismal and brown from age and neglect. There were no photos of her or anyone else.

She looked back at Ben. His face was pale, his body surprisingly warm. She checked for a pulse but didn't really need to. She already knew.

Next to the bed was a box with her name on it. Inside was the next installment of her Brittanica series, C/D. She ran her fingers over the gold letters, tracing the slight raise, feeling the smoothness of the leather, smelling the freshness of the pages, like a new pair of shoes.

She sat there a minute, the heavy book in her lap, the dead man next to her.

She picked up the receiver. It was dirty, smeared with black goop and fingerprints, and thought about who she could call. A neighbor? Her aunt? Her boss? He seemed understanding—perhaps he would come and help. He could bring Nina with him. The three could have lifted him off the bed, laid him outside, and waited for the ambulance together. Even if things had gone differently with Lilly, she couldn't have called her. This would have been too much to ask. She could request an ambulance but realized as her finger pressed "O" she didn't want to take the responsibility or claim ownership for a man that may or may not be her father.

She was hanging up when she heard the bells. For a second she thought she was imagining the sound, then realized they were coming from the old grandfather clock in the far corner. They reminded her of the ones at work and out of respect or habit, took a moment of silence. It was just enough time to notice the matches and cigar lying on the far side of Ben. She reached over for them. They were the nondescript, generic kind from any given diner. The ashtray was clear and probably stolen from some fleabag hotel he was staying at while traveling on the road.

She lit a match, watched it burn in her fingers before tossing it in the ashtray. She missed and it fell on the bed an inch or so from her desired target. It burned out on the dingy blanket, leaving a small, brown mark. She struck another, flicked it toward the ashtray, also missing. She hated this room. Hated the familiarity. The smell of old boxes. Of dirty, musty clothing and thick damp air. The paperweights and napkins and the pens with the naked ladies on them and her life and everything that existed in this sad, pathetic house.

She struck another, then another until the book was empty and a small pile of smoldering sticks surrounded the clear, cheap glass. If she squinted, the ashtray looked like a carnival game, the one where you won a goldfish if you got a Ping-Pong ball into the small opening of a bowl.

She searched for more matches on the nightstand and found several packs in the drawer. This time when she lit one, she fed it to the others and watched a blaze of fire rip across. She flung the book and it fell a foot or so away from the far end of the queen-size bed. She was about to quit when the blanket started to smoke, the tired wool burning easily. She looked around for something to feed it with and when nothing caught her eye, she flipped open the encyclopedia to a random page and ripped it out. She crumpled the paper into a loose ball and added it to the smoldering area. She watched it catch fire, then tossed another page. By the time she hit words that started with D, the room was smoky.

When she could no longer breathe, she gathered herself up, put her hand on Ben's face, and cupped it slightly. It felt dry and old. Warm. She leaned in and kissed his forehead, careful not to get too close to the fire. She kept the photo of the couple and closed the bedroom door behind her.

Shannon sat in her car, the motor purring, until she heard the distant roar of a firetruck.

Then she pulled away.

SWIMMING WITHOUT ANNETTE

The guy in the blue scrubs slides Annette out from the wall. The sound is jarring, like the clanking of loose silverware in a kitchen drawer. The thick white sheet that covers Annette's body is removed. From my angle, it looks as if someone has smeared eye shadow all over her neck.

"He must have come up behind her and grabbed her like so," the medical examiner says, reenacting the scene. He inserts his hand under her. I hear his fingernails scrape against the metal slab as he scoops up her head and wraps his hand around her throat, placing his fingers over the large bruises. I take a picture with Annette's camera. He looks up at me, startled.

"You know, I could lose my job."

I smile flirtatiously, like my mother taught me during a time when she still had high hopes of me being with men, and rest my hand over his. "You have really nice hands," I say. His face eases. I stroke his ego and his index finger at the same time. "So soft," I add. He smiles and pulls away, leaving me holding Annette's neck up by myself. My fingers just touch the bruises, my hand too small.

"Anyway, you can't tell anyone you've taken these." He suddenly looks like a young boy, his body thin and shrunken. The blue medical uniform seems out of place against the steel-colored room. I remove my hand, place Annette's head gently on the table, focus the camera, and shoot. The clicking and fast-forwarding sound reverberates off the sterile walls. Everything feels hollow and heavy at the same time.

I want to bend down and kiss Annette, stroke her hair, run my thumb back and forth over her forehead above her eye, like I did in bed when she'd have a headache from working in the darkroom too long. Even dead, she looks beautiful, her pale skin like a half-baked apple pie. Her body is cold and stiff, her eyes fixed upward. I close them, my hand brushing over her face. My fingers touch her dry lips, caress her cheek. The bruises—bright blue, brown, and yellow—almost glow off her body. I lean my ear down toward her mouth as if I expect her to say something. To whisper his name. Say mine. Utter the word *love*.

I identified her body three days ago. I was flying in from LA. Some of the shirts I design were being photographed for *Elle*. Annette was supposed to join me but a work conflict kept her in New York. Instead, I watched a movie starring Meryl Streep by myself, her seat unoccupied on the plane, my hand kept company by stale pretzels and a bitter Bloody Mary. I called the apartment when I landed, then tried to reach her on her cell. I wasn't alarmed until I saw the squad car perched in front of my awning. Even then, I thought they were waiting for someone else. On the way to the coroner's I kept thinking, how would Meryl handle this? She's always so controlled.

Annette's face was dirty and bloody, her clothing damp. I wanted to lift her off the table and take her home. Soak her in a hot bath with scented green-apple soap, dress her in my favorite flannel pajamas. I would have brought her back, warm and clean.

The police wouldn't allow me to stand closer than six feet.

The medical examiner hadn't arrived yet and everything was considered evidence. I pleaded with them to let me bring her a change of clothing. Crumpled to the floor and begged. They picked me up, walked me out, and put me in a car. One of the rookies drove me home, the siren off. I sat in the back seat and watched the handcuffs that hung from the gate swing back and forth, knocking against the window.

"We better go," the examiner says.

I nod and take a few more photos. I think about developing them myself. Annette taught me how, but I haven't been able to go into the darkroom yet. Instead, I deliver the film into a one-hour photo place near NYU. I tell them I'm taking a forensics class and that the photos are a bit gruesome, then ask, "Do you give student discounts?"

The pounding of house music from the nightclub above is light enough to be annoying, but not loud enough for me to make out the song. There's an uneasy hum; the clicking of cups against saucers, an occasional stir of a spoon against ceramic, the sound of the waitress's croaking voice asking if I want a refill, all seem distorted. The diner takes on a ghostly feel, as if waiting for something to happen. As if time has slowed down. Even the air seems to move cautiously.

I glance at the clock above that register: 10:05 P.M. For the past six hours, I've been waiting for my lover's killer. I have decided to look for him on odd days of the week, those being Mondays, Wednesdays, and Fridays.

Annette was here a month ago. Sitting in this spot, perhaps, pre-Christmas gifts on one side, photography magazines on the other of the padded booth. It was outside this restaurant where he grabbed her, threw her down, his hands ripping at her neck, his fingers pressed into her skin, nails cutting her flesh. It was in this alley where her body lay sprawled on the cold pavement. Blood mixed with loose negatives, rolls of undeveloped film, lipstick and wallet tossed like shells on the beach. In my mind I visualize the approach, see him needing help of some sort, maybe asking for directions or claiming he was sick. I picture him with thick, dark hair and sharp features. He's tall and broad, with clear skin and charming good looks.

We met at a party in SoHo five years ago. I caught sight of her walking in a few minutes after me. Her eyes were magnificent, iridescent, and her hair had a silky, ash-colored glow. We stood a few feet away from each other at the bar. I remember wanting to slide my hand over to hers and see what her skin felt like. I wanted to stand close enough to smell her perfume, her breath, anything. I wanted to be her.

We gave each other knowing glances until she slinked over to me, pulled at my sweater, and led me off to the side, not a word spoken. We sat in worn-in velvet chairs, smoked her Parliaments, and drank chocolate martinis, syrupy and sweet. We stared at each other and listened to the jazz quartet made up of women who performed on stage.

Annette had the most beautiful lips, soft and full, like feathers or white daisies. We kissed outside the bar, the cold air sobering us up. She'd put her arms around my back, brought my hips close to her, and for one moment, a brief second that you can't grab on to, I was whole and immortal. Almost nothing. We stood there, embarrassed, in the street. People stopped and stared, jealous of our affection, disgusted by our display.

The door opens. Cold air catches me off guard. A man walks in with another woman. Her arm is hooked through his and they laugh as if they've just come from a ritzy cocktail party and are sharing an inside joke. They take a seat off to my left. He's tall, broad, and terribly attractive in a Gatsby sort of way. He's wearing a dark green trench coat. I write all this in my notebook.

I sit here and wait.

I drink my coffee. I watch others. I think of a plan.

The first victim was a married gynecologist who'd bought three pairs of shoes from the store next to the diner. They found her several hours later in the stairwell of her walkup, a patent leather flat crammed into her mouth, her neck broken. The second and third were club kids from the after-hours lounge a few blocks from here. A matchbook from the diner was tucked into the cellophane wrapper of the Marlboro package in one of their pockets. They were spotted on the street, arms linked together, bodies flopped over like Raggedy Ann dolls. People assumed they were homeless kids who'd passed out on the street after a night of partying. In their laps was loose change from well-meaning strangers. The fourth lived across the street. She had just brought dinner from here. I imagine the food still hot, the fries greasy, bun getting soggy, cheese on the hamburger turning hard as she struggled to open her door. Maybe he came up behind her and offered to help. Maybe he said he was visiting someone and she let him in. The police found her body propped up against her elevator gate, aluminum take-out container opened and placed purposely in her lap.

The prints the police pulled from the victims are useless. Computers came up without a name or a lead. There are no hair follicles, no clothing fibers, no skin embedded under any of the women's fingernails. Still, the cops have assured me they're doing all they can. They have round-the-clock surveillance, detectives in unmarked cars positioned outside, an undercover cop dressed as a homeless person in the alley where Annette was found. They look at me funny, eyes shifting away from me when they tell me this, their impatience elevating each time they see me at the station. They are no longer interested in my write-ups or my photos of restaurant patrons. At first they took them with interest. Now they sit in a folder at the bottom of a pile of Manila envelopes on someone's desk.

The pungent odor of unwashed hair and sweat floats by. It belongs to the biker boy who wears a thick chain and combination lock around his neck. It clinks as he walks past me. One leg of his nylon workout pants is scrunched up at his knee, the other hangs down over his sneaker. Gold rings decorate most of his grimy fingers; the largest one reads *fuck me*. It's time to go.

I walk out the door, dazed from the thick air of the diner, and almost get knocked over by people hurrying home, anxious to get out from the cold, their winter coats and furs pulled up against their ears, faces hidden by scarves and earmuffs.

Cars buzz by, the street light changes.

At home, without Annette, I look for a place to sit. A place where my body will fit comfortably into the crevices of emptiness. There are traces of Annette everywhere, tangible evidence that prove I once lived with someone: Special K cereal, a camera bag, her photographs. The light, dizzying smell of her burns through the walls, like cooking aromas from the neighbor next door. I've had the rugs cleaned and repainted the apartment. After two months of her absence, she still hangs in the air.

Photos of her body are spread out everywhere, along with the police file and autopsy report, making my apartment look like a detective's office. I've collected a mass of folders, too. Lists of specialists, orthopedists, criminologists, and therapists, along with printouts from Internet sites dealing with murderers, profiler gurus, and unsolved FBI cases, are stacked in neat packets on the floor. The wall next to the dining room is decorated with her as well. I've replaced Annette's beautiful photographs with large bulletin boards. They display fingerprints, hand charts, and the photos I took at the morgue. When I can't sleep, I stare at them. I resurrect her voice, re-create her laugh, place a mental picture of her in the antique chair we bought together at the Twenty-sixth Street flea market, and ask her to tell me what happened.

I think of her smile as I run my hand over one of the blown-up photos of her face. I place the tip of my index finger over one of the bruises and trace the outline of her neck. This is the part of her I miss most. The way she'd toss her head back when she'd laugh, her ash hair spilling over her shoulders, over her eyes. She'd take her fingers and run them just above her scalp and pull the hair away from her face. I inch my thumb over her lips, aching to feel them on my mouth. I miss her teeth. The light clicking of enamel when we'd kiss, the sucking of her lower lip, the feel of her tongue. When she worked late, and I was already in bed, she'd slide in next to me, smelling of silver chloride and fix bath, place her lips just over my earlobe, and say, *I'm home*. We'd lie in bed, our bodies intertwined, our voices just above a whisper, while the glow from the TV illuminated the room.

A heavyset woman thuds into a booth. I catch her reflection in the window. The double chin makes her look deformed. Her face is tense, her eyes glassy. She looks as if she's going to cry. The staff calls her Lindsay.

"Need a menu tonight?" the waitress asks, placing a Rolling Rock in front of her.

Her arms are so large that her watchband digs into her wrist. It looks as if the thin leather strap will snap at any moment. I wonder what kind of mark it leaves at night, if she takes it off, if she lets the suffocating skin breathe. I wonder if he's watching her and if she will be next. Maybe it's me who's caught his eye. Maybe it's my name on his list.

Knowing he might be here is all I have. It's the only thing I can hold on to. The only thing I can do to help. So I wait and watch and listen and stare and observe.

I came here every day in the beginning. Dragged Annette's parents and my brother here, too. Both appeased me. We sat for hours, nursed bad coffee, ate tuna melts, and picked at fries.

During the third month, the waitress asks if I've gotten a job nearby since she's noticed me eating here so often. I nod yes. I'm surprised it's taken her this long to ask.

"What do you do?" she inquires, setting silverware in front of me. She's dressed in a black-and-white waitress uniform. Her name tag reads *Doris*.

"I'm a clothing designer. I make T-shirts."

"Oh," she exclaims, her face opening up like a flower bulb. "How exciting."

I smile politely and pull at my sweatshirt, trying to remember what I'm wearing underneath. Something I've made or did I merely throw on a white T from The Gap? Sometimes I wear whatever I've slept in.

This morning I awoke from a terrible, wonderful dream. Annette and I were in bed, making love. For the first few minutes I was unable to tell what had actually occurred and what was from the deep crevasses of sleep. I placed my hand in the spot where I thought she was to see if it was warm, to see if she had been here. I called for her, thinking maybe she was in the next room reading the paper or dressing for work or making coffee so we could sip it together, both sharing one mug. I slinked out of bed, walked into the next room, and found it empty. The whole apartment was. I expected to smell her perfume but I think that would have been too much for me to handle.

In the booth to my left is a professor who works on a laptop. He's balding and wears wire-rimmed glasses and bites his thumbnail in deep thought. I call him "The Nibbler." I've categorized all the men, defining them by a code system only Annette would appreciate. "Trench-coat Man" isn't well. I've watched the way he holds a cup of coffee. His hand shakes when he lifts it and I wonder if he has Parkinson's. I cross his name off my mental list. "Bad-Hairpiece Man" doesn't seem to have the stamina or the personality for killing someone. He became hysterical last week when a roach crawled over his spoon and under the table. "Biker-Boy" is still a suspect—so is one of the waiters who lost his temper last Friday over a small tip left by a group of teens. I look around for new people. I look for Annette, half expecting her to bounce through the diner door and yell *Surprise*.

I visit Macy's. They're having an after-Valentine's Day sale on men's gloves. I test myself to see how good I've gotten at measuring size. I ask the saleswoman to take out several different pairs. She lays them out on the glass counter. I finger the soft leather, asking, "7 ½?" She looks inside and nods. I go down the line like a game show contestant or circus act, each time giving the correct size. The last pair is a 9 ½, an inch bigger than the killer's. I try them on, want to see how my hand takes up the space inside. They're warm and soft and my fingers feel lost in them.

I interview an orthopedist who specializes in hands. "He's tall—six-two, six-three," he says. His voice is crisp and he keeps looking at his watch instead of at the crime-scene photos. "You can tell because of the angle and the position of the bruises." His phone rings, but he's kind enough to ignore it. He raises his voice to talk over the trilling. "He's probably a righty. He pressed harder on this side of her neck. See?"

I go to a palm reader, a proclaimed psychic, and show her the same pictures. I lay them out like tarot cards.

"This man is angry. Very angry." She looks up at me expectantly, waiting for a reaction. When I don't say anything, she continues. "He is filled with rage." She drops the photos as if looking at them is channeling too much pain for her. "You should stay away from him," she advises as she sticks my twenty in the pocket of her flowered housecoat.

Annette and I had our first date a week after we met. She showed up with expensive wine in a pretty bottle, its true color hidden by its protector. Our conversation was smart and witty. It poured out from our lips as it became an extension of us, a sexual desire to share information. Annette, a lightweight, got tipsy on her second glass and passed out on my couch. I sat with her head in my lap as one of my hands ran through her hair, my other rested on her arm. I inched my finger underneath her spandex sleeve, felt the softness of her skin, the firmness of her muscle. The smell of her perfume was so calming to me that I sat there for hours listening to her breathe.

I saved the glass she drank from, her lipstick mark imprinted perfectly on the crystal. I refused to wash it and placed it in the bar where it was kept company by the other glasses. It became a running gag when she moved in three months later.

"Would you wash this thing already?" she'd say, handing me the glass when we'd do spring- or fall-cleaning.

"You're soooo sentimental," I'd coo, taking it from her grasp and replacing it in its rightful spot. "It's all I have to remind me of our first date."

"I'm living with you. How much more of a reminder do you need?"

When friends came over, it was always mentioned. Either someone would ask about it when they removed glasses to help pour wine or they'd notice it sticking out among the others. "Karen's made me immortal," Annette would joke with inquisitive guests, holding up the glass for all to see. "I'm a bona fide rock star." Everyone would laugh, and I'd blush and sip wine quietly on our couch.

The last time someone mentioned it, Annette teased that I was planning to auction off her photos and the glass on E-bay. "Maybe I should sweat on something or drool on a napkin? Perhaps I should just go around the apartment kissing things?" Then she waltzed over to me and kissed my cheek, leaving the shape of puckered lips etched on my face.

I remove her unwashed glass from the bar, hold it close to my chest, and think about putting my lips over hers.

The diner is unusually crowded, packed with high school kids in sports uniforms. Their varsity jackets and scarves are clumped in a seat. I scan the restaurant, see the regulars, make a few mental notes. "The Nibbler" is typing away in the back, "Pinhead," a man whose head is smaller than the rest of his body, is off to the side, eating with a woman who looks like a hooker. "The Hamburgler" is here, too. He only orders hamburgers smothered in mayo and drinks three or four beers with each meal. I don't see "Biker-Boy" or "Mustache-Man." A thin, sickly looking guy is eating chicken pot pie in the corner. I've had my eye on him for some time and he acknowledges my presence with a nod and a half grin. I return the gesture while eyeing his dry blond hair; his lips are thin and red, like those of a girl.

I spot an empty stool by the counter next to an attractive woman who's smoking and playing with the ends of a salad.

Normally I sit in the back, which enables me to see most of the diner. Other times I take to the front where I can watch people pass by outside and still see customers inside. At the counter, my back is to most of the patrons. Even though there's a long mirror across from me offering a panoramic view, teas and cereals are stacked on the shelf, cutting into my sight. Plus, a large refrigerator which houses the desserts—generic cheesecake, chocolate cake, apple pie, green Jell-O, and a bowl of fruit, Saran Wrap past its clinging stage—intersects the left side of the restaurant.

"Tuna on whole wheat?" Catrina asks, already scribbling something down. The waitstaff knows me by now. I almost look forward to seeing them.

"I think I'm going to break out of character and order an omelet with tomato and feta."

Catrina nods, erases what she's written, and starts over. She tears off the slip, sticks it on the ordering thing, and yells to the chef in restaurant short-talk.

"That's always a safe bet, though the food is rather decent here," says the woman sitting next to me. She smiles and tilts her head to one side.

My stomach hurts and I'm not sure I'm in the mood for conversation.

"Hope," she adds, blowing smoke out of the right side of her mouth.

"For what? Not getting food poisoning?"

She's incredibly pretty. Reddish hair, soft green eyes, and full lips painted a tawny-brown. She looks about thirty-eight, maybe a few years older than me. I study her face for a second. She scrunches up her nose and narrows her eyes in a playful way as she flicks her cigarette and leans into me.

"No, my name is Hope."

"Your parents must have been very optimistic."

We laugh and stare at each other. I'm about to look away when she reaches for my face. "You have something, an eyelash," and brushes her index finger an inch or so under my eye.

No one's touched me like this since Annette's funeral and it feels as if I'm watching a movie, as if my skin isn't real. She moves back to her original position.

"What's dinner without a little wine?" She taps her empty glass and holds it up to Catrina. "And one for my friend." Then back to me, "I always feel better having a partner in crime."

"It's been a long time since someone bought me a drink," I say, fidgeting with my napkin.

"Well, I'd be more than happy to buy you another when you're ready."

Hope rubs her index finger around the edge of the glass a few times, seductively, like I remember my mother's friends doing at dinner parties. It makes a high-pitched sound and I wonder if she's flirting with me. Annette had terrific gaydar. For a lesbian, I seemed to have been overlooked in this department.

"I'm Karen." I eye Hope's Ultra Light cigarettes, suddenly longing for something to occupy my hand. "Which is a stupid name. It sounds like I'm a carry-on bag."

She giggles and tosses her head back, just like Annette would do. Then I remember why I'm here.

Catrina sets the food down. The well-done omelet, the golden brown French fries prepared just as I requested, all make me nauseous. I take one bite, feel full, and start to cry. Hope leans in closer to me and strokes my hair, warming me like the hot coffee from the diner.

"Can I do anything?" Her voice is as soft as a cashmere sweater.

I shake my head no, and, in an effort to stop the tears, look up toward the door. I see "Bad-Hairpiece Man" walk in. I click back into professional mode and take out my notebook.

Today, I'm sitting at the table closest to the register. Taped to the wall are glossy school portraits and some pictures of children sitting on other children's laps. A calendar displays the month of March with a picture of snow-covered mountains. Two fake roses in a tiny bud vase are on each of the Formica tables. They're a new addition, a small attempt to make the place cheerier. Three elderly ladies sit gabbing to my right. I can smell their perfume, heavy and too sweet, their voices as shaky as their hands. They talk about their grandchildren, their pets, their lonely lives. Men in overcoats sip coffee, their jackets still on, cell phones resting on the tables.

The diner is uncomfortably quiet and I haven't seen Hope in three weeks. A small hole has been created since our evening together. It feels as if she, too, has disappeared. I've thought about calling. We exchanged numbers, but the paper sits folded on my nightstand.

"Trench-coat Man" is here again, sitting beside me. So is "The Hamburgler." Lindsay slouches off to the left, face buried in the paper, her fat hands clutching the uneven ends. I asked if she wanted to sit with me, but she said no, her voice so soft I could barely hear her.

I've started conversations with strangers. Invited myself to join single men for lunch or dinner. Inched my body into the seat next to them, claiming the restaurant is too crowded or that I work at home alone and that the presence of another person is so important even if we don't talk, which we eventually do, because everyone in New York is lonely and sad and needs to speak to someone. Anyone who will listen. And I do. I become all eyes and ears. I learn their stories. I pry without looking as if I am. It's not hard—people are eager to share. I stare at their hands as they rest on the table or hold a fork, grasp a plastic glass, each time mentally measuring them. Then I go home and compare my hands to the life-size posters in the apartment.

Last week I finally spoke to "The Hamburgler," whose real name is Lincoln.

"As in log?" I had joked with him, his fingers gooey with mayo. We were sitting a few stools away from each other.

Tonight we make polite chitchat.

He's a construction worker in the city. So are his two brothers, but none of them works for the same company. His father's a retired cop, his mother's a social worker. He owns a jeep. He's cute, tall and broad, but has too much gel in his hair. Most impressive are his arms. They're toned and muscular like the beer poster where the guy's shirtless and is holding a cat in one hand, a Bud Light in the other, a red bandanna around his neck.

"Anyway, that's my deal." He wipes his mouth with a wet napkin and stands up. "It was good talking to you." I watch as he tosses a few dollars on the table and walks slowly up to the register.

I wonder how tall he is.

"See ya," he says.

"See ya," I echo.

He pays the bill and sticks the remaining cash into the back pocket of his jeans.

"Where you going?" Lincoln yaps when I walk outside. He's standing by the pay phone.

"Home."

"Where's that?" He hangs up the receiver.

"Mercer and University."

"Walk you there?"

My mind races. I try to picture his hands. "Sure." I try to think of something else to say. "No cell phone? Isn't that a pre-requisite for living in New York?"

He laughs. A warm, rich laugh, like a game show host, and for a moment I think, I must be wrong. No one could kill anyone with a laugh like that. I'm disappointed and confused, but we keep walking, his stride equal with mine even though my legs are shorter.

"It's broken. I finally learn how to work the damn thing and it dies on me." He smiles and shrugs, shy and sly at the same time. I feel dizzy and start sweating. Perspiration drips down my back, the kind my mother complained about during her menopausal years. We reach my corner. The diner is only a few blocks away but it feels as though we've been walking for most of the night.

"So," he clasps his hands together, "it's still kind of early. Want to get a drink?"

"Sure." I search his face, looking for clues. His eyes seem kind. He has nice ears. "I'd like to change first. You want to come up for a sec?" I finger Annette's metal X-Acto knife in my pocket, the one she used to cut negatives with.

He lifts his eyebrows and leans his body forward, rocking onto his toes, hands shoved into his coat.

We're quiet in the elevator; neither of us has anything to say until we get to my floor.

"Nice building. You own?"

I can't tell if he's staring at me or past my head, like the police do when they want me to leave and have more important matters to take care of.

"Yeah. I've lived here for eight years." I unlock the door; the sound of the metal cylinder reverberates in my hallway, the smell of beer on his breath and hamburger on his clothing is enough to make me gag. I wonder what the fuck I'm doing as I hit the lights and walk in.

Like an expectant mother who's packed a suitcase and placed it in the hall closet waiting for the exact moment it will be needed, I, too, am prepared. I've hidden a tape recorder in each room set to voice activation. The police reports, files, and journals reside on the top shelf of my closet. The photos have been stripped from the walls, and Annette's work put back to its original spot— black-and-whites from our trip to Vietnam, a picture of a street vendor which appeared in *The New York Times* a few years ago, the series she did on sharp objects which won her a Guggenheim, hang on the wall with pride.

"Do you want to take off your jacket?" I ask, hanging mine up in the hall closet, my back toward Lincoln. I feel him come up behind me. A hand slides over my waist and around my stomach. His foul breath on my neck feels locked in my hair. I place my hand over his and, like a blind person, search for a size. I feel as if I've spent my whole life waiting for this moment. He squeezes my ass lightly with his free hand and playfully brings his body closer to mine.

"You smell so good," he whispers, his lips just touching the skin under my ear.

I lead him into the living room. More mirrors. Better angles.

He leans forward and kisses my lips harshly, knocking me momentarily off balance. My hip collides with the edge of the dining room table.

"Sorry. You okay?" He looks concerned. Maybe I'm wrong. I should stop this now.

"Fine." My hand reaches for the bruised spot, but his hand gets there first. He rubs at my hip in small circles. Then he bends his head down toward my neck and starts to kiss me. With each kiss he backs me up closer and closer to the wall. I want to move. I want to push him away, tell him this is a mistake. That *I've* made a mistake.

His lips are at my ear when he utters, "What are you think-ing?"

"How nice you feel." I can stop this now. Ask him to leave. Tell him the truth. Anything.

"Really?" He smiles and grabs at my arm, clamping it against the wall up near my ear. He takes his other hand and caresses my breast, then squeezes my nipple.

"Let's take a breather," I suggest, my mind racing.

"Why?" His voice is even-toned, like a golf announcer, void of any feeling; he leans into my pelvis.

I think of the last time I was in this position. Annette had pinned me up against the wall in our hallway, spread my arms up above my head like a policeman frisking a criminal, and kissed me on my neck, my ear, my arms.

Lincoln's whole body rests on me, causing the knife in my pocket to dig into my skin. I try to maneuver my hand down to adjust it but he's got his leg pressed into my crotch. He leans in harder, one hand still holding down my arm, his other moving up to my throat, right under my chin.

Lincoln lifts up my jaw, like a chiropractor working on a patient, his thumb and index finger at each ear. I feel my vertebrae elongate and a slight pulling starts at the base of my spine. I see his forearm, make out the edge of his watch. I flash to Lindsay's fat arm, think about how hard a time he'd have holding her down. As big as his hands are, they might not fit around her neck.

I try to smile and look as if I'm enjoying this. "I like it rough." My voice is hoarse. I move my free hand to his thigh and massage him, then inch toward my pocket.

"Do you, now?" he whispers.

I feel a wet spot on my leg, feel the blood staining my pants from the open knife, and wonder if he'll notice.

Above my head is a photo of Annette and myself. It's a small picture set in a silver frame. We were at the park reading the paper and our friend snapped the photo. I stretch my hand up, thinking if I can cause the picture to fall he'll have to move, but his grip is too strong. My fingers reach, but feel nothing. I see his eyes glance up and over my head. He looks from the photo to me, a smirk forms on his lips, his eyes like slits.

"She's pretty. Your sister?"

"Girlfriend."

His smile widens.

I can feel my body shaking. A numbed, prickly sensation comes over me as I envision Annette fighting for her life, trying to scream or hit him with her camera.

"Ever done it with a man?"

I want to swallow—it's hard with his fingers gripped around my throat. My free hand searches for something, anything.

"Have you?" I croak.

He pulls at my sweater, bringing me to him, then shoves me harshly into the wall. My head snaps back. My eyes try to focus. I become aware of several things: my jerky movements, my breathing, the smell of hamburger. I look around the apartment in quick bites to see what I can grab on to for protection. The glass vase on the dining room table, too far away; the phone wire to twist around his neck, too complicated, too many movements. I reach out on the wall, feel around on the bar, looking for a bottle of gin or vodka to whack him on the head with, or the wine opener to pierce him in the eye. My hand comes up empty until it feels glass. I grasp whatever it is and smack it against the wall. He turns away from me to look at what I've found. I hold the stem, jagged shark teeth, and plunge it into his neck. He backs away screaming, an earsplitting shrill. I look for something else to protect me. I drop to the floor to pick up a large chunk of glass and see Annette's lipstick imprint, almost perfectly intact. He surges at me, and I shove the glass pick into another spot, slide away as his head rams into the coffee table.

His body hits the floor.

All is quiet.

I kick him in the head. Watch a mat of black hair sweep my floor.

No movement.

My foot juts out and I strike him again, same spot. Still nothing. I turn him over. I think he's breathing, or maybe the breathing is mine. I can't tell. Pieces of Annette's glass are sticking out of his throat. His eyes are bulging. Blood oozes out from his body, staining my Indian rug. I bend down closer, place my hands around his neck. My fingers attack his throat, searching for the exact position. Like hands on the keys of a piano after endless hours of forced practice, as if they remember, each creating their own private musical sound, they grip tighter and tighter as he gasps for air. I feel his pulsating veins, see his protruding eyes get bigger. Blood is seeping out of the deep puncture on the side of his throat. Pieces of glass dig into my skin. I pull back. My hands are thick with blood, like I've been finger painting. I slink back to the wall, lean up against it for balance. Then I notice something, the light reflecting off the large piece of glass still stuck in his neck. Annette's smudge-proof lipstick insignia, a trace of bright red. And from my angle, it looks as if she's kissed him.

STILL LIFE

She won't remember much. The falling and the flying, as if both are happening at the same time. Their first kiss, wet and breathy. The way his ring would feel up against her skin. The thick, bitter taste of Italian coffee, the pungent smell of turpentine, the wishing she could start her life over. The desperate need to understand who she was before.

And the wanting.

She will remember the wanting.

Aside from the hum of the fan and the occasional ringing of the phone, the gallery is quiet.

Natalie likes to be the first to see the exhibits, as if the people in the paintings have been waiting all day for her to visit. Actually, it is Natalie who waits, heart pounding, anxiety rising in her chest like a soufflé baking in the oven.

The girl who works at the gallery was late again this morning, making Natalie's head ache. At 10:08 she was still a no-show. She checked her watch over and over, wondering where the young woman with the dyed red pixie hair, the combat boots, and the shoulder bag made out of straw could be.

Natalie sits on the bench in the middle of the room, memorizing the gallery's list of upcoming events. She makes mental notes for which days she can go, and which receptions and openings she can't make. She has inquired about renting studio space, each time leaving cryptic messages on broker's machines, telling them not to phone her back, that she will try them again later. She's looked into classes at the Y and the New School but has been unable to register. Brandon keeps throwing away the brochures and gallery announcements. At night she scavenges through the trash, wipes them down, and removes bits of food and coffee grinds stuck to them. She saves each one in an envelope and hides them in the back of her closet as if they were drugs. They're kept in a suitcase filled with clothing, photos, a passport, and her mother's jewelry.

Natalie stares at the art, at the walls, at her hands. They don't look like hers. They are pale, clean. She tries to peel off her ring to see what it would feel like not to be married anymore, but her fingers are swollen. Layers of skin bunch up at her knuckle, making it impossible for the ring to come off. She licks her finger, feels the cool gold and smooth diamond against her tongue, hears it clink on her teeth. Then, with a harsh tug, she rips the ring off her finger. It skittles to the floor, as if it were a rock skimming across a pond. Her hand looks so clean and untarnished that it makes her long for days when paint was embedded in her nails, her skin dry and raw.

She looks up at the woman in the painting. She reminds Natalie of her dead mother, face gray and fading, eyes cold and hollow. So much of her wants to return to her old house, curl up into a ball, and lie on the floor in her mother's closet like she did as a child when she and her fraternal twin, Lena, played hide-and-seek. Natalie remembers how comforting it was to inhale the mix of Chanel No. 5 and leather while her mother's expensive clothing concealed her body. She'd give anything to suffocate her thoughts in the cellophane garment bags that hang in her own closet.

Natalie bends down, searching the floor for her ring, though she is tempted to leave it here. She imagines the pixie girl happening upon it as she cleans up for the night. She sees her slipping it on her finger and modeling it for her friends at a random bar after work.

Two months ago, she sat in a lawyer's office off of Fifth Avenue. He was a fat man who wore a bad toupee. "Nowadays, people get divorced for all sorts of reasons," he said, taking out a yellow legal pad. "What's he done?"

Natalie can't pinpoint the exact moment Brandon changed. There were small, insignificant signs. "It was as if someone were removing a spoonful of sugar from a five-pound bag," she told the lawyer. "At first it goes unnoticed because the missing amounts are minute. Then you decide to bake cookies or brownies. When you reach for the bag, you notice how light it feels. You look inside and realize all the sugar is gone. And you're confused because you don't remember using it."

He looked at her nervously, his fat face turning into a frown. She watched him shift uncomfortably in his dilapidated leather chair, as she noticed his degrees hanging above his head in thick, black frames. He put the pad back into his desk drawer, cleared his throat, stood up, and extended a clammy hand. Natalie didn't tell him there were clumps of mustard embedded in his mustache and when he nodded at her, his toupee shook.

"Why not send me a retainer?" he said. "I'm sure he's done something to you. I'll brainstorm on my end once I receive your check."

She was tempted to mail him her old retainer she'd kept from her orthodonture days in high school. If memory served, it was still housed in the blue plastic case, caked with saliva. It was then that she opened a bank account, depositing twenties and fifties when able. She began charging expensive items at department stores, and then returning the merchandise for credit. All night she planned her escape.

Natalie steals into the padded booth of the restaurant. Her three friends are waiting, chatting about fake fur.

"Sorry," she offers, catching her reflection in the aluminum paneling. "I got a late start." She stares at the image looking back at her, a distorted woman with pale skin and harsh, red lipstick. She takes a paper napkin and quickly wipes it off, leaving her lips blotchy. She breathes slowly as she waits for the dizziness to stop and the throbbing in her temples to ease. She fakes her best good-girl smile and tries to join the conversation. The concern that has stretched across her friends' faces starts to disappear as Camille talks about her anniversary party. Her other two friends, Molly and Sarah, both wives of Brandon's business partners, are listening with great interest and nodding in unison. Natalie wants to contribute but feels two steps behind, as if her brain isn't focusing.

Please let this be a virus, she begs silently. Wasn't her neighbor sick last week? She could have picked something up over the weekend in Connecticut when she went to visit her in-laws. After all, how will she fit into the new clothes Brandon insisted she purchase in preparation for summer: signature cream pants from Ralph; thin crepe suits in rose and sand from Calvin; gray pin dots from Armani. She'd already taken them to the fitters for alterations. She'd be unable to return them, and as far as Natalie knew, there was no maternity policy, no unexpected pregnancy clause which would allow her to credit them to her account.

Off to the left, someone's child is wailing. As if at a tennis match, the four women turn their attention in that direction. Seated at the adjoining table are two ladies in their thirties with their offspring. One child is crying. Natalie watches the mother. Watches the way she shovels food into the baby's mouth, not waiting for her to swallow the mush so that more oozes out than stays in. Natalie wants to tell the rushed mommy to slow down, almost yells this command from across the table, over the buzz of conversation and the clamoring of dishes in the kitchen. Can't she see her child hasn't finished? Isn't the other woman watching?

The mommies make exaggerated faces, distorted tics, while patrons and the owner of the coffee shop all stop to fuss over the small people, acting like quacking ducks fighting for a tossed piece of crust. Some stop to offer comments and advice, others want to touch the little golden beings, as if their aura will bring luck, like the holy water at church.

The waiter brings oval ceramic plates with salads, omelets, and sandwiches resting upon them to the table. The heat from the kitchen, the heavy air, the constant clattering of silverware, all make her think she will be sick.

As her friends eat, her attention is drawn back to these mothers. If she looks hard enough, Natalie can still see who they once were—eager, passionate, perfectly styled from head to toe. Now they look drained, large rings residing under their eyes and worn on the appropriate fingers like trophies, their purses replaced by oversized diaper bags with Peanuts and Disney characters on them.

Molly is talking about something. Then she is laughing. Her other friends do, too, so Natalie smiles and cheats her way through it. She wants to contribute to the conversation, only she doesn't know what the subject is. She is sure they're past Camille's party by now.

"Would Friday the twenty-fourth work for everyone?" Camille asks, flipping through her pad of notes. Natalie watches her friends take out their datebooks, lizard Filofaxes and Hermès day-timers, to check if their schedules permit another social event. They nod and it has been decided. This only adds to her unbalanced state.

Perhaps a party is what she needs, perhaps this is what good wives do. Natalie feels as though she is living someone else's life. As if these women have become strangers to her, the situation surreal, the restaurant a cardboard cutout, the patrons, actors.

They were living in Nantucket. Natalie was painting then, and Brandon worked at a small brokerage house when Merrill Lynch offered him a job. A month later they sat on the runway, their plane fifth in line to take off. Natalie looked out the window and wondered what she would do in New York. She remembered Brandon taking her hand, remarking how all great artists lived there, and while he was at work, she could paint in the SoHo loft he would buy her.

Those were the selling points. But there never was an art studio or time to paint. Natalie's schedule was filled with dinners with Brandon's clients, days of shopping, tracking down the exact items he felt should be in their home and in her wardrobe.

"You can't go to Daniel or La Goulue in this," he'd say, holding up her overalls and paint-stained T-shirts. She should have fought harder. Looked closer at her life.

On her wedding day, Natalie dragged Lena onto the hotel's roof for a smoke, she in her white gown, Lena in a light blue bridesmaid's dress.

"I could always jump," she joked, flicking ashes away from herself.

"Do you love him?" Lena asked, motioning for the cigarette.

She watched smoke escape from Lena's mouth, wanting to say "yes," but the word sat in her throat like cotton.

For the past year, Natalie had written a list of positive qualities she felt Brandon possessed. She kept it folded in her bag, adding to it every now and then, taking it out and reading it to remind herself of his good points: calls his parents, wants children, takes out the trash . . . that was love, wasn't it?

At first, Natalie enjoyed the cocktail parties. Being home all day and not knowing anyone except her sister made her grateful for the company. The painfully long business dinners started to happen twice a week, followed by corporate dances, mandatory weekend events at clients' homes in the Hamptons and Connecticut. Then came the charity fund-raisers she planned with the other men's wives, all of whom were having babies and didn't need to work. Within a few months, Natalie became part of Brandon's job, an external component as important as his cell phone or Palm Pilot.

Now she sits with these women, having lunch and talking about nothing.

A pair of mommies walk by as a little boy runs ahead of them. Space is cleared for the women with strollers, like Moses parting the Red Sea. As he passes, Natalie is sure she can smell baby powder and wet diapers. When his mother catches up to him, she grabs harshly at his arm, losing her temper, and yells at the three-year-old, who lets out a piercing cry. Like live theater, the restaurant is a captive audience to this spectacle.

Natalie thinks back to when her mother chased her down the street, screamed at her for running ahead, jerked her arm so hard that it popped out of its socket. The rest of the day was spent in the hospital waiting for the specialist. The white-walled room, black-padded table swirl into images of the sobbing boy in years of therapy, lying on a succession of leather couches, surrounded by walls painted in calming, subdued colors of browns and tans. She cringes at this.

"What are you thinking?" Sarah asks, her new diamond earrings reflecting off the large fluorescent lights of the glorified diner. A recent anniversary gift, they are too big and look fake. Every time Sarah moves her head, she creates her own laser show.

"Nothing," Natalie replies.

Under the table, she slides her hand over her abdomen. She swears it feels larger. Rounder. She rests it there in hopes of stopping the nausea; then, in sudden frustration, she slaps it as hard as she can without crying. Even though she winces, she cleverly contorts her face into a fake sneeze.

"Maybe you are coming down with something," Camille says with concern, resting a soft hand on top of Natalie's. "All of Carol's kids are sick."

Camile pulls her hand away and for a moment Natalie wants to reach for it, have something to hold on to. "Make it go away," she whispers, so softly, so lightly that no one can hear it but her.

She passes by Lee's Art Supplies on her way home. Like a junkie, her body remembers, even craves the smell of turpentine. She misses the scent of fresh paint. The wet, slippery feel of the colored oils. The person she once was in college.

Dressed in men's oxford shirts and black jeans, she'd carry brushes and paints in her knapsack rather than a bag filled with paint and brushes for her face. She had not entered the world where women wore Papagallo shoes and matching headbands or turtlenecks with whales on them. She hadn't learned that sorority parties were a lifeline, that your last name and a bank account were all you needed to advance in this world. That you could lose your identity.

Natalie knows she can already say good-bye to the long afternoons spent at the museum, which she lies about to her other friends who only know she disappears in the latter part of the day.

"Bridge lessons," she tells them. "Brandon thought I should learn."

Brandon will be ecstatic. After all, his mother, Ruthann, has practically set up a room for an imaginary grandchild. Natalie herself has been groomed for the position since they announced their engagement five years ago. Now, with a baby, there will be no art tours, no classes. And Brandon doesn't believe in sitters or nannies, insisting *he* never had one.

"My mother managed," he announced. He was standing in their living room in his boxers, hands on his hips. His boss's wife was expecting.

"My sister has help," Natalie countered, her voice escalating to match her husband's.

"She has three children. When we're on our third, you can have as many nannies as you want." Then he smirked, a pathetic, patronizing grin. "Besides, my mother would be available to sit anytime you wanted."

She had to control her laughter. She'd get her tubes tied before she handed her child or anyone else's over to Ruthann.

Natalie clutches the Duane Reade bags filled with pregnancy tests, each bought at separate, unfamiliar drugstores, as she shops at Zabar's. She thoughtfully chooses appropriate goodies for Brandon's dinner—thinly sliced string beans in ginger sauce, stir-fry vegetables, new potatoes with sautéed onions, and grilled chicken. This will make him happy and make her the wife she's expected to be.

She thinks back to last month. They had come home drunk from a cocktail party. She recalled Brandon stopping at the Korean market to satisfy a sudden craving for ice cream. He returned home with chocolate Häagen-Dazs and a bag of Raisinets. He fed them to her, still in his tux, as she lay naked on their satin sheets. She vaguely remembered reaching for her diaphragm and Brandon taking it out of her hand.

The pregnancy boxes all looked similar, each promising ninety-nine percent accuracy results in three, four, or five minutes. And each came with an added bonus: buy one, get one free; win $5,000 instantly in family savings bonds; complimentary Lubriderm lotion. Natalie does not know what she will do if the tests show up pink, one of her least favorite colors. Or if the line is black or a circle appears or whatever shape or object forms within the allotted time.

She had dressed incognito, scarf tied around her head and large, dark sunglasses over her eyes as she wandered down the aisles of the stores.

"Which one is best?" she asked the saleswoman in a fake French accent at the first store. The girl didn't know and called her friend over. The two talked loudly, asking other workers their opinions. The second drug store kept the tests behind the counter. Like illegal paraphernalia, they stood alongside condoms and cigarettes, making Natalie feel as though she needed a written note from her gynecologist in order to purchase one. The third and final stop was the worst. She was in the middle of pulling out her wallet when a friend walked by.

"Nat? Is that you?" Kelly said. "I almost didn't recognize you with the scarf. Bad hair day?"

Natalie saw Kelly's eyes move from her to the test lying on the counter. "For you?" She beamed.

"No, my sister, Lena."

"Oh."

"She's been feeling sick all week and hasn't had a chance to run out. She didn't want to get Richard's hopes up, so . . ."

"Oh, of course." Kelly winked. "Your secret's safe with me."

. . .

She enters their apartment and stands in the doorway, frozen. She hates this room. Hates the first moment when she walks in, the hard objects, the unsettling feeling that something terrible has taken place without her knowledge. Even hates the smell of the housekeeper's cheap perfume.

Before they officially moved in, a decorator was hired at Ruthann's forceful suggestion. Natalie had wanted the job. Wanted the chance to use her skills, show off her talents, but Brandon said she was doing them a favor. Ruthann, too, said Natalie would be silly not to agree. They had fought about it for a few minutes, Ruthann's face getting red, Natalie swearing she would be strong and not back down. She reminded Ruthann her degree was in design. Ruthann made a tsking noise with her tongue which sounded like air escaping from a tire.

"What woman wouldn't jump at the chance to have someone else handle everything? Besides, Natalie, you know, problems arise and you're not very confrontational. You don't want someone to take advantage of you. That's why you need a decorator."

And so it was decided. The apartment took six months longer than intended and after the unveiling, she realized that nothing she and the decorator had agreed upon was in the room. Now everything seemed unfamiliar. The paint, the furniture, even the moldings looked foreign.

She runs her fingers over the Baccarat vases and Christofle water bucket—gifts from Brandon's business associates and friends of his parents—wishing she could replace them with sharp marble sculptures, ugly and noxious.

She unwraps each test, revealing long thermometer wands, small plastic cups, and cardboard discs. While she waits for her results, Natalie paces, flips on the TV, takes a Valium.

When she first met Brandon, he was wearing a white shirt, khakis, and suspenders which hung off his pants. He shook her hand, then put his left one on top of hers, like a warm cheese sandwich. She fell in love with him right there in the dorm room.

With a little coercing, he would model for her. One time she talked him into posing naked in the TV lounge, his sleek, lanky body leaning up against the vending machine. She loved to make him laugh, loved watching his muscular body move. He would tell her stories—some real, some not—and make her guess which were truths while she painted. For a treat, and when Brandon was very well behaved, she would feed him M&M's and Raisinets from the very machine he was hugging. No one had told her people change. And she's learned memories are no longer enough to hold on to. Even though she has tried, her picture has blurred. So slowly that it's tricked her.

She is rummaging through Brandon's desk drawers for cigarettes and is about to light one when the clock beeps. She hurries into the bathroom and sees the tests aligned like estate items at Sotheby's. Two pink lines, indicating "yes," appear brightly on the middle test. As she tries to catch her breath, a pink "P" emerges on the heart-shaped cardboard disc closest to the window. Natalie doesn't even bother to wait for the third. She walks hurriedly to the incinerator and tosses them down the chute, wishing she could hurl herself along with them.

Hours later, she and Brandon eat dinner. Over the Zabar's food she swears she can hear the baby breathing between bites of chicken and the clicking of the fork on Brandon's perfect teeth. She wants to reach for his hand, look into his face for redeeming qualities and see the boy he was in college. *If he smiles at me*, she thinks, *if he asks me how my day was, I'll tell him about the baby.* She pretends to reach for the salt, hoping he will cup her hand in his, kiss it gently the way he used to, or pass the salt without her having to reach too far for it. She almost cries when her fingers feel the cool metal and her hand wraps around the shaker. She grunts slightly, falling back into her chair, her husband never taking his eyes off the TV.

Natalie has a recurring nightmare where she cuts Brandon open, hoping his former, younger self will pop out like Athena exploding from Zeus' head. In her dream, he is on an operating table. Natalie is dressed in one of his Armani suits, a mask on her face, large metal clamps in her hands. She cracks open his chest, spreads his rib cage apart, and reaches deep inside his body. She removes paint brushes, swatches of canvas, scholarship letters, and awards she won in college. Last to come out is a part of her own heart. All things Brandon has digested. Now, unable to sleep, she lies awake at night, listening to Brandon's even breathing. It's his harsh voice, the way he sounds like his father on the phone so that Natalie can't tell if it's her husband or her father-in-law calling, that keeps her awake.

The sky is overcast when Natalie meets Lena and her three nieces in Central Park. Rather than run into Natalie's arms, they head for the swings and the slide. Lena gives her sister a cumbersome hug, her arms laden with diaper bags, juice boxes, and toys. She feels smothered in between them.

Natalie knows she is flawed. Realizes she is missing a Mommy gene as she observes her nieces, their blond hair bouncing up and down, their tiny, lean bodies running back and forth, chasing each other. They are so very breakable. One wrong move, one small mistake, and Natalie's damaged them for life.

Lena was always more maternal, even as children, almost as if she got Natalie's share in the womb. When they played house, Lena always wanted to have four kids, two girls, two boys. Or Lena would be the mom, Natalie her child. Natalie preferred chemistry sets, Legos, and Smurfs. Boyish things, her mother would call them.

She's tried to bond with her nieces, has spent hours playing tea party and Candyland, hoping a maternal instinct would emerge, wet and glowing, ready for caretaking. But it never did. The girls would eventually cry over something and Natalie would feel utterly helpless.

She watches Lena, looks at her enviously, desperate to understand, even share the secret of motherhood. She wants to tell her sister about the thing growing inside her, explain why she cannot keep it, and ask that she accompany her to the 4:15 appointment with Dr. Briskel, the kindly old man who delivered both of them.

Brandon is wearing the new suit he bought last week at Paul Stuart. He looks like a brown pear. Natalie thinks about this as she is introduced to Mr. and Mrs. Sager, client friends of her husband. He is an investment banker, she owns a stationery boutique. They have just had a baby boy. Pictures of him are everywhere, artsy black-and-whites, and bright colors: him sleeping, nursing, drooling.

The Sagers' home, a grand duplex on the Upper East Side, is decorated in whites and creams. White marble on the floor, cream couch, ivory walls, even milky-white lamps. The only color in the apartment is from the beautiful paintings. Natalie aches to touch them, run her fingers over the raised paint, talk about the artists, but every time she starts to use her voice, another overlaps hers.

They sit down for dinner. A white walkie-talkie device is on the table next to cream placemats, bone plates, and a small crystal bell used to summon the server. The gentle hum coming from the speaker suddenly turns to staticky crying.

"Guess who's up?" Mrs. Sager excuses herself and after a moment, returns with a small bundle in her arms wrapped in a white blanket.

"There's my boy," Mr. Sager exclaims. "Who's Daddy's best boy?"

"Say, 'I am,' " Mrs. Sager says, her voice high-pitched and singsongy. It reminds Natalie of the way Brandon's mother talks to her.

"Do you have any children?" he asks, lighting a cigar.

"Not yet," Brandon says, answering for his wife, "but soon." He winks at Natalie while reaching for a cigar. She nods back.

"Would you like to hold him?" asks Mrs. Sager, putting the child in Natalie's unprepared arms. It lies uncomfortably on her chest, fidgeting and wet. Her body is so tense she is sure the child can feel this. She wants to stroke the soft, tiny head but is afraid. What if she were to drop it? Break its neck from holding it incorrectly? What if they leave her alone with the infant?

The baby starts to cry.

Mrs. Sager wrinkles her face and leans in to remove the sobbing child, who is instantly put at ease in its owner's arms.

"He doesn't take well to other people," she offers apologetically.

Natalie can see the woman is embarrassed for her and for Brandon. What a shame, being married to such an inept girl. She visualizes this episode being spread in their social circles. Brandon is not happy, either. He rolls his eyes to show his disappointment in his wife, the one who cannot hold an infant, the one who is barely functioning herself.

Opting not to go to her gynecologist, Natalie sits in an abortion clinic with three young women, or children, she can't decide which. Posters that shout free choice and safe sex hang all around her. The walls, which look as if they were once white, have now turned into a dull yellow as if they started out entirely different and have faded little by little, becoming something else entirely. Like the mommies in the restaurant, if Natalie stares long enough she can just make out the original color, find small patches of white behind a couch.

She fills out several forms while seated in the nondescript chrome chairs with gray padded seats. Magazines—*Parenting, Parents,* and *Child*—form a patchwork of color as they mix with informational pamphlets on VD, STD, AIDS, and other diseases.

Natalie reminds herself not to touch anything and to use her own pen rather than the one attached to the clipboard. There are to be no fingerprints. Nothing to prove she was here. Like her trips to the museum, there will be no evidence. Her receipts and admission tickets are always thrown out on her way home.

She is in the middle of writing down the name *Jane Summer* and creating a phony family history when she notices one of the girls is crying quietly to herself. Her long, dark hair hides most of her face but Natalie can still see her eyes, red and glassy. Natalie aches to sit beside her, hold her hand, stroke her hair and tell her not to worry, that she is doing the right thing, that she is being responsible. She longs for the someone to say these same words to her.

Natalie finds herself towering over the girl, extending a pretty flowered handkerchief she has retrieved from her purse. "Here you go," Natalie says, smiling softly. Before the surprised child has a chance to thank her, Natalie is out the door. She can just hear the receptionist call her phony name as the door closes behind her.

During the cab ride home, she shakes uncontrollably. She watches the meter jump every few blocks as she tries to catch her breath.

At home she changes out of her carefully chosen "abortion outfit" (brown cardigan sweater set and gray flannel pants) and into one of Brandon's white oxfords. On days when she feels most detached from Brandon, she lights his cigar, parades around the house in his trousers and tie, stands in his loafers, and pretends to be him. Today, she retrieves her old jeans smattered with paint from the suitcase in the closet and slips them on. They fit snugly over her abdomen. She lights a cigarette and puts her hair up in a ponytail secured by a rubber band found in the kitchen drawer. She then asks Jose, her most favorite of the porters, to escort her down to the storage room in the basement.

They ride the elevator in silence. Natalie smells the sweat on him, longs to run her hands over his muscular body. Have him hold her in his thick arms.

"Are you and Mr. Finer taking a trip?" he says, unlocking the door.

The room is musty and dank. "No, I'm redecorating and wanted to see what we had down here."

He nods and pushes the metal luggage rack toward a large, narrow rectangular box marked *Property of 12E, Finer*, in bright red marker.

Natalie opens the box carefully, removing the first object. She gently tears off the plastic and tissue paper to reveal an oil picture of a dilapidated farmhouse in a handsome silver frame. She repeats this motion, feeling empowered by the repetition, by the heat of the storage room, by the way Jose is helping her.

It doesn't take long for them to remove the eight pictures from their temporary home and set them gently on the rack. Jose looks at the one positioned nearest to him. It's an abstract painting of a face. The long nose, angry eyes, pale colors make the ghostly image seem to pop off the canvas. Another reveals a woman's face, eyes sad, mouth hanging open, as if she is screaming. Last is a painting of Brandon. He is naked and lying on a sofa. In one hand he holds a newspaper, a lit cigarette in the other. An ashtray is balanced on his stomach.

"I like this one, Mrs. Finer," he says, taking a step back to admire the work. "He looks half dead, half living."

He stares at her and Natalie can feel herself blush. She nods and thanks him.

Upstairs, she puts on the stereo, removing Brandon's *Best of: Famous Instrumental Hits of the 90's* and inserts Fleetwood Mac's *Rumors*. She lets the velvety music carry her back to her Vassar days while she carefully takes down the expensive artwork which dominates their walls. She uproots the Warhol, the Max, the Haring, signed lithographs, and originals of useless objects: a can of soup, a building, an orange figure. All that remain are black outlines. Natalie runs a finger over the marks. Then, slowly, purposely, she replaces the empty spots with the paintings that are leaning against the front door.

She stands in the middle of the room, looking at her life. Each wall bears a small piece of her soul, a fingerprint. She looks from wall to wall, making quick, swift movements as her head snaps from one side to the next. Before she knows it, she is turning, fast, like when she and Lena were little and would have contests to see who could spin the most without falling down. She spins until the apartment becomes a dizzying blur of her work and the carefully chosen items that have been intentionally placed around the apartment. Her masterpieces merge with coffee-table books on boats, dead presidents, architecture. With furniture she hates. With everything that doesn't belong to her. They all congeal, fusing into unrecognizable shapes. When she has had enough, she walks drunkenly to the terrace, desperate for air, steadying herself as she makes her way past the swirling room, forcing her eyes to focus.

She slides open the glass door, walks out feeling the cold breeze and the aroma of winter. She leans over the railing and peers down. She spits, watching her saliva as it travels through the air, free-falling to the cement, leaving a small speck of wetness.

Natalie spots twelve children waiting on the street corner with their teacher for the light to change. Dressed in their school uniforms, standing in two perfect rows, they look like the little girls in the *Madeline* books. She sticks a foot through the thick bars and pushes herself up for a better look. If it's a girl, she would read those books to her daughter like her mother did to her and Lena. Natalie leans out a little further, still dizzy, hands wet with sweat. Desperate to catch a glimpse of her future, she slopes her body forward. She can just make out the name of their school. She smiles, comfort moving through her as her hand slips from the brass railing.

THE JOY OF FUNERALS

I'm in the elevator looking as if I'm having a panic attack.

I press the first-floor button, knowing that it won't make me drop down any faster, but it gives me something to do. Next, I race out of the building and run across Fifth Avenue and head west, faces turning as I brush past them. I can tell they're wondering if an emergency has occurred, if something's the matter. I weave my way through the swarm of people, maneuvering in and out like a cockroach running alongside the linoleum on someone's kitchen floor. I dart into the subway, retrieve my MetroCard from my bag, swipe it through the turnstile, and jump into the car as the doors start to close.

I'm a pro by now. Got it down to a science.

On the train I calculate the number of stops and the fastest plan. If I see the uptown express, I'll transfer cars and get out at Seventy-second Street, then walk the five blocks to the chapel. If I stay on the local, I'll exit on Seventy-ninth and walk two blocks back.

Moments later, I snap my head out from the underworld, shooting up like a groundhog looking for its shadow, and enter the coffee shop on the corner. I make a beeline for the bathroom, the aroma of French fries and grilled cheese triggering hunger pangs, reminding me I've not eaten this morning.

I slip into the empty stall and pull off my shirt. Beads of sweat drip down my back as I remove a fresh linen one from my tote. I dry my underarms with the first, then seal it in the Ziploc bag I've brought along. I strip off my stockings, toss them in the trash, put my shoes back on, and tuck my new shirt into my skirt. I shove a piece of gum in my mouth and chew for a few seconds before spitting it out. *Breathe. Breathe.* Foundation, lipstick, and powder are applied and hair is gelled back. I glance at my watch. "Not bad," I say to my flushed reflection. Nothing in my teeth, hair looks decent. Not perfect, but passing. Dab a little perfume under each ear and—*voila!*

I take another deep, cleansing breath, slip on my glasses, open the door, and proceed out of the diner like a normal person.

The weather is outstanding, warm and beautiful. Clear. I'm sure Edna is thankful for this. I'm sure everyone attending Archie's funeral will comment on what a gorgeous day it is.

People are predictable. In the winter, they stand in a huddled mass of tears, matted down in thick wool coats, scarves wrapped tightly around necks, hands in leather gloves. In the summer, the warm air rings of sorrow and mourners sigh in sadness as cotton jackets and black dresses blow in the breeze. To me it doesn't matter what season a funeral takes place; I enjoy them just the same.

I stride into the chapel and attempt to hide my pride. While searching for Edna Siden, Archie's wife, I nod and exchange sympathetic looks with others. I stick my hand into my pocket and finger the obit from the paper, hoping the words will magically transfer into my subconscious. I feel the coarse paper, think about the heavy black ink rubbing off onto my skin, as if the dead's souls are rubbing on to me. This one reads: *Archie Siden, 82, beloved husband of Edna, father to Jack, and brother to Maxwell, passed away on Thursday due to complications from a heart attack.* Archie was a handbag manufacturer and the first to design the Audrey Bag. It looked like a small, round hatbox turned sideways. Audrey Hepburn donned it in the movie *Breakfast At Tiffany's.*

I take a quick scan, survey the mahogany-colored room, make some mental notes—emergency exit, bathroom, coat rack—before seeing if anyone looks familiar. Though the chapel is crowded, I'm able to pick Edna out instantly. Grief is inked onto her face like a large red birthmark. A temporary tattoo of sadness for the permanently widowed.

Edna is a small, plump, gentle-looking woman who appears to be in her seventies. Several people are at her side. They have formed a protective ring around her, ready to catch her should she fall over, should her body finally register the shock.

I approach slowly, making my way through her line of bodyguards.

"Hello, I'm Zoe."

Her face is still. Frozen.

"You don't know me, but I worked with your husband years ago," I tell her. "In fact, Archie gave me my first job." My palms are still wet from racing and I wipe them on my skirt before reaching for her gloved hand to hold in mine. She looks into my eyes and her tears start. "He was a very kind man. Always ready to listen, always had a smile on his face."

She tightens her grip, half smiles, thinking about what I've just said. I can tell she's recalling a past memory, flipping through a catalogue of moments when Archie was especially sweet. She gives me a firm, quick squeeze as someone takes her arm, ushering her along. The rabbi opens the doors to the chapel and we all file in.

. . .

I sit in the back pew with strangers.

A lonely, eerie silence envelops us as the smell of wood and other people's perfume mix together. I let the organ music drift through me as I stare at the mourners, captivated by their closeness, by the bond they all possess. I watch as they enter and take a seat in the chapel: husbands and wives who sit close together, hands gripping hands, one the supporter, one the consoled; gay men who clasp each other, hands around backs of heads, and tight hugs; small children who long to run up to the casket and are restrained by their parents. But mostly, I'm envious of sisters who sit so close together that they look as if they are trying to become one body, a mush of memories and history congealed like a thin strand of popcorn hung purposely on a Christmas tree.

In order to fight the nervousness, I count heads. Other times, I'll play a mental game: number of women versus men; people wearing black versus other colors. Sometimes, I'll think I see someone I know, or someone who recognizes me. A pounding begins in my chest as I hold my breath. A buzzing fills my head as everyone becomes a blur, a slurry mass of familiar faces and features. I feel my body shut down, organ by organ, and wait in utter silence.

Sitting in the back is sometimes alienating, but when it's full like it is today, it's often the best place. Apologetic latecomers slide in, guilt-ridden, hoping to go unnoticed, whispering to me, asking if they've missed anything. Or they sometimes feel inclined to share the reason why they're late. *Traffic was awful*, the wife will say. Or, *We sat on the FDR for an hour.* I fill them in quietly, explaining who has spoken, what they've missed, talking about the deceased as if he were part of my own family. Only after I've introduced myself and connected with them on some significant level can I rest and breathe a sigh of relief. I have been defined. I have proven I belong. I have earned a right to stay.

Archie's brother, Eli, is first to speak. He clears his throat and grips the edges of the wooden podium. He talks of a big brother who protected him from school bullies, who took him in during the Great Depression, gave him a job at the factory, and eventually made him a partner when the market crashed and brokers were out of work. He speaks of a supportive, smart, family man. Someone I'd have liked to know.

As he continues his eulogy, the audience forms a chorus of sniffles and sighs. The nodding of heads, the holding of hands, and the drying of tears all happen at once. I want to reach for someone, but I'm alone.

Later, Edna introduces me to others as one of Archie's favorite employees from the old days. She beams like a proud parent as her lady friends ooh and ahh, telling me how nice it was for me to pay my respects, how happy it would have made Archie to know he was so well remembered.

"You never forget a man who does so much good," I say.

They nod, eyes glassy.

For the most part, I stay silent. I listen to others who tell stories and share rare glimpses of the recently deceased. I eavesdrop, collecting pieces of random information, all of which I will use to compose my own story, braiding it together into a tapestry of fabricated memories.

Something is to be said for the relative who can embellish on a tale or two about someone when they were six or seven, or call them by an old nickname they have outgrown, or embarrass them with information privy only to an insider. There's a level of understanding and forgiveness that can't be re-created with anyone else. They are bookmarks in each other's past as they reminisce about the only thing they have in common. Conversations pick up exactly where they left off years ago. And as they share stories, something magical and intense happens. A small puzzle piece slips quietly into a fading picture. Slips quietly into me.

Before people leave for the cemetery, Edna goes out of her way to find me and asks if I have her address. She and Archie's family will be sitting shiva. Do I want to stop by?

"I'd love to come, but I've got to visit my father at the nursing home," I tell her.

She smiles. "Such a dear," she adds, putting her hand on my cheek. It rests there for a moment, soft and warm. Then she leans forward and kisses my forehead ever so gently. For an instant, I'm five years old, standing on a stool with my name on it, leaning over a porcelain sink, looking into the mirror in my grandmother's bathroom. I smell Edna's rosy perfume as it merges with the scent of Ivory soap, which my grandmother used. Her hands, smooth as silk, would lather up my dirty face, rinse it clean, and pat it dry. Afterward, she'd lean in and kiss me right above the bridge of my nose. My grandmother's lips were tender and warm, like Edna's gloved hand. Then she would press her cheek to mine.

For a moment, I can't catch my breath. I just want to stand here for the rest of my life with Edna Siden's hand on my face. Unexpected tears well up in my eyes. I do my best to blink them away. Real tears are not usually allowed during these processions. They are reserved for the quiet darkness of my apartment, shed over cold TV dinners and empty take-out containers.

Edna removes a handkerchief from her pocket. Red petals line the corners; patches of lipstick are smattered in the middle. From my angle, it looks like a small abstract painting. She dabs her eyes. "Oh, sweetheart, don't cry. He would be so happy you were here."

All I can do is nod.

. . .

I return to the office. My absence has clearly not been missed. I highly doubt my father's firm would collapse if there weren't enough pencils, Post-its, or coffee. Technically, my job is shopping for office supplies. Thank God I went to college and got that degree in fine arts.

As a child, I loved coming here. Found it thrilling to watch my father scurry around, make important phone calls, and hold meeting with his colleagues in the room that held all the big, daunting books. Now I work here. It's a pity job. Everyone knows it.

I enter the bathroom and find Lilly, one of my co-workers, already doing a makeup check. Her blush, eye shadow, and powder are sprawled on the marble slab. I reach for her blush brush and sweep it across my face. I don't need to ask if I can use it. Here in the bathroom, everything is community property.

She's mid-sentence as the chimes from St. Patrick's Cathedral interrupt our space, filling the air with gongs and bells. I watch her expression change to delight as she proceeds to do her best Shannon imitation. She gets very solemn, puffs out her cheeks, puts a hand in the air, and in a low, singsongy voice, says, "People." Then a little louder, "People. Can I please ask you all to settle down? I would like to have a moment of silence."

We both laugh at this and for a minute, I am a bad girl. The cool, rebellious member of my family. Lilly knows it's safe in here with me, mimicking our co-worker, because I'm her ticket to freedom. Her "Get Out of Jail" card.

It's hard to fire the boss's daughter. Harder, still, to make friends. People are nice to you because they have to be. Conversations stop when you walk by. Lunch offers are few and after-work drink invites nonexistent. I don't keep in touch with many people from college and hardly anyone from high school. The friends I made as a child have moved away, relocated to warm states like California, Florida, and Texas. Others have married and now have families of their own. The office is all I have.

I smile and clap. "Well done." This is how people bond at my father's firm, sharing makeup and poking fun at others. But in the back of my mind I'm wondering who else has died, what the body looked like, and if I can pull a double.

I glance at my watch.

"Nina, can you get your father to order new chairs? The ones we have now hurt my ass." She looks from her reflection to mine, her face in mid-freeze, the bright red lipliner an inch away from her lips. "You must have some pull or something. Right?" Even though Lilly is Asian, she has no accent and is more American than I.

My foot does a little tap on the bathroom tile. I need to get back to my desk. I'm sure I've carelessly left the *Times* open and circled the obit announcement in red, as if I were looking for a job.

Lilly's mouth is still moving. She's saying something about a party she went to, then talks about a new Hermès bag she's bought and finally comes full circle, focusing on the office chairs.

I wish she'd shut up. My head is going to explode if she doesn't.

Officemates say a restrained hello, or they smile as I pass them en route to my father's office. I stand in his door frame and wait to be noticed. His glasses are perched on his nose, blue contract pages are in one hand, manila folder with pink and white papers are in the other.

I take stock of his belongings; coffee mug, bottle of water, ink blotter, leather couch, the crisp shirt that hangs on the hook, and though I can't see it from my angle, I know a clean, fresh "courtroom" suit is in the closet. A black, lacquer-like basket on the floor holds magazines and newspapers: *The Wall Street Journal, Newsweek,* and *The Law Review* are his afternoon reading.

"Nina," he says, surprised, as if I've just dropped by the office unexpectedly, as if he hasn't seen me here every day, or even two hours ago.

It's still sunny when I leave. Labor Day comes late this year and Manhattanites are taking advantage of the last long weekend. Lexington Avenue is littered with people waiting for the jitney bus to take them out to the Hamptons. The young ones sit on their weekend bags, talking on their cells, reading paperback books. The older ones lean against the buildings for support, their dogs in LV carrying cases.

I think about Edna as I unlock my door, as I hang up my clothes, as I open the plastic bag that still houses my damp shirt and release it into the laundry hamper.

I linger in the closet, looking at all the bags. Each outfit is sealed in plastic to save the smells. Like flashes from firecrackers, the scents ignite my memory as they come flooding back. I unzip the bag that holds my navy suit. It smells like bagels and lox. Instantly, I recall the Saperstein funeral. The prairie skirt with Indian motif smells of ham and beer, the O'Mara wake. That time, they let me help out in the kitchen and I got to dance in the dining room. One of the cousins held me close and told me I was pretty. That he wanted to kiss me but his brother was watching us, and it would have been inappropriate. My gray slacks and matching wool sweater reek of cigar smoke. I remember sitting in someone's library with several men and laughing at one of the stories a friend was telling about the deceased. I take a deep whiff of the flannel pants, feel slightly satisfied, and zip the bag closed.

When I can't sleep, I read through the scrapbook of funerals I've attended. A hundred and three, to date. All entries get the obit, plus a description of the event, the people I've met, and the soundings. Sometimes I lift a napkin or a matchbook. Other times, I'll snap a picture with my spy camera or take a Polaroid outside the chapel the next day. *Click*—I've immortalized them. Like the people I visit, I can never forget. My favorites are the letters of thanks I've received from devoted wives, lonely husbands, orphaned children, and friends of the deceased—souvenirs of the lives I've touched and the lives gone.

This is why I go to funerals.

. . .

Today the *Times* reports on a man who was killed in a terrible car accident. He was thirty-eight. Young. Only four years older than I. His wife, Leslie, is an advertising executive. Her husband, Dr. Larry Shappell, was Chief of Staff at Mount Sinai Hospital. He was the youngest person ever to hold that title. The picture of him in the paper, a black-and-white photo taken in his office, shows him shaking hands with the president of the hospital. You can see his plaques on the wall, his organized desk, and a frame with a photo of his wife. He and his wife have a home in White Plains. They have no children.

I fantasize that he's my husband. Visualize him coming home from a double shift at the hospital having operated on a young girl or a sick teenager with congenital heart failure. His hands would be red and raw from scrubbing all day, his eyes tired and heavy. I stare at the second picture of Larry in a turtleneck and slacks, standing next to his wife, who's dressed in a classy black suit, sweater thrown purposely over her shoulders. A silver pendant hangs around her neck. They look as though they're posing for a Banana Republic catalogue. These are people I should be friends with. People my mother would be happy to see me shuttling off to visit in the Hamptons or spending long weekends with on the Cape.

My choices for funeraling are very systematic. First, I race through the pages looking for familiar names—friends of my parents, old classmates, mothers and fathers who let me stay in their swanky apartments on Fifth and Park Avenues, fed me home-cooked meals, incorporating each food group element, let me call them by their first names, included me in games of Monopoly, Sorry, and Clue, talked to me, made me feel wanted, and let me be part of their surroundings. I check for business associates from the jobs I've held or haven't been able to keep, for friends of my grandparents, friends of friends; these are all level one, first hand connection. If I don't find anyone whose name rings a bell, I move to level two, personal association. Like betting on a horse, I choose a name I like, one that reminds me of a fond memory. Thelma, the name of my third-grade teacher, or Steven, the first boy I kissed. Next is level three, movie and musical references. Last week I went to Rupert Pinner's wake because it reminded me of Robert De Niro's character, Rupert Pupkin, from Martin Scorsese's *King of Comedy*. And finally, four, the riskiest of the bunch—eeny, meeny, miney, mo. I rarely get to four and have only attended two funerals from that category: Shechal's, a taxi driver who was shot in the head by a fare, and Svetlana's, a Russian immigrant who died of streptococcus.

I've gotten lucky with Larry. He's perfect. I rifle though my crammed kitchen drawer for scissors and carefully cut out his photo. I reach for the glue stick and come across old prescription slips I haven't filled. I fan them out, think about collecting enough to wallpaper my bathroom but stuff them back into their place. I stick Larry's photo into my scrapbook along with the obit.

These drawers are normally clean and organized, my house spotless. You never know when a visitor will pop by or when you'll meet a neighbor in the hallway while throwing out the trash or riding down in the elevator to get the mail or to see if you have a package. Sometimes I hang out in the lobby, talking with my doormen, telling them I have a leaky pipe or that the intercom isn't working or I've made too much pasta for dinner, would they like some? We chitchat as I eye the door, hoping one of the tenants I know will walk in, cheeks rosy from the cold, too many packages in their arms. Or they'll be walking their dogs, the kind that jump on you and give licks to anyone who will pet them. A therapist I saw for a few weeks in college told me I reminded him of a cocker spaniel, always looking for someone to play with. At our last session, I barked on my way out.

The Shappell funeral is Friday at the White Plains Memorial Chapel. I usually attend those within the five boroughs of Manhattan, though I make exceptions for special ones like Larry's. I like the train ride. Like the feeling of having somewhere to go. People are extra-friendly. You can strike up a conversation with the person seated across from you or ask for directions.

The night before, I surf the Web to learn about heart problems. Perhaps I can have a murmur or a nasty case of asthma that's left me with a weak heart. The good thing about murmurs is you can look fine and still have one since they're hard to detect. Some don't require surgery and can be treated with medication. I find the perfect disease, Marsocoma, the slight breakdown of the vascular organ. A drug called Trilladon strengthens the valves and

THE JOY OF FUNERALS

blood flow along with the tissues. I practice saying my disease and
print out the information from The Heart Association's home site.

I'm wearing a chocolate brown suit today, one of my better ones,
and sophisticated glasses. The chapel is only eight blocks from the
North White Plains train station. I got great directions from the
fat, balding man who sat next to me. I trudge up the hill, look
at the street signs, and follow the instructions until I see cars
parked from three blocks away.

The chapel is packed. There are easily over 450 people here.
Not one seat is empty. A tingling of excitement starts in my pelvis
and I feel as if I've had too much coffee. Everyone is young and
pretty and perfect. The seats are filled with doctors and hospital
staff, people from the ad agency, friends, neighbors, and family.

"This is truly a turnout," I say to a thin woman standing next
to me in the back.

She nods. "It's criminal what's happened."

"Awful. I was scheduled to see him for a checkup next week.
I, I just can't believe he's gone."

"Were you one of his patients?"

I press my lips together, sigh deeply. "Yeah. He was the first
to detect the murmur." I look her right in the eyes. She's wearing
a brimmed black hat, tilted theatrically to the left. Her lipstick is
too red for her complexion and makes her look like a female
version of Dracula.

"We should find you a seat." She takes my hand and pushes
her way through a mass of people until she reaches the last pew.

"Howard, would you mind giving up your seat? This girl . . .
woman," she corrects herself, "was one of Larry's patients." Then
she lowers her voice, "She has heart problems."

I don't accept at first, then when he insists, already on his feet, I obey. "He was a wonderful doctor," I say, inching into his warm spot, careful not to move too quickly. "One of the best and believe me, I've been to enough to know."

I stick out my hand, shake his, then reach for Dracula's. "I'm Sally Deven. Larry was the first one to diagnose my murmur."

Everyone within earshot oohs and nods.

"You have to meet his wife," she says. "She'd love to talk with you."

I get a ride to Leslie's house from Troy and Betty-Ann Morris. Troy and Larry were racquetball partners. Their car is an SUV minivan and has a child's seat strapped in the back. Betty-Ann clears a place for me, tosses some toys and books over to the left, and emerges with white paper bags and an empty Starbucks container in her hand. "Sorry it's such a mess." The back smells vaguely of Pampers and coffee. I finger the stuffed pig and stare out the window, watching the streets turn into a blur of green and blue.

We pass the cemetery on the way to Leslie's home. Several cars are already there. I see Leslie get out of one of the limos, make out her black sunglasses and matching outfit.

"Sally, you can hang your coat up in there." Betty-Ann points to the first door on my left as I walk in.

The house is beautiful. Large and roomy. Modern, yet warm. The floors are a gray-blue marble, the walls a soft white. A large flower arrangement rests on the glass table behind the couch while another sits on the Lucite coffee table. Blues and creams accentuate the shiny silver-and-chrome furniture.

"It was really sweet of you to offer to help. You sure you're up to it?"

I nod and follow her into the kitchen. "Larry said," I stop and look at the floor for a second, then back up at Betty-Ann, "he said as long as I take my medication I'm fine. Of course roller coasters are out."

She laughs, introduces me to a neighbor and the housekeeper, then hands me a platter of cold cuts. "That can go on the main table."

For the next hour I move around the house as if I've lived here my whole life.

As people start to arrive, I duck into the upstairs bathroom. I look in the medicine cabinet and take inventory of the small soaps shaped like shells. There are guest hand towels and a candle from L'Occitane. I open the cabinet underneath the large porcelain sink and find more soap, a basket of travel shampoo and conditioner bottles stolen from hotels, and a box of tampons. Something catches my eye. It's a mini sewing kit with a big "W" on it. I reach for it and slip it into my pocket.

By the time I come out, the room has filled up. The men are in dark gray suits, the women in slender black dresses and jackets, pashmina shawls draped over them. Others are in cashmere sweaters. All clutch black leather handbags.

I search out Leslie and see her walk in. Someone takes her coat, someone else hugs her and leads her into her own house. I watch from against the wall, paper cup filled with coffee in my hand.

Leslie Shappell is one of the most attractive women I have ever met. She looks like Jaclyn Smith when she was an Angel and the show was really popular. If I didn't know what she did for a living, I'd have thought she was a model. Her eyes are reddish but not glassy, and there are no tears as of yet. I wait for her to walk around, check on things, and finally settle into the family room. Someone brings her fresh coffee, someone else a plate of crackers and cheese, another a glass of wine.

The family room is my favorite. It's filled with lots of chairs and cushy couches, a large TV, and a fireplace. The smell of wood fills the air. There are huge glass windows that reveal a deck, a pool covered by a large green tarp, and a lovely garden. I visualize a golden retriever or chocolate lab in the kitchen or locked in the bedroom until all the guests have left.

Leslie is distant but approachable, and I listen for a few minutes as others express their condolences. I watch her accept their words, unmoved. Bored.

I inch up to her.

"I'm sure you've heard this all day, but he was a wonderful doctor. I was misdiagnosed three times before your husband found the problem." I see her eyes wander off to the front door. "To be honest, I had a little crush on him. He changed my life." I think I've lost her with this so I add, "The whole thing really sucks."

She snaps her gaze back to me. "It sure fucking does."

We wait in silence for a second.

"Thank you. If one more person told me they were sorry for my loss, I think I would have puked."

"That would have sucked, too."

She laughs and I know I've scored humor points somewhere on an invisible chart of likeability.

Betty-Ann and Troy come over. Others join us, too, and for a moment I feel privileged.

"Who is she?' the woman with the fat lips asks Betty-Ann.

"She's a patient of Larry's."

"Oh."

Suddenly, all attention is on me. I nod and smile slightly.

"How did you get here?" one of the guests asks—a neighbor of Leslie's, I think.

"Betty-Ann and Troy drove me."

"No, I meant to the funeral."

"I took the train."

Leslie rolls her eyes in my direction as if we're old friends.

"Sally, what do you do?" Troy asks.

"I collect circus memorabilia," the words spill out. "I work with film companies and theater productions."

More people gather around. My head spins and my heart speeds up.

"Do you smoke?" Leslie whispers in my ear.

I lift an eyebrow.

"Follow me," she says, pulling at my sleeve.

I accompany her out of the den. She leads me down a flight of steps into her basement. Even though the floor is carpeted, the room is still cold. There's a washing machine and dryer, a work-bench, TV, some odds and ends, mismatched furniture, and a few shelves that hold detergents, bleach, and other cleaning solutions. A large basket of dirty laundry is on the floor.

She props open a small window and pulls out a cigar box from behind the dryer. "If Larry knew I did this, he'd kill me."

She jumps up onto the washing machine and opens the box. I follow, easing myself up against the dryer and sit next to her. She takes out a joint, followed by a lighter. I watch the flame catch the tightly rolled paper, watch her inhale, see the smoke leave her mouth. I watch her get stoned and ache to tell her how beautiful she is. How her eyes sparkle, almost dance under the basement light.

Years ago I developed the missing-gene-link theory. The internal need for a sibling. Like looking for my husband, I look for the perfect older sister, the one I have fantasized about having since I was five. Unobtainable, unavailable, standoffish women all in a row. Who will be next? Who will fit the profile? Slightly cold, lightly damaged, mostly injured, all for the asking.

She passes me the joint. I put my lips around the wet paper and breathe in. I let the smoke fill my lungs, feel them expanding inside my chest, and hand it back. I blow smoke out of my mouth and start to laugh. "You know you've come a long way when you don't need to put a towel under the door."

She smiles. "Are you sure it's okay for you to do this?"

"It's fine." I take another puff, pass it back into her waiting palm. "Fuck if I let a murmur dictate my life," I say, talking like she does.

"Fucking right."

She takes another hit, then leans in as if she wants to tell me a secret. I can almost taste her breath, eat her perfume. We are so close and we giggle like schoolgirls. I want to reach out and take her hand, see what it feels like in mine, and ask her to share her memories from childhood. I want to know her whole life without her having to tell me. I want to be the one whose number she calls for lunch, who she goes to the movies with, who swirls in with ice cream and videos and cheers her up as we both curse the guy she's seeing, someone named Mark or Hank or Sid. I hand back the joint and notice how massive her hands are, a fat paw, the kind that could smother you. I want to get lost in them. Her fingers touch mine. It feels like nothing and everything at once. Something moves inside me, painful and deep, as if I'm digging into bone, making me long to tell her how much I need her.

She eyes me. "Sally? You okay?"

I'm afraid to look at her because I think she sees me as I really am. I'm afraid to look away and break the intensity that's linking us together because I fear I will never get it back. I will never have this moment again. I blink and it's already gone.

"Sal, are you all right?"

"Yeah."

There's silence now, broken only by the knocking of her heels against the dryer and the occasional tapping of her wedding ring on the metal top.

"My sister-in-law is driving me crazy. I know she means well but she's killing me. I didn't like her much before, but seeing her like this is making me lose it. She keeps handing me tissues and telling me to let go. If I really let go, I'd smack the shit out of her."

We both laugh hysterically at this.

"And she's a terrible crier. Her whole body shakes and her nose gets red and drippy and the whole thing makes me ill."

"She's the one dressed in the blue-and-white-striped thing?"

Leslie nods, rolls her eyes.

"She looks like a circus tent. Maybe I should buy her outfit off her and add it to my collection."

Leslie laughs so hard she starts to cough. I pat her back; tears fill her eyes and for a moment I can't tell if she's laughing or crying.

"You know, I never cheated on him. Not once. My friends had flings with their bosses or their friends' husbands. They've met random men in Manhattan, drove in during the day for quick fucks in midtown hotels . . ." She shakes her head, stares out. "I was always the faithful, good girl. Even during his internship when I never saw him and spent every fucking night by myself waiting for him to get home."

I nod and stare out, too.

"I wanted him to take the day off. I begged him to play hooky with me. He had rounds, so we compromised on a 4:30 movie."

"You had no way of knowing," I say, my head feeling light, my eyes heavy. I rest my hand on her upper back, feel her shoulder blade. "You want to blame someone, blame the asshole who was driving."

She nods, joint resting in between her large fingers, her hands on her leg, her eyes staring off somewhere. "Four days ago I had everything—now I have fucking zero."

"You have so much," I say, my voice a whisper. "Just look around."

I think about who would attend my funeral. A few shrinks I disliked. My parents, perhaps a neighbor or two, some random friends who never understood me. Maybe some relatives I haven't spoken to or seen in a decade will show their faces, then do some shopping at specialty stores they don't have in their area. "Everyone here seems to truly care about you."

She wedges the end of the joint into the corner of the ashtray, then dumps it into the cigar box and throws it behind the washer. "Everyone here is useless."

She jumps off the machine and walks past me. I hear her heels clicking on the steps, hear the intense anger each time they meet the cement. I slide off the dryer and wait, glaring at the empty spot that's just encompassed her body.

The door opens on the top step, then it closes.

I've just ruined whatever relationship we had.

For the next hour, I stand by the window wondering how I can redeem myself and win her back. I wish it was winter and that we were in the middle of a blizzard or a rainstorm. Something to keep me here. "Snow. Snow," I keep saying to myself.

In the country, snow collects quicker and clumps together like sticky rice. I picture myself pouring wine for Leslie. If I got her too tipsy she wouldn't be able to drive me to the station. Perhaps all the taxis would be busy, the wait too long. Perhaps it would get so late that she'd just let me sleep over, dressed in her pajamas. Bagels for breakfast, fresh coffee, and the Sunday paper with nothing important to do. The next day stretched out like a grassy field. But the day is beautiful, slightly windy and sunny, the trees heavy with bright green leaves and just a hint of color.

One night is all I want. One night to know I'm not waking up alone.

Betty-Ann and Troy drop me off at the station.

On the ride home, the train is empty. There's no one to talk to except a drunk black man who's passed out in the last seat at the back of the car. I watch the station get smaller and smaller and eventually disappear.

. . .

The first funeral I went to was for my grandfather, on my father's side. I had just turned eleven and was told he died of leukemia. I remember not having to go to school, even though it wasn't a holiday, and wearing my good black velvet dress with matching tights and patent leather Mary Janes.

We held the sitting and the service at Campbell's chapel on East 81st and Madison Avenue. I asked if it had anything to do with the soup company. I visualized people milling about, standing over a coffin, clean white bowls in their hands filled with red tomato soup as tears fell into the thick broth.

Though the casket was closed, a large photo of my grandfather standing by the fountain at his Florida home sat on top in a silver frame.

The viewing room was comprised of three large connecting areas and was filled with familiar faces: my parents' friends, my schoolmates' parents, and people who I was later introduced to as relatives of mine. It was like a party. A sullen, boring party without music and caterers.

Everyone was extremely nice to me. My mother's longtime girlfriends gathered around me in a circle. They sat on gold-colored folding chairs with matching velvet padding and leaned forward, a little closer than normal, their faces open but serious, their legs crossed. Their recently polished nails clicked against stout glasses filled with water or long-stemmed glasses holding red or white wine. I was telling a story about my grandfather, something that had to do with a trip to FAO Schwarz, and everyone smiled and nodded. I was holding court and I felt very grown up, very important.

Most exciting was reconnecting with family members I hadn't seen in years, and being introduced to others I'd never met before. In these circumstances, everyone is included; everyone deserves a chance to say good-bye. The word *family* was tossed around so freely. I was suddenly labeled. Defined. *This is my cousin, . . . This is my niece, Nina.* I sat on people's laps and got hugs from total strangers.

An hour in, I was hooked.

The funeral was mesmerizing. We went to temple and my rabbi talked about all the good things my grandfather had done. Several of his children from his first marriage spoke, followed by co-workers and old friends.

I loved hearing the stories. Loved finding out about a man I hardly knew.

When the service was over, we piled into a smaller room where people who weren't coming to the cemetery could express their sympathies. After that, family and close friends assembled into waiting black cars and like a street parade, we left together, one following the other.

The second funeral I attended was for Mr. Marshal, one of my father's clients, who was at the zoo when he met his fate. He fell into the glass of the insect house and died on impact.

Over the past few years I had heard stories about how weird and outrageous he was. That he'd owned a cemetery, and every Halloween he'd invite me and my parents to go trick-or-treating with him and his two daughters, Gail and Gwen. On holidays and as "thank-yous," he sent my father horror movies and true-crime novels as gifts. My father would bring home the movies and we'd watch them together, popcorn between us, lights dimmed. The books sat unread on a shelf in his den.

My father was the executor of the Will and it was important for him to be there. Good for business. The church was old and musty and we were overdressed. My mother stood out in her black pantsuit and my father was the only one in a tie. We sat in the middle pew, though I'd wanted a front seat. I wanted to see Mrs. Marshal and her two daughters. I wanted to know what kind of man their father was.

Neighbors and friends told endless stories about him, each more funny and bizarre than the next. One guy remembered the time Mr. Marshal had insisted their neighbor was a mass murderer. He and three other men held a two-day stakeout. Aside from his army experience, those forty-eight hours were the most bonding ones he'd ever had.

Mr. Marshal made the neighborhood colorful, said one man. He was dependable, eccentric, comical. But in all his weirdness, all his oddities, he was a good friend. His son broke his leg and it was Mr. Marshal who made the splint out of plywood and masking tape. When his wife died it was Mr. Marshal who was his drinking buddy.

Another man joked about the dried food Mr. Marshal ordered in, preparing for a war. "If a tornado hit, you'd bet we'd be running over to Herb's, eating powdered, freeze-dried ice cream, watching *The Mummy* or *The Blob* in a huge, cozy underground house."

I leaned forward in my seat, captivated.

Finally, Gail spoke. She talked about how her father was her best friend. That he was unconventional and imaginative. Months were spent planning their Halloween costumes. Hide-and-seek games went on for days. "I'm not going to cry because I think he'd tell me to tough it out. That he's happy wherever he is." She looked up, then down, then back to us. "He's probably laughing and playing tricks on someone or organizing a heaven Halloween ball, or pulling a prank on . . ." She stopped. She opened her mouth several times, but no sound came out. I held my own breath, felt the muscles in my chest go tight while mentally encouraging her to continue.

"I loved him very much. I miss you, Dad." Her chin moved slightly and I had to lean closer to see if she was crying. Her speech was terrific. Honest and moving. I was jealous she'd had such a wonderful time. A sister she was close with, a father who did things with her, a mother who was there. When she finished, I wanted to clap and almost did but caught myself.

"This isn't a show, Nina," my mother said, her hand firmly placed on my arm.

Next, Gwen brought up a large tan bag. Gail explained each object she removed from the sac before putting it into her father's coffin. They took out a Swiss Army Knife, a flashlight with new batteries, several bags of his freeze-dried food, money clip, deck of cards, garlic cloves, a cross, and a bottle of Jack Daniel's. "This is the first comic book he ever bought—No. 2 Superman—and a copy of *Abbott and Costello Meet the Mummy*."

We were encouraged to say our good-byes to Mr. Marshal individually and a line formed immediately. I walked up with my father and peered in. He looked like a wax dummy. His face was cut up and the objects Gail and Gwen had shown were placed around his body. Everyone thought it a joke. Mourners expected him to jump out and laugh. I did, too. I waited a few minutes, staring at him, looking for breath or for his chest to move up and down, or for his lips to crack a smile. Nothing. He was really dead, my father insisted. He wasn't coming back.

My parents retired to Mrs. Marshal's house while the kids from the neighborhood hung around. I had the best time. Gail showed me her father's collection of horror memorabilia: comic books, movies, and action figures. She lead me on a tour through the morgue, boasted that her father had owned one years before but her mother made him sell it. She was sure her father had hidden something else for her in the house—a note or map—and we spent the day searching for it, snooping through the cob-webbed basement and stifling hot attic.

Hours later, dirty and hungry, we emerged and found my parents waiting outside on the porch.

"Nina, we've been calling for you for the past two hours. Where the hell have you been?"

"On a treasure hunt."

"We almost left without you," my mother proclaimed.

"Come on!" She marched to our car, almost tripping on a rock in her high heels.

I waved good-bye from the window, looking like one of those kids getting hauled off to boarding school.

I never saw Gail or Gwen again.

. . .

I love it when the funeral I'm attending is for a shrink. It's like live theater. The Freudians stand around smoking, rubbing small objects, looking inquisitive and authoritarian; the behaviorists congregate by open windows or door frames, always prepared to make an escape; the analysts take to the couch, finding comfort in the cushions. I enjoy playing the "friend, foe, or patient game." Generally, I can pick out the clients from those who actually knew the deceased personally, not professionally. I tend to fall into the latter.

The first therapist I saw, my parents sent me to. I was twelve and pudgy. My mother thought I was overeating and one of her friends suggested we find out why I was feeding myself so much, what empty place I was trying to fill.

I was forced to go for one year.

The doctor was an older man, a true Freudian, and rarely talked to me. When he did, he made preposterous statements, as if he were testing my reactions. One time I was touching the edge of his beat-up couch and the top plastic thing fell out of my hands—I had a habit of pulling it off and sticking it back on. He turned to me and said, "Your actions say you want to have sexual encounters with me." I told my mother this in the middle of our hallway, my coat still on, my face blotchy from embarrassment. She insisted I was lying. She came with me to the next session and asked if this were true. Freud sat there motionless and stoic for several minutes. Finally, he crossed his legs and asked my mother why it was that she didn't believe her daughter.

I didn't have to go back.

A turbulent senior year at Lenox, a private school on the Upper East Side, brought me to Dr. Gitler, a young, well-meaning woman who was more repressed than I. She sported long skirts and long-sleeved shirts and never showed an ounce of skin. I told her about my analysts and all she did was make lots of notes.

Her hands were always busy, scratching the paper, tearing out sheets, clipping them into folders. Her pens were constantly running out of ink and she'd shove them angrily into her enormous yellow knapsack and pull out another dried-up one until she eventually dumped the contents of her bag out onto the floor. There was so much crap I couldn't believe it. Crumpled-up dirty tissues, Juicy Fruit gum wrappers, lipsticks, rubber bands, paper clips, a beeper, wallet, checkbook, huge ring of keys, and her hospital badge. If she was so disorganized in *her* life, how could she straighten out mine?

I bought her a box of blue Bics and presented them to her at our next appointment, but she told me she didn't accept gifts from patients. I explained they weren't a gift, more of an offering. Watching her frazzled state was annoying. We spent the next four months talking about how that made me feel.

There was one I saw in college who told me I remind him of a dog; the one who wanted to talk about my womb experience; the fresh-out-of-grad-school psychologist; and Maggie, a doughty, kindly woman who looked like Aunt Bea from *The Andy Griffith Show*. She was soft-spoken and chunky with swollen ankles and a thick neck. She was the nicest of the bunch. She asked lots of questions and nodded. When I cried she leaned forward, looking like she really wanted to help. Her approach was not for pills but for tissues. She took no notes, just sat and listened. She sighed a lot and her eyes read pity, not sympathy. She never made a single statement and I never felt we made any progress. After eight months, she gave me Marty's number and thought I'd be more comfortable talking to a male doctor whose therapy was more progressive and "hipper."

Marty was my last.

He was extremely attractive in a young-father kind of way. Of all the shrinks, I liked his waiting room best. Liked the magazines he had to read, the people who sat waiting for their appointments, the structure it gave me.

He shared the space with several other therapists so it was always bustling with people, like a club or coffee shop where you saw the same familiar faces. I thought about asking one of the patients out once, for a soda or after-work drink. He was scruffy and lean and always wore sweats or fleece. He looked like he'd come from the gym or had played racquetball with his buddies. I figured, at least he's here working on his shit. He had the language down, the special words, understood the importance of open discussion. I had asked Marty if it would be all right. He was pleased that I felt "safe" in the surroundings, but was concerned I was attaching myself to unobtainable men. "I'm not sure it's inner office protocol. I have to ask my associates and get back to you." Then he added, "Besides, you don't know what's wrong with him. I'm not keen on you dating some passive-aggressive psychopath."

I couldn't tell if he was joking.

And there was something a little sleazy about him. I always felt like he wanted to sleep with me. I shared this with my mother, a proclaimed therapy believer who insisted lying on the couch twice a week was the only way people functioned in this world.

"Everyone thinks that, Nina. That's part of the process. That's how you know it's working. It's called *transference*."

Marty loved drugs and prescribed endless prescriptions. "The cocktail of champions," he called it. At thirty-three, my kitchen counter looked like a pharmacy. None worked. The Elavil made me dizzy. I couldn't string my beads or read a newspaper. Words danced around the pages of books. All I could do was look at fashion magazines. Prozac made it impossible to pee, Zoloft made me groggy—I could function, I couldn't think. I tried to tell him about my need for connection, the longing for human touch, but he seemed disinterested. Eventually, I stopped going.

I missed the office more than Marty.

Sometimes I resurrect all of my therapists, place them in my living room, and make them talk to each other. They share morning coffee and muffins or scones, or they gather in the early evening, make Cheever-like drinks, and discuss me outside on an imaginary front lawn or back deck. They chatter away, misdiagnosing me, making general assumptions about my childhood. "She clearly wasn't breast-fed," the Freudian spits out in between puffs on his pipe. "Nina suffered from narcissistic parents," Aunt Bea would hunch. "It started in the womb," chimed in the reclaimer of the inner child. "She wasn't fed emotionally from the start. Her mother barely helped push her out. All cesareans suffer from this."

If only one of them would have asked, *What can I do for you, Nina? How can I help you? Tell me what you want and I'll give it to you I promise,* all would have been fine. I could have told them about my needs. About not feeling my life. But they never asked. They never offered anything. They just watched me, watched the clock, and gave me quickly scribbled bills and carelessly written prescriptions. Now I go to funerals. It's cheaper and I can choose who to talk to. I can see who needs me and who I need.

Marty's funeral was nice—two of his colleagues spoke, and his roommate from grad school. I didn't see anyone from the office though I looked for the scruffy gym guy. Not that he would come—Marty wasn't his doctor.

Marty's wife, Faye, greets each visitor warmly at the door, a smile on her drawn face. She is well-poised and appears tired and bubbly at the same time, as if she's thrown a tremendously successful party and is ready to ask the guests to leave.

She doesn't ask how I came here or how I know Marty and I don't render the information. I don't want to be pegged for some crazy patient, at least not yet.

I take a customary lap. The apartment is rather big by Manhattan standards. Three bedrooms, a large living room, dining room, walk-through kitchen and connecting pantry, housekeeper's room that is used to store bikes, ski equipment, and two of Faye's furs, and two and a half bathrooms. People are sprinkled throughout the apartment but most congregate in the living room and dining area. The group is mostly professionals, mid-to-late forties, and older professors and doctors who mingle with many of what look like Faye and Marty's neighbors.

I find an empty seat on the couch and sip Diet Coke and pretend to look busy as I eat cold macaroni salad and build a lettuce, ham, and Swiss sandwich.

A woman clutching a small gold bag sits down next to me. Her shiny blond hair has been perfectly highlighted, her blue eyes remain tearless. She looks as if she's stepped out of a fashion catalogue in her brown shawl, matching skirt, and white silk shirt. She glances at the walls, then over to me.

"Hi, I'm Gina." I extend my hand. She lifts hers, goes to shake mine and, noticing my bracelet, reaches for that instead.

"I'm Helen. How lovely. May I?"

I move my arm closer to her. Her fingers run lightly over the misshapen turquoise and round silver beads. She slides two fingers inside the bracelet and places her thumb on top, then presses together. She rubs her finger back and forth, as if trying to steal some of the magic.

"It's so pretty."

"Thanks."

"Can I ask where you got it?"

"I made it." It didn't take long. I strung together three separate strands and connected them with several silver-plated pieces and a matching clasp.

"Really?"

I nod, beaming.

"It's really nice. I would have guessed Bendel's or Bergdorf's." Her fingers are still caressing the stones. "Do you sell to them?"

"People have suggested that. Mostly I make them for friends, give them as gifts."

I think about asking if she wants me to make her one. I could take her wrist measurements and inquire what kind she'd like. I have virtually hundreds of beads at home, sitting in different-sized, clear boxes, waiting for a purpose, eager to be used.

I'd design jewelry for a living but, as my mother has pointed out, if I can't hold down a real job, I shouldn't be putting my efforts into self-employment. My parents thought it best I work for my father while sorting out my problems in therapy. While Marty's drugs played havoc with my emotions and mental status, I did menial duties for my dad. I went in some days, stayed home

others. He doesn't care if I'm there or not. Sometimes I go home
with him and we have a family dinner. We usually enter to find
my mother still in her suit, a headset permanently attached to her
ear. She represents musical prodigies, agent to tomorrow's young
Glenn Goulds and Midoris. Their head shots and photos of them
holding their instruments, looking serious and sophisticated yet
young and impressionable, are stacked in piles on her work table
in the den. Their press clips, reviews, and articles are kept in
Lucite holders.

I was forced to take piano from age six to fifteen. To this day,
all I can play is "Celebration" and everyone's favorite, "Chopsticks." I'm convinced that this fact alone is my biggest disappointment to her. It's hard to rep other people's children when
your daughter is tone deaf.

All of Helen's fingers have inched their way around my wrist
as she inspects my craftsmanship. She looks up at me. Then something behind my head catches her attention. I watch her eyes leave
my face and rove up and left, toward the mantel where Marty's
remains are housed. I'm about to ask for her address when she
drops my wrist and stands, zombie-like. She pauses there for a
moment, then takes small steps closer to Marty. I set the paper
plate down on the coffee table and am in the middle of standing
when another woman slips in and starts conversing with her. I
watch the two speak, wondering what they're saying, if they're
talking about me. I'm inches away from Helen and am ready to
take off my bracelet and lure her back, offering it up, when the
other woman turns around and faces me. She takes me by the
arm sharply and whispers, "She'd like a minute or two alone."

After we've taken several steps away, she adds, "I think she's
one of Marty's patients. Faye invited them."

I nod earnestly. "I had no idea. How kind of her."

The woman leans in closer. "You know, Marty used to tell

Faye about his sessions. I believe she's a shopaholic. Spends thousands each month on clothing and what-have-you."

I stop short, wonder which of my secrets he would have shared, what theories he told his wife but withheld from me.

"Really?" I say in mock shock. "She does look especially put-together."

"Of all the sicknesses to have, that's the best one, don't you think?"

We both decide this is so, and resume walking toward the dining room with the mission of retrieving some cookies and marble pound cake when a shrill is heard. I know in my gut it belongs to Faye. We rush with others to the kitchen area and find her crumpled on the floor in deep sobs. Like ants migrating, everyone flocks to surround her.

Faye's sister bends down, others do as well, but she raises a hand, a silent indication to retreat. And they obey. Everyone takes one step backward while the sister slinks to the floor and cradles Faye in her arms. Suddenly, I wish to be both. I want to be the holder and the holdee. The personal fight of which side to take, of which person to be, makes me dizzy. I stand, paralyzed, and watch with other spectators, as if we are witnessing a car accident. It's so real, so raw, I want to cry. I look up at the guests' faces. They are either horrified or slightly saddened, lips pressed down-ward, eyes droopy. Some bring their hands to their mouths, trying to muffle a cry, while their eyes spill with tears. Others cover their faces completely. The way everyone is looking at Faye makes me sick. I stifle the urge to ask them to leave. Can't they see she's gone through enough? She doesn't need an audience. Her husband is dead.

Her husband is dead.

"Honey," the sister's voice is light and cooing, but urgent, "let's go into the bedroom."

Faye is crying so hard she can't hear or move.

"Help me get her to her feet," commands the man standing next to me. Another, a woman in a tweed suit and patterned scarf, suggests giving her some water. I watch two other women fight as they reach for the same glass. Someone else insists they get Faye up and walk her to an open window. The sister just sits and holds her, calm as can be, as if this is a daily occurrence.

"Shhhhh, I'm right here," she says while stroking her hair, "I'm here. It's okay."

I'm feeling a little disconnected and turn back to look for Helen. I search the entire room—nothing. I look for her in other parts of the apartment and when I don't find her in the study or in one of the bedrooms, I start to panic. I remember she's a patient and think maybe this is all too much for her. Maybe she, too, is having a breakdown somewhere.

I hurry back into the living room, hoping to find her there, seated in the exact spot on the couch. But no. People are still clumped together in the kitchen doorway but Faye is standing now, held up by her sister and another man. They move her slowly, one on either side, down the hallway. In the distance, she looks like a star football player with an injured knee, her arms hanging loosely off their shoulders, the carriers' arms wrapped tightly around her waist.

It's then that I look toward the mantel, up at the urn. Except it's not there. I look around the room, thinking someone has moved it. Look to the floor to see if it's fallen. But it's just not here. It's vanished. As if it got up and rolled away on its own. I half expect to find small fragments of Marty, like a little trail of crushed-up bone and skin mapping out where he's gone off to.

Helen is nowhere to be found and I wish I had gotten her address or a last name. I would have sent her a bracelet. She's the exact type of person my mother would love to see me with: classy, well-dressed, WASPy enough to look society-esque and be photographed in all the important monthlies. Then she'd finally have something to show to her friends. "Did you see Nina's photo in *Avenue*? Oh, she was at that charity event. Stood right next to the mayor . . ."

I don't feel like saying good-bye to anyone so I take my raincoat and leave.

I walk through the park, looking at the foliage. The greens are transforming into bursts of color, the sun is saying good night a little earlier. I wish I had someone's hand to grasp. A boyfriend in a crewneck sweater and wavy, dark hair with nothing but the rest of the day drawn out for us to rent movies and order in Chinese.

. . .

Beth Resnick looks as if someone has sucked the color out of her face. She's thin and pale and appears terribly lonely. Her skin is ivory-white with just a hint of peach eye shadow and matching gloss on her lips. Her eyes are a soft brown and her chestnut hair is twisted back in a loose knot. She's dressed in a long prairie skirt with a white shirt sticking out from under a gray wool knit sweater. The sleeves are long and cover most of her hands. Only the tips of her thin fingers are revealed.

There are maybe twenty people at her mother's funeral, making this the smallest one I've been to in years. The group, made up of women in their late fifties, are bridge friends. I know this because several people have been describing their card hands and talking about club tournaments and how many points Marion had when she died.

The chapel is a one-stop shop. Reminiscent of the old kind that would sell you the casket, perform the embalming, take care of the makeup, even hold the reception afterwards. The Rockwell Funeral Parlor does it all.

Surprisingly, the casket is open. I'm tempted to take a photo of her but the room is so small that I'm positive someone would notice. The clicking sound would surely give me away.

Marion is exquisite, like a porcelain doll. Her face has a healthy, rosy glow, like she's been sunning in Miami. Her lips are full and red, her eyes, perfectly blended. I half expect them to flutter open. One of the ladies said she was wearing a wig but I couldn't tell.

When the service is over, I wait in line, eager to talk to Beth, drawn to her loneliness. It's a scent she wears. I know because I wear it, too. It sits like a pretty bottle on my dresser and clings to my every movement. I wonder if we all smell the same.

Beth receives a few sporadic hugs, but mostly the ladies touch her arm or reach for her hand. She nods, wraps a piece of fallen hair behind her ear, and fiddles with her pearl earring, twisting it with her fingers. She keeps her lips pressed and smiles thoughtfully, glasses on her nose, a beautiful pin on her sweater. She frequently clasps her hands and raises them to her face, cupping them together as if trying to inhale the wool. Perhaps she's trying to capture someone's scent that lingers on her after a hug. The men with too much aftershave, woman who have over-spritzed their perfume. Maybe she's smelling herself to make sure she's still here.

I wait to catch her eye, to see if I should approach, to see if she notices me.

Beth didn't cry once during the eulogy and has remained dry-eyed since the proceeding started. This is rare behavior. Many people put on good show, running around as if they're producing an event. Others are so transparent, you can actually see them faking their crocodile tears behind their big black glasses. Some are a complete mess, making you wonder how they will ever get through the next five minutes, let alone a lifetime. Most, however, are in shock and the grief hasn't hit yet. But Beth is none of these. She is gentle, soft-spoken and meek. There is an honest and exposed sadness about her which makes me feel terrible for lying and I'm sure when my time comes, God will punish me for this. For going to all the funerals, for taking advantage of people's good intentions and kind offerings.

As I wait in line to express my sympathies, I search through an invisible list of lies I've concocted for such occasions. But today, I'm at a loss. What can I say? That if I lived in this neighborhood, too, our mothers would have been friends? I visualize Beth and me at school, sitting next to each other in the cafeteria, trading sandwiches. Her tuna for my chicken salad. Her turkey on white for my pb and j.

A nervous, tingling sensation starts inside my stomach as my eyes catch Beth's friends. And I know as I approach, Beth doesn't need another one. The gaps and voids she has have been filled. There is nothing I can offer.

I'm about to leave when a chunky woman, dressed in a long black shirt and a lace skirt that reaches the floor, pops in front of me. Every ounce of skin is bedecked with turquoise jewelry. Her earrings are clunky, her necklace is overpowering, and almost every finger sports a ring. Even her watch strap is encrusted in stones.

"Are you a friend of Beth's?" she asks. She looks like a lost gypsy.

"Yes."

"From school?"

"That's right. It's been a while since I've . . ."

"What do you teach?"

I look at her blankly. "Drama."

"How lovely." She looks off in Beth's direction. "I'm sure she'd be glad to know you're here. Come say hello."

She puts an arm around my shoulder and tries to steer me closer to Beth.

"No, that's okay. I really just wanted to be here for the service."

The line is moving faster now.

"I was . . ."

"I'm Georgia," she announces, interrupting me for a second time. "I did her mother's makeup."

I freeze, then twist to face her. "Really? She looked fantastic, if that's not too forward for me to say. It's just that my sister-in-law is ill, and I was wondering if you had a card or something." I'm stalling. Then I make my eyes water. "She's very vain and I know she'd feel much better if there was someone to take care of her."

"Of course, darling. Anything I can do to help."

I smile shyly and look up in time to catch Beth and her friend staring at us.

I wave, then mouth the word *sorry*.

They look confused. Beth's face scrunches up and the friend whispers something in her ear. Beth shrugs and starts to walk forward.

I look back at Georgia. "I've got to go. My kids are waiting."

"Honey, it'll be but a few moments more."

I have maybe one, two minutes to get out of here.

"Please, Georgia, I must catch a train." My voice is pleading and I hear the urgency.

"You came all this way and you can't spend a few minutes with her?"

What is she, a goddamn cruise director? Beth is several feet away, her hand is already starting to extend. I pull free and holler,

"Beth. I'm so sorry." As I back up, I bump into two people standing behind me. "I'll call you later tonight and check in."

I stumble a bit while spinning around and cut hurriedly toward the first doorway I see. I don't know where I'm going—it could be the room where they sell the coffins or the place they do the embalming, but I can't worry about that now. There's always a back door or an emergency exit somewhere. Worst case scenario, I'll use the window. We're only on the first floor.

The hallway is dark and it takes my eyes a few seconds to adjust to the quick change in light. Voices fade and my breathing becomes louder. The good news: my shoes are muffled, thanks to the carpet. Bad news: I can't tell if someone's following me.

The end of the hallway reveals a set of steps leading down, and a door. Steps, as a rule, are a bad idea. I wrap my hand around the knob and pray it turns.

The room is tiny and bright. Several candles are lit on a wooden table. Something smells acidic—no, of sulfur. I close the door behind me, but there's no lock. A smaller door is on the opposite side of the room and I see myself as a twenty-first-century Alice in a twisted version of Wonderland.

The next room is an old kitchen decorated in faded aluminum. On the counter is a plate of sugar cookies and pre-sliced pound cake. A metal tray holds two large pitchers of water, a Styrofoam cup with wooden stirrers, a bowl of sugar, and a box of Sweet 'N Low. Suddenly very thirsty, I look for more cups, but come up empty-handed.

There are no windows, so I walk deeper into the kitchen and finally see a screen door. I grasp the handle sharply, authoritatively, and proceed through.

The street is unfamiliar. As far as I can tell, I'm in the back of the block. Disoriented, I walk through a gated area, past an empty lot, and finally arrive at the corner of Spruce and Hempstead. I have no idea where I am. All the streets in Rockville Centre look the same. I can't even see the front of the chapel. In the distance is the sound of a train. I walk several blocks until I feel comfortable enough to ask for directions.

As I wait for the 4:05 to take me back to Penn Station, I swear to myself this is the last out-of-town service I will attend.

I'm still shaking when I get to the bead store. Like the headstones at the cemetery, the beads are divided into rows and rows. Large, small, round, square, shiny, frosted. Greens become blues, blues to purple, and all the way through the rainbow. Blacks, silver, and gold reside in the last few columns. The orderliness calms me. The smell of sandalwood incense is soothing. I even enjoy chatting with the young Chinese women who own the small establishment. They greet me warmly even though they are constantly forgetting my name. I overlook this because their salutations are genuine, their big, round faces open and accepting. They ask me what I'm working on every time I'm here. They look at each other, nod, and make exaggerated expressions.

On my way out I check the large bulletin board filled with school information and people looking to sell glue guns and tables and such. I think about signing up for a class at The New School or Parsons School of Design, anything artistic that I can do with my hands. I write down some numbers and take several brochures, a Learning Annex catalogue included.

At home I sift through the material, hoping something will jump out at me. There are classes in everything: *Stringing with Wire* at Parsons sounds interesting. *Working with Metal* at The New School piques my interest. A class on blowing glass beads is offered at the Y. I call to see about availability but it's already full. The Learning Annex has the most bizarre offerings: *Sex Tips from a*

Dominatrix; Connecting with Your Angels; Contacting the Dead; but the course that sells me is a weekend getaway to Macon, Georgia, where a rambler, a person trained in storytelling and factual history, leads a tour of the Rose Hill Cemetery.

The woman at The Annex tells me I'm very lucky, I've gotten the last spot.

"You'll love this," she assures me. "Since Halloween is only a few weeks away, this course has become very popular." She takes down my credit card number and tells me to have a wonderful time.

I mark "Rose Hill" on my calendar with a red Sharpie Pen, then count the days in my head till I leave.

. . .

Men act completely different at funerals from women. They clump together, lean on walls, or stand in door frames. They huddle in small groups, hands shoved deep into their pants pockets or arms crossed over their chests. They talk about sports, the market, the recently deceased in memory, not emotion. They rarely cry. Sometimes I go just to see if there are any eligible bachelors.

I've met a few men through these gatherings. Even brought one home once. But they never stay long and not many of them enjoy going to funerals with me.

I have a fantasy about finding a husband or at least a boyfriend here. A male version of myself, who pays shiva calls, sits at wakes, and longs to be part of something whole. We could start a family, or I'd be adopted into his, where appearances at holiday functions would be mandatory.

Clive was nothing more than someone to talk to. I met him three years ago at a funeral for a dog trainer. He had a goatee that was somehow charming and an Irish accent. He sat very close and every now and then whispered in my ear. I couldn't understand him but the accent was such a turn-on it didn't matter. I just nodded and laughed and followed his expressions. If he looked angry, I frowned. If I turned to face him and found him smiling, I did, too.

To get through college he worked the night shift at a morgue. As a lad in Ireland, where he spent several years hanging out and finding himself, he dug graves for cash. He seemed to enjoy funerals as much as I did. He attended a few here and there, found them eerily titillating and had fantasies about banging a girl on a coffin or doing it in one of the graves he'd dug.

At first I thought, I've found the perfect man. We could go to funerals together, become the flawless his-and-her team. "How did you two meet?" people would have asked. "At a funeral," we'd answer, and then we'd laugh, an inside joke for us to share. We'd hold hands and smile, say something like, "See, good can come from something terribly sad." But he was clearly disturbed. Even I could spot that. I wanted someone searching for the living—Clive was more concerned in finding the dead.

We went on one date. I felt disconnected with him as we walked to the restaurant; and he was fidgety through most of dinner. He tapped the pads of his fingers on the table as he talked. I could see him wondering how much longer he'd have to sit here, pretending to be interested.

There is no photo of Richard D. Stein in the paper, just a seventy-word blurb, a Cliffs Notes version of a man's life encapsulated in nothing more than cherished so-and-so, adored this-and-that.

The guys I meet at his service seem like boys rather than men even though most are in their mid-thirties. They are fraternity brothers and office buddies who travel in a pack, smoke cigars, and drink heavily. They work hard, play harder. They are good-looking boys in suits and ties, polished loafers, freshly gelled hair. They believe in staying out late and taking spur-of-the-moment jaunts to Miami and Atlantic City. Few are married, fewer still are ready to settle down. But they are cute and I want to find one, take him home with me, and make him fall in love.

The service is predominantly testosterone-driven, though a few women are sprinkled in the mix for color. Some are from college, others are cousins, but mostly they are Richard's mother's friends. Seeing there's not much competition, my chances here are good.

The parents' friends convene on one side, the thirty-five-and-under on the other. It reminds me of my first boy-girl social at school where no one wanted to cross to the other side and ask a classmate to dance.

Usually I search for someone to talk to. Anyone whose face looks open and accepting, or who is sitting alone and appears as if they, too, are hoping to connect with someone. Next, I ask myself, can I be helpful? If the answer to this is still no, I look for a body to comfort. It's easier to befriend someone who needs you. To grab them in their dark time, and create a bond when they are weak and low and tired and suffering and extra breakable. But since Richard's service is mostly men, these rules don't apply. Instead, I go on attraction.

An Asian man with jet-black spiked hair catches my eye. Too pretty. Next to him is a bald man with glasses in a fitted turtleneck sweater. Too prissy. Third from the left of the entranceway is just right. His full face looks freshly shaven and moon-like. He has a mess of black curls and wears wire-rimmed glasses.

I pass though the door frame, accidentally knocking into him. "Sorry. Good thing I'm not drinking."

"You might be better off if you had a few," he retorts.

I smile, girlie-like.

Dean tells me how his fraternity brother, Richard, was found dead on the steps of his town house. How he still can't believe the news and thinks the whole thing absurd.

"The police aren't doing a fucking thing to help. They're completely useless. All they confirm was that he was drunk and stoned. Christ, I could have told them that."

He fills in the pertinent information: parents' names, where Richard worked, that he was very good at his job—no one ever tells a negative story about the dead—that he loved to fish and was known for spending hours at sea on his boat. His nickname was "Ishmael" and upon seeing him, friends would quote lines from *Moby Dick*. *He was a mammoth of a whale, gray and black.* He explains how Richard was the favored child. That his younger brother had a nervous breakdown and was institutionalized for a bit but seems much better now. When he asks me what my connection is, I explain about the necklace Richard had commissioned me to make for his mother, an early birthday present. I gamble on that one. I was going to say holiday gift, but December is still two months away. I don't want to ruin this, so I stay pretty true to real life.

"We'd been working on the present for a few weeks—it was going to be a surprise for her. Anyway, we got friendly. My father owned a boat years ago and we talked about that and I showed him my fly-fishing photos. He was fun." I shrug. "We talked on the phone a bunch of times. He was going to trade some stocks for me . . ." I pause, smooth out the creases in my skirt. "I didn't know whether to bring the gift for his mother or not. It was already paid for. He was really pleased with himself for designing it. I just thought she'd want to know what a sweet son she had."

"You've got to give it to her," Dean says excitedly, as if we're both in this together. "She'd totally want to know."

Three friends from work and two from childhood give truly touching speeches. They are well-thought-out and share different snippets of who Richard was. His brother talks for a short time, never once removing his hands from his pockets. He leans forward and speaks so close to the microphone, his voice sounds staticky and muffled. Each time he opens his mouth, he looks as if he's going to eat the electronic piece.

After the service, everyone is invited downstairs where the blessing of the bread and catered dinner occur. I'm introduced to many of Dean's friends and we sit at a large, round wooden table, drink wine, and talk about Richard.

People ask about the necklace, what made Richard decide to call me, how many times we got together, did I bring it with me . . . I tell them I thought it would be inappropriate to give it to her now, but ask if I should mail it or mention to her today that I have it. We take a vote deciding to tell her about the gift, and rather than mail it, drop it off in a few days.

Every time Dean gets up to refill his glass or use the restroom I look for a clue—a hand on my shoulder, a thoughtful gaze— to know if he likes me. I receive none.

Hours later, only a handful of us remain. I'm one of two women surrounded by twelve men and the plan is to proceed to Live Bait, a bar six blocks away on East Twenty-third Street, for a final drink/toast.

We walk, a gaggle of black and gray, to the bar. A large

fish and tackle box hang outside, above the doors.

Inside, it's smoky and dark. We occupy several tables in the corner and drinks keep coming—pitchers of beer for me and the boys, a vodka tonic for his mom, and bourbon, straight, for his dad. The brother is nowhere to be found. When I ask about him, Dean tells me not to bring him up. It makes the parents too sad.

I'm glad to have worn my black skirt and matching jacket. My legs look good in it and I seem like a fashion-conscious gal, the kind they'd want to bring home to Mom. The type to cook solid, hearty meals, but not better than hers. Someone ambitious, but not too successful. Someone smart who doesn't outshine her beau.

I don't know whose idea it is to take the Circle Line around Manhattan but the last lap is at 11:00 P.M., in fifteen minutes. With Richard's love of boats, it seems like a logical step. Suddenly, someone is on the phone reserving a block of seats, someone else is doing a head count. I hold my breath, wonder if I'll be included. Dean's head nods, then he turns to me.

"You in?"

"Sure."

Dean turns back to the counter and points to me, then holds two fingers up which transforms into the thumbs-up sign.

I'm dancing inside to have been asked and Dean holds the door for me, touches my hand a little when I go through.

We assemble as a mass and spill into the street. His parents don't make it to the boat with us. Rather, they say their tearful good-bye on the corner.

Our twenty has become twelve.

We climb into cabs where I'm scrunched in between Dean and Paul, with Charlie on the end. Kyle is in the front. I'm almost in Dean's lap, but he doesn't seem to mind. Beer permeates the car. Someone belches, everyone laughs.

Our cab is last to pull into the dock. Dean and I walk up the metal plank and onto the boat, where we're high-fived by Richard's friends. A beer is thrust into my hand and we stand by the bow, hugging the railing, hugging each other. Someone emerges from the other side, shaking a bottle of beer with his thumb over the neck. It sprays like champagne. Suddenly, everyone is doing it. Me, too. And Dean and I laugh. Kyle makes a toast, ending with, "May you sail safely up to heaven." Another friend chimes in, "And catch some big fucking fish on your way there." We hold our bottles, clink glasses, and drink.

The sea air is cold and Dean takes off his jacket and places it around my shoulders. Whenever I shiver, he squeezes me tightly. My body feels so good next to his, my face nuzzled in the crook of his neck. He smells of beer and aftershave and wind. I feel his chin rest on top of my head and I wonder if I smell good and if my hair still has that freshly washed scent of conditioner and if I should invite him over and if he'd stay, and if we had sex, would he leave right after or wait it out, and if I could have a future with this man.

The boat docks at midnight. People hug me good-bye. Strangers I've spent the past five hours with now seem like close friends.

Dean and I take a cab home and only one address is given, mine. I don't know if I'll invite him up until the last minute. The thought of sleeping alone in my bed, of coming home to a barren apartment, is overwhelming. I don't want to lose our intensity, or hear the empty promise of asking for my number and the waiting for him to keep his word.

The ride home is bumpy. I'm tired and a little seasick. Too much beer, too much food. I wonder if he's the kind of man who'd rub my stomach when it hurt or kiss my belly if a child were inside. Would he place his hand in mine during movies?

Take long baths with me, massaging my shoulders sore from being hunched over my bead table? I want to ask him this now. Almost announce how nauseous I am to see his reaction. Will he roll his eyes and push me away, joke about opening the window? Or would he slide his hand over my stomach and move it slowly back and forth? How can I expect this when I've only known him a quarter of a day? Instead, I rest my head on his shoulder. Not heavily at first. I don't put all of my weight on him until I'm sure he's okay with this, until I'm positive he hasn't stiffened. Then I let my head drop, weight and all. My temple thumps lightly, almost indistinguishably, against his arm. I push the envelope and put my right hand gently, softly, on his upper arm, inches away from my chin. He places a hand on my thigh. I breathe in deeply. I decide right there to ask him up. No second address needed. My eyes watch the meter jump as I listen to the cabby talking to someone, maybe his wife, as he coasts up an empty Madison Avenue.

"Do you want something to drink?" I ask, once inside my apartment.

We both stand awkwardly in my small foyer. I've made a beaded lampshade and it's the only light on in the apartment, a test to see if he'll ask about it. To see if he was listening to me earlier.

"What you got?"

"How about brandy?"

"Great."

He stretches out on my couch while I get two snifters and an old bottle I received from my father's client last Christmas. I sit next to him and let Dean open the brandy so he feels manly.

We take sips of liquor.

We wait.

The apartment is quiet and comfortable. I let my left heel drop first, listen to the thud it makes as it hits my carpet. The right shoe follows and I curl my legs into myself, knees pointed toward him. He moves his hands to his neck to loosen his tie, realizes it already is, and takes it off instead. He hasn't asked about the lamp but I slide my pantyhosed foot up his leg anyway.

When he finishes his drink he places the empty glass on my coffee table and leans into me. His mouth tastes like brandy. So does mine. He's a good kisser, sensual without being sloppy. His tongue moves slowly, as if feeling its way around my mouth, familiarizing itself. The tip just touches my teeth. He puts a hand on my cheek, another behind my neck, then kisses my ear, my chin, my eyes. I like his hand on my face, like the way his lips feel on mine.

Later we hover in the door frame to my bedroom, both anxious. I watch him undo his trousers as I unzip my skirt.

I wake up when my foot feels something in my bed, another foot which belongs to a body. Relief passes through me. It breaks the morning fog, almost overrides the pounding in my head. The taste of brandy is still in my mouth or is it Dean's mouth that tastes like brandy that's in mine?

I stare at him in my bed, his body tangled in my sheets. I watch his eyes flutter, copy his breathing, thank God he is next to me.

For the next five minutes I watch him sleep. I inch my finger over his bare shoulder that's peeking out from the comforter. I move it down to his elbow lightly so I don't wake him, and yet I want to talk to him. I want to see what he has to say in the morning. If we have something, anything in common except for last night. I slide an arm under my head and memorize his features. My eyes travel up over his head and scrutinize my wall. Cracks in the paint. If he were to stay over on a regular basis I'd repaint the apartment.

I decide to make Dean breakfast, hoping that will keep him here a little longer. Fix him bacon and eggs, frozen waffles, or bagels. A hungry man's meal worth staying an extra hour or two, maybe spend the day. Help occupy the space between morning and evening. His breathing alone fills my apartment, takes up residency.

The table is set and coffee made. The Advil is starting to work. The sizzling sound of bacon is like snakes hissing. It's too loud and makes me a little sick, but it's worth it. After all, I am making Dean breakfast. I am wooing him with food.

Ten minutes later, a disheveled man appears. His hair is standing up on his head and I can tell his tongue is sticking to his mouth. His boxers are white and blue striped. He's a little pudgy and his nipples look like mini flying saucers surrounded by bursts of hair.

He glances around the apartment as if seeing it for the first time. "How long you been up?"

"Not long." I extend a mug in his direction. "I made coffee."

He seems confused and surprised. Unsure of what he wants to do, unsure of how he got here and who this woman is standing with a plate of bacon in one hand, coffee mug in the other.

I'm wearing a cream-colored silk robe with pink petals and light green leaves on it, worn on occasions such as these that never seem to come up. I wonder if the robe or breakfast is what's throwing him, or is it me. The pressure to stay sits on his chest like indigestion.

He reaches for the coffee, then makes the toasting sign and

says thanks. The line of us toasting Richard with the bottles of beer on the boat ride appears in my mind. I wonder if he's thinking of this, too.

Dean looks for his shirt and spots it hanging on the doorknob. He places the coffee in the exact spot the brandy snifter was hours before and slips it on, followed by his trousers, which sit folded on the arm of my couch.

We eat silently. The food filling him, his presence filling me.

"Richard would love that I met you at a funeral. It just sucks that it was his." He laughs a little, mouth full of waffle. "It's the kind of thing I would have told him about. The first call I'd have made would've been to him in the taxi. We'd have met for breakfast at some twenty-four-hour diner, still drunk or stoned from the night before."

Suddenly, I'm someone's story.

"He'd get a fucking kick out of this whole thing." He's laughing harder now, has trouble swallowing what's left in his mouth and he reaches for the coffee. "Man, he'd have relished this."

I nod, place my fork next to the knife. "He'd get a kick out of it." I have an urgent need to get up, to move away from Dean.

I put my plate in the sink, turn on the water, and pretend to be busy. Dean comes up behind me and surrenders his plate.

"This was great," he says. His tie has magically materialized around his neck, and it will be seconds before his hand is reaching into my closet to retrieve his coat.

We stand in the hallway outside my apartment door and wait for the elevator. I'm hoping one of my neighbors will hear us talking and pop their head out to see what's going on. See me with this man.

"I had a really nice time," he says, fiddling with his wallet, checking to see if he has cash. For a minute I think he's going to take out a few twenties and shove them in my hand. "Got cab money. I'm good." He looks up at me. "Let's do this again."

The elevator doors have barely opened but he's already slipping inside. His last few words are lost in the closing of the doors. It sounds like "I'll cold eew."

. . .

I've lied to my mother about where I'm going.

She thinks I'm traveling to Nantucket for a wine-tasting expo, but instead my ticket reads Atlanta. From there, a van will pick up me and nine other people and drive us an hour to Macon, the slums of Georgia. I haven't gone anywhere in years and this is the first time I'm traveling without visiting someone I know.

My parents think it's a wonderful thing for me to do. Not only has my father allowed me to take time off from work, he's offered to pay for my trip, an unprecedented decision.

My mother and I meet on neutral ground, the fifth floor of Bergdorf Goodman, and have tea sandwiches. It is here where she tells me how excited she is I'm taking this trip, insisting it's good therapy. She is unaware my shrink is dead, that I am med free, and that as much as I hate to admit it, still need her in my life. So I meet her for cucumber and egg salad sandwiches and we drink iced tea and I let her be excited and buy me clothing I will never wear: a red leather shirt/jacket, a jean skirt, and a teal knit sweater that zips up in the front. I allow her to make me into the daughter she'd like to have rather than the one she's got. I want to know if this makes her happy. Almost lean over the table, motion to her as if she's got a fallen eyelash on her cheek or a small hair out of place, and ask if she'll still love me if I never marry. If I never give her grandchildren.

. . .

The Learning Annex has promised a "fascinating and cultural experience for anyone wanting to learn about Georgia's history and is intrigued with historical homes and cemeteries." We leave on Friday afternoon and return Sunday evening. The brochure says you can point to any of the 10,000 headstones in the Rose Hill Cemetery, the oldest on the East Coast, and the rambler can tell you about the person, how they died, and who their family was.

Ten of us are to meet in the boarding area at Delta. We've been mailed orange folders and nametags and it's suggested we wear them out in the open so we can tell one another from the other passengers.

I'm one of the first to arrive. The folder/nametag trick works because I spot Brian immediately. I wave the folder lightly and point to my tag. He greets me with a warm smile and tells me he's a professor at Binghamton who teaches Historical Southern Culture.

An hour later, I find myself in the windowseat sitting next to Myrna and Fred Shultz, a retired couple in their sixties who do travel writing—he takes the photos, she does the text. Sitting across from me are four married women who graduated from Tulane together. They wanted to take a quick getaway from their husbands and children and chose this because, as Barbara, the ringleader of the pack, said, "They just couldn't look at another spa." Behind me are two Gothic teens who haven't said much except they're filming this experience, hoping to have the next Blair Witch project. Their video cameras have been on since we boarded.

We are, at best, a motley crew.

Brian, who is seated directly in front of me, had his head in a book before takeoff so it wouldn't have mattered if I'd gotten to sit next to him. The ring on his finger is the biggest disappointment so far.

The inn is surprisingly lovely. Old and creaky, it was built in 1812 and is one of the only homes still in its original foundation that wasn't destroyed in the war. My room is called the Marigold and it has a canopy bed, fireplace, antique furniture, and small deck. The bathroom is comprised of marble. Two large palmetto beetles that appear to be having sex are free of charge.

On our first night, we sit in the parlor and have mint juleps and cheese puffs with artichoke mousse dip. Dinner is served on the porch, where we're serenaded by an insect operetta. The night is sticky and balmy, the food rich and heavy, just as southerners like.

The college foursome doesn't split up. Rather, they sit in a row with the boy Goth across from me. Rhoda, spirit of the earth, is on my left, leaving Brian and the retired couple on my right. The owner of the hotel, Walt, and Thomas, the rambler, sit at either head.

Thomas is a real southern boy. His sandy-blond hair is tousled; he wears a white shirt, suspenders which hold up his khakis, and brown buck shoes. His accent is charming, but reminds me of the rooster from the cartoons. Every time I hear him say, "I reckon it's so," I have to stifle a laugh.

Breakfast is an exact replica of dinner. It's as if we've slept in our seats, only our clothing selection has changed. Homemade cheese biscuits are waiting for us along with hot grits, scrambled eggs with bacon and sausage, and thick French toast with fresh strawberries.

The male Goth and the retired couple talk about camera

equipment. Myrna wants to go digital, Fred fears technology, or as he puts it, "A CD is something I buy at the bank." He laughs as if this is the funniest thing anyone has ever said. The college gals push food around on their plates, each commenting how fattening everything looks. The one in the middle requests yogurt be added to tomorrow's menu.

I had wanted to sit next to Tom, thought that arriving a few minutes early would ensure this, but his seat remains empty.

At 10:43 A.M. Tom appears with a megaphone attached to a small gray box which he carries over his shoulder.

We take a trolley car to the cemetery and stand camera-ready by the massive black gates. Tom raises the sound piece to his mouth.

"Can everyone hear me?"

We all answer, "Yes."

"Do we really need this?"

"No."

Tom smiles as if this is part of his routine. He puts the instrument down by the entrance, explaining that he'll pick it up on the way out, unless a spirit wants it.

"This tour started fifteen years ago. Rose Hill was founded in 1840 and stretches sixty-five acres." He suddenly sounds very professional. "It is home to 10,000 people, including three governors, two U.S. senators, thirty-one city mayors, and eight congressmen."

The cemetery is bright in the sun, which reveals its true weathered appearance. Even in its dilapidated state, it's beautiful. We pass by a white wingless angel, a little stone girl in a long dress wearing ribbons in her hair, and an owl. Outdoor works of art enclosed in an open-air museum. The earth is super dry and the grass is brown and dying. Nothing lives here but red ants that suck your blood and can kill you. This is what Tom is saying, not to touch or kick the small mounds that spring up every few feet.

"The first thing to note is the typical Italian Angels and allegorical pieces that reign above or seem to protect a specific plot. The details are delicate and finely carved but many are broken or are missing appendages," Tom explains. "Footstones and headstones are chipped, beaten by Mother Nature. These monuments were once ornate and ostentatious. Elaboration was the rule. But in 1954 a tornado did horrible damage and many vandals have had their way with them."

Tom is doing a splendid job. He practically glows with life, a living spirit walking amongst the dead. I catch him gazing at me, probably because I'm most attentive. I try to nod and flirt while he speaks, but I'm afraid of distracting him too much.

"We begin the first ramble at the confederate section, home to 600 men. Here you have very little space between plots. It looks as if the men were stacked on top of each other."

The sun is beating down on us and my skin feels as if it's burning. The college girls are drinking Evian water they brought with them from New York. Brian is taking notes and the Goths are still filming. The retired couple is arguing over camera shots and angles.

"Note the typical Southern granite and gray marble," Tom says, hand extended. "Now, if you give your attention to this plot, you'll notice it belongs to Lt. Bobby, a terrier. He was the men's mascot and a cherished pup. His owner, Captain Harris, died on a Monday. The dog took sick and passed away exactly one week later, an hour to the minute that Harris died."

Everyone seems interested, so Tom continues.

"This is the Woolfolk household where eight members of the

family were axed to death in their beds in 1887. Mr. Flint D. Woolfolk's son, Bill, was charged with the murders. The only one to survive, Bill was found wandering the streets of Macon, bloody and disoriented."

Tom appears sexier as he leads us deeper into the land. His voice gets creepy and quiet during suspenseful parts.

"Here, a fireman's hat, coat, and belt, all made of stone, are draped over the headstone of Kit Tobias, the four-year-old son of a fireman."

The plot is maybe three feet long, outlined by stone planks to show that the resting place belongs to a child.

"The irony of this story is that he died in a fire in his home while his father was at work, unable to save him," Tom adds.

By the third ramble, which overlooks the Ocmulgee River, the college posse seems bored and tired, the Tim Burton wanna-bes are running low on batteries, the older couple look like corpses, dehydrated and pale. Even their umbrellas can't blot out the sun. Brian is taking notes and asking too many questions. I feel like telling him extra credit isn't being given.

Two hours later, we collapse onto the trolley and head back to the inn, where fresh lemonade, cookies, and mini cakes are waiting for us. We look like wilted flowers in dire need of water.

After dinner, Tom and I stroll the neighborhood and I ex-plain my fixation with cemeteries. I walk close to him, knock-ing my knuckles into his, hoping at some point he'll reach for my hand.

I wonder what my life would be like if I moved here, just inhabited the simple, slow way of living. I could be a rambler like Tom or I could show historic homes, talk in a Southern accent, and make perfect grits.

This week, I am Shelly, a dental hygienist who works on Park

Avenue. My brother is a lawyer and my sister, who is married with two children, Jannie and Eric, is a stay-at-home mom. On Sundays we have brunch with my parents, an art dealer and a book doctor. In Georgia, I can be anyone I want.

Tom has a sweetness about him, an innocent, untainted, American feel. I see all these characteristics in his face as we stand on the stairs of the inn. A light above our heads is all that illuminates us and attracts every bug in the neighborhood. I try not to swat them away while we talk, afraid of ruining the romantic moment.

When he kisses me good night, I close my eyes. The sound of crickets magnifies as I try to hold on to the moment.

Tom doesn't appear for breakfast and I feel stood up. I'm sure he'll surface at one of the historic homes we're touring, but he remains a no-show. I keep eyeing the door as the woman—who's dressed in nineteenth-century garb—makes her opening speech. Distracted, I catch every few words, so I know she's talking about Sherman, the battle of something, and then I see her point to a small black object the size of a softball. "This is the original cannonball that grand old Sherman fired in the 1800's."

The second house is from 1855 and looks like Tara. The theme to *Gone With the Wind* plays over and over in my head as I picture myself drinking mint juleps, dressed in a poofy, lacy outfit standing on the porch, a fan in my hand, searching for my Tom to come home—on horseback—and waltz into our eighteen-room estate and make passionate love to me on our wooden bed. I think about this as we exit the house, as we board the plane, as I stand in the baggage area, eager for the Goths and the college girls to reclaim their belongings—everyone one else did carry-ons.

A car is waiting for the college group when we exit the airport. The Goths decide to shuttle it to the subway; Myrna and Fred live on the Upper West Side and cab it home. Brian is taking Amtrak back to Binghamton but offers to drop me off.

We don't have much to say during the ride home. We agree the trip was interesting and well organized, that we were lucky to have had such lovely weather, that we're glad to have gone, but neither of us has the desire to return.

As we pull up to my awning, I brush his cheek with mine, a bold move on my part, and thank him for being a gentleman.

My doorman lifts an eyebrow when I enter.

"So, did you get any?" he asks, as the cab drives off.

"Yes. He's got a tremendous penis, really amazing."

Andrés hands me my mail. It's a measly stack—a few catalogues, bills, *Allure* and *Elle* magazines, guilty pleasures. He doesn't look me in the eyes. I've embarrassed him.

I call my mother in the morning to tell her I've arrived home safely, but when she answers, her voice sounds odd. It's scratchy and softer than normal.

"What's the matter?" I ask.

"Your Aunt Delia died while you were away."

"What?"

"Massive heart attack. She was sitting in a restaurant, waiting for Jerry. She was thirsty, asked for some water, and by the time the waiter got back to the table she was dead."

"When did this happen?"

"The night you left." Her voice is even-toned.

"Why didn't you call me?"

"We wanted you to enjoy your trip. Anyway, the funeral is

today, if you want to go. Your father is meeting me there from work."

If I owned a cat, I'd be holding her.

"He wanted to go in for a few hours. Who am I to stop him? Maybe it's the best place. It will keep his mind busy . . ."

"If I hadn't called would you have even told me about this?"

"Nina," her voice is impatient, "don't do this to me today. You know how I feel about your father's family. I have nothing to wear and I need to go to Greenberg's and Eli's and pick up the desserts."

"Forget it." My voice comes out harshly, surprising both of us, and I hear my mother suck in air at the other end of the phone. It sounds like a balloon losing helium. "Just give me the information and I'll meet you there."

I go to the office to take my father to the funeral parlor. Everyone expresses their sympathy, many say they'll meet us at the chapel, then ask if we need any help. I accept their kind words while doing my best to appear upset.

In the cab my father stares out the window, one hand holding the black leather strap attached to the door, the other clutching the *Times* and the *Journal*. He hasn't said much. He's just thanked me profusely for picking him up.

At Campbell's, I have no need for a scarf or hat, no use for glasses. Today, I get to be myself. I can't believe no one recognizes me. I'm always shocked when not one employee asks why I'm here two or three times a month.

As we enter the viewing room, I expect to see my childhood. I think perhaps time has stopped and everyone will look young and healthy. I'm horrified instead. They've either gotten smaller and fatter, or have lost hair in some spots and gained more in others. The vain ones have stopped the aging process altogether. Their faces are tough and tight, their foreheads raised too high.

Many are unable to frown or move their brows.

I search out my aunt's children, David, Robert, and Vicki, but can only find their offspring—toddlers who have morphed into real people. They now range from gawky, acne-faced fifteen-year-olds to five-year-old blond, Ralph Lauren-like models. Some are new to me altogether.

It is in this spot where I want to start over. Reenter the room when I was eleven and we were all here for my grandfather's service. I close my eyes and remember the memorial, hear the rabbi's consoling voice in my head, recreate the soft gold chairs my mother's friends sat in.

I catch David at the entrance, greeting people. I have to keep myself from running over and giving him a hug. It's hard to be distant and affectionate at the same time.

By the fifth person I've kissed hello, I feel as though I'm at a party. Perhaps my aunt is in the bathroom somewhere or is running late like my mother, and hasn't arrived. I try to tone down my enthusiasm but I'm on a high, from the people, from the word *family*, and from how good and awful it feels to be here. No matter what happens, no matter how terrible and aloof they might be, they are still relatives. And in that fact, I'm comforted. It comes over me like a quiet hush.

Since my mother's running late, my father and I sit in the viewing room. I tell my father who's who, giving sound bites and short bios as my mother would, as if we were secret agents. "That's Lenny," I whisper to him as a tall man in a hat sits down next to us. "He's married to Anita. He works for J.P. Morgan."

My father pats my leg. "You're a good kid, Nina."

I play with the bracelet on my wrist, think of Helen, wonder if Marty's ashes ever turned up. My thoughts jump to his wife, Faye, and what Marty could have told her about me and our sessions. Then I wonder if I can call her and get Helen's number, perhaps send them each a bracelet.

I haven't seen Vicki, Robert, or my uncle yet, and I keep my eyes on the door until they enter.

My uncle is a broad, hefty guy with an unusual angry, teddy-bear quality. Today, however, his eyes are bloodshot and he moves slowly. A shuffle. Vicki trails behind, talking loudly on her cell phone, dark glasses over her eyes, tissues in her hand. She's dressed in a green suit that's too tight and too short. She looks as if she's falling out of it. I want to cry at how bad she looks and must quell my desire to take her by the hand and lead her into Ann Taylor, which is across the street, and buy her an outfit that fits. I want to greet her, tell her how sorry I am about her mother, but she's too absorbed in her call to notice me.

My father and I stand when my uncle approaches and I watch the men hug, patting each other on the back. Then my dad starts to weep. It's a terrible sight. His whole body shakes. His face becomes ruddy and his jaw drops open, as if he's having a stroke. Falsetto moans follow, like those of an injured animal caught in a trap.

We sit in the third row from the front. Orchestra seats, up close and personal. I stare at the red carpet that has white snowflakes embroidered on it, an odd choice for a temple.

Five minutes later, my mother saunters in. This is after nineteen people have asked me where she is, why she's not here, and what in God's name she could be doing. She dons her funeral pearls and they bounce off her chest as she hurriedly walks over to us. As she bends down to kiss me hello, I smell fresh shampoo and realize she's had her hair done. The pearls just miss hitting me in the eye.

. . .

My father doesn't want to speak, though I encourage him to utter something, anything. A last good-bye, a missed moment, but he refuses.

My oldest cousin, David, tells of the wonderful relationship his parents had. A stay-at-home mom whose main concern was for her family. Delia was involved in the PTA, directed plays for the kids at school, and was always available. He adds that his father, who traveled constantly for business, would fly or drive home so he could sleep in his own bed, wake up next to his wife every night. "Best friends," he concludes, shaking his head side to side.

This is a lie. I know for a fact she and my uncle were having problems and spoke endlessly about getting divorced. But David gloats and praises the relationship, the connection he had with his mother, the honor of being the firstborn.

He tag-teams with Robert, who is accompanied by his wife, Abby, and they stand together at the podium looking like a statue on a wedding cake. Both share stories about my aunt, about how gracious and accepting she was, making Abby feel like part of the family. Abby adds that her mother died when she was little and years later my aunt filled that role for her.

Vicki brings up the rear, talking openly about their turbulent relationship, about the heavy partying, the loose behavior, the unreasonable demands she felt her mother was making, and has only recently come to appreciate. At forty-one, she feels she was just starting to understand her mother and enjoy her company.

The grandchildren speak next. David's three kids, then Robert's two. They cling to each other as they walk to the stage, Xeroxed letters in their own handwriting, originals buried inside with my aunt. My little cousins take such care of each other. They hug as one finishes and the next delivers the speech, mirroring their parents' actions. When one comes down from the podium, another gets up to meet the first halfway. Robin takes a hand to Jodi's face, brings her close and soothes her for but a second. There is no differentiation between David's children and Robert's. The lines have smudged regarding who belongs to whom. Two sets of mothers, two fathers. They will always be taken care of, will always have people to call in emergencies.

I catch my mother crying, and feel suddenly very much alone.

Afterward, we regroup and I'm reintroduced to my little cousins, who don't remember me. I am who? The cousin they never see. Their faces show faint recognition; they turn to their parents for confirmation, for added information.

"You remember Nina," says David. "She taught you the spoon trick? For your sixth birthday she sent you an Eloise doll?"

It's a slow, foggy process. They want to remember me but can't.

I've missed much.

The cemetery is cold and the walkway is littered with colorful leaves. It's extremely breezy and the rabbi has to yell over the wind. He's a good-looking man who is too stiff and uneasy with the position of power he holds.

"Delia wasn't one for words, so we'll keep this short and simple as she would have wanted," the rabbi says. It feels as if we're doing a *Reader's Digest* version. Everyone seems uncomfortable, myself included.

Earlier, there was a big discussion about where my aunt wanted to be buried—in the mausoleum with my grandparents, or alone in the plot my uncle bought. After much debate we watch in silence as she's lowered into the ground by the silver pulley system. Three Spanish groundskeepers oversee this process. They're dressed in Hawaiian floral shirts, which remind me of the fallen leaves, and jeans. The contrast is an odd mix to our sea of blacks and blues.

The rabbi concludes by explaining the shoveling procedure. Our first mitzvah is coming here, to help escort the dead to their final resting place. The second is to drop dirt on the grave as a way of letting the soul leave peacefully.

Mounds of dirt, which sit on sheets of asphalt with three shovels standing upward, are on the left. The rabbi takes the first scoop and we line up in order of importance. No one delegates or directs; people seem to have an innate sense for cemetery etiquette. My uncle is at the head, followed by my cousins, their spouses and children, my father, me, my uncle's brother, his friends, and more family from my uncle's side.

Each of us takes a turn.

The sound of shovel to dirt, dirt onto coffin, back to mound of dirt, builds into an odd rhythm. Familiar, yet non-placeable. My hand grips the round handle. The heaviness of the shovel compounded with the dirt is empowering. The feeling magnifies with each scoop of soil I take. "Rest in peace," I say under my breath as the clumps fall into the hole. "Who were you?" is what I ask when my second scoop drops on top of my first.

I watch the line move, notice the smattering of dirt that clings to the men's pants as they walk away. Proof of their involvement. When the last person has gone, David and Robert resume the work, appearing like a mechanical assembly line. Vicki ventures forward and takes the remaining shovel and the three move in silence. Dirt. Drop. Dirt. Drop. She is masculine and muscular, half man, part woman, maneuvering in an unspoken competition with her siblings. Someone asks if she wants to stop but she refuses. She is intent on scooping up every last bit.

We go to my aunt's home and I breathe in the Perlman/Wasserman smell. It's been over a decade since my last visit. Like Campbell's, the Wassermans haven't redecorated in eons.

As I hang my coat up in the closet, my grandfather's shiva flashes before my eyes. I remember being here and serving drinks and cold cuts, offering coffee to some of my mother's friends, picking up dirty napkins and empty paper plates and bringing them in to my aunt's kitchen.

Vicki is on her third drink by the time I hit the living room. My uncle is yelling at her to slow down on the vodka as he reaches for the bottle of Johnny Walker and pours himself a drink. I find David and Robert in the den watching TV, their children playing with Legos and cars on the rug next to them. The wives congregate in the kitchen. Friends and family are sprinkled throughout the first floor.

I want to say something and almost clear my throat in order to gain everyone's attention. I have worked on this speech since I was twelve and have never found an appropriate time to use it. Now is wrong, too. I can't spew about how hurt I am. I can't tell them I have never been made to feel like a member of this family and won't someone please explain what I did that was so awful for me to have been excluded all these years. Party after party that I was not invited to. Get-togethers and weddings and showers and bar mitzvahs and holidays and school plays . . . but there never is a right time to deliver my rehearsed words because I am never with my family when it's not a funeral.

While everyone is eating and crying and milling about, I sneak upstairs.

Paying respects at a relative's home is like finding a secret stash of candy. I can't help but inspect each room, search through cabinets and dresser drawers, look through scrapbooks and photo albums filled with old Kodak memories: my grandmother and her siblings sunning at the Breakers Country Club, my father's twelfth birthday party, my aunt and uncle's wedding photos, my cousins playing in the sand. Snap. A moment is captured. Tangible evidence of time. Proof of existence. Validation.

I snoop in the hope of finding answers about who they are; I search for something which will connect me to them.

I enter Vicki's room first. The bed and carpet have been replaced but the bulletin board and mirror over her vanity table still ring of her adolescence. The mirror is smattered with moments from her college years, the bulletin board proudly displays ribbons from horseback riding competitions and swim meets. I run my hand over her dresser. A slew of old tapes and loose change are in a basket, a stack of holiday cards held together with a rubber band is in the drawer. *To a wonderful daughter on her birthday, Happy Valentine's Day from Dad's favorite girl, Congrats on your graduation.* Two decades old, these things still prove this is her room. There are other clues, too. An old wallet with foreign currency, school yearbooks, a box of old lipsticks.

At my grandfather's funeral, Vicki was out of cigarettes and let me tag along with her in the car to get more. The convertible was a mess. Cigarette butts were spilling out of the ashtray, bright red and pink lipstick marks on the tips. There were empty soda cans strewn about, paper bags from fast food drive-throughs, and lots of used napkins. Books, clothing, and boxes littered the back seat.

I sat in the car, motor running, while she paid for the smokes at the convenience store. I was about to look through the glove compartment when she came back. Like a well choreographed number, she hit the car lighter with the palm of her hand, un-wrapped the box of Parliaments, tapped the packet a few times on the dashboard, and removed a single cigarette in perfect time for the lighter knob to pop out. She rolled down the window, puffed on the cigarette, and started to cry.

I didn't know what to do or say. I didn't know why she was crying. I didn't think it was over my grandfather, considering the fact that no one liked him. I just sat there watching her as she flicked ashes out the window. Then I reached for her hand, the one that rested on the clutch. I placed mine on top of hers, no-ticed her iridescent, salmon-colored nails were all chipped and that her skin was dry. She wore silver rings and the tops of my fingers rested on them. I closed my eyes and leaned my head against the seat.

"You want a puff?" she asked. I couldn't believe she was talk-ing to me.

"Sure," I said, and placed my lips directly over the mark her lipstick had made. Visible instructions. Then she told me to breathe in and swallow a little smoke, which made me cough. She laughed while she shook several cans of Coke, searching for one that felt half full, and handed it to me.

Before we reentered my aunt's house, Vicki ate Mentos and reapplied lipstick. She caught me staring and when she was fin-ished, tossed it to me.

She leaned forward and for a second I thought she was going to help. Instead, she flipped down the mirror above my head. I ran the iridescent pink color over my lips, careful not to press too hard, careful not to break it. It hurt to hand it back and I remember thinking if she really cared about me she'd have let me keep it. She would have given it to me as a gift and I would have carried it everywhere and never used it except on special occasions. But she extended her hand, an unspoken gesture to return it.

Once inside the house, she went into her parents' room and locked herself in. I stood outside for a moment, ear pressed to the door. I heard her pick up the phone. Heard her talking to someone. Heard her slipping away.

I look for the Revlon lipstick she let me use years ago. Velvet Rose is here, as if it's been waiting for me. I apply it quickly to my lips.

David's room is next. His has been turned into a work area/gym. A treadmill is in the corner, along with dumbbells and a rolled-up exercise mat. Robert's room has been converted into the guest room. A masculine version of Vicki's, without the personalized items.

The hallway wall is a time line in pictures. My aunt and uncle's wedding day, them at my parents' wedding, Delia pregnant, Delia pregnant with Robert, David and my uncle standing beside her, and on and on. The children playing in a pile of leaves, the children at a graduation, more marriages, more births, more family moments.

The attic is too dusty to tamper with so I head back downstairs and join the land of the living. My aunt's friend is talking to my mother and when she sees me, she motions with her hand to sit down next to her.

"When my husband died, I told our maid I wasn't coming home until everything sickness-related had been removed from the apartment." The woman takes a deep breath. "I wanted his medication thrown out, the sheets stripped and gone, I wanted flowers in every room so that when I walked in, nothing of my husband's illness was there. I only wanted to be surrounded by happy things." She slaps the top of the coffee table. "Remember only the good." Then she beams as if she's said something fantastic. She nods to others for approval, a hint of understanding.

"You're right, Lanny," my mother says, placing a hand on her thigh. "You took care of him for years. You should only be surrounded by pleasant objects."

I get up and excuse myself. I can feel my mother's eyes on me, assessing my outfit, my hair, feel her disappointment burn through my shirt and onto my skin.

I walk into the kitchen, open the refrigerator, look for something—I'm not sure what—and when I come up empty-handed, shut the door. I saunter back into the living room and realize something has happened in my absence.

My uncle has leaned forward and is resting his elbows on his knees, one hand covers his eyes, the other holds a shaking glass. His brother is sitting next to him, his hand pressed firmly on his back. David comes over and removes the glass from his father's hand. I watch my mother bite down on her lip and shake her head. My father stands behind her and rests a hand on her shoulder. For the first time in years, I see her take his. She pats it first, then grips his fingers. Everyone is very still, as if a photographer has said *Hold please, now say cheese.*

I find Vicki outside in a lounge chair, a wool blanket wrapped around her. She's crying in between puffs of smoke and sips of vodka. I stand a good two minutes, watching her, before I open the screen door and walk out onto the deck. I sit down next to her, drape my coat over me, my arms in backward. I'm allowed out here today when normally someone would tell me to leave her alone. But I have earned this right from birth, from the very minute of conception. No matter how left-out I am in real life, today I have privileges.

She passes me her cigarette, then her glass. I accept them graciously. I've graduated from soda. We both have.

. . .

The days slip and melt into each other. Moments pass like breaths. Hours, like the blinking of an eye. I have nothing to hold on to, nothing to prove anything has happened.

Each morning I wake to a familiar sadness. I look at the calendar, count the days to my period. I'm not due for another three weeks. This melancholy is attributed to something else entirely.

I've been nibbling on Halloween candy all week. It's in a big glass bowl by the front door. Even though cartoon characters, forest animals, and not-so-scary-looking monsters will ring my bell in two days, it sits ready for the asking, the stash disappearing little by little.

The days are getting cold and the sun seems to be vanishing unfairly earlier. In another month, families will be bonding over glazed hams and Butterball turkeys, sitting at elongated tables with their pants unbuttoned.

I flip channels endlessly, hoping to catch something entertaining.

I'm tired of being alone. Tired of watching the clock change from 10:52 A.M. to 10:53 to 10:54, excited only by upcoming TV shows. Those are the people who know me. The cast of *ER* and *Law and Order*. Those are the people I spend my day with. They keep me company. They are dependable. They show up on time.

I walk around my apartment, look at the clock: 8:38 P.M., and stare out the window. I look through my address book for people I can call. I have a few actor friends from college who live in LA. Perhaps I could visit them. I could call Tom or Dean. I miss them. Miss the feel of a body next to mine, the vision of someone in my bed. I scan the White Pages, which has now found a permanent spot on the kitchen counter, for a name. Everyday I look for another, write it down on a sheet of paper titled "emergency numbers," and tack it to the fridge.

I love the White Pages. So many people. So many people who don't know me. People I could meet. I fan the book, run my fingers through the tissue-thin pages, and think of who I could call. I close my eyes and ask God to lead my finger.

"Let me pick a good one."

I run freshly painted nails down the endless names, my eyes closed, till something inside says *Stop*. I look down and have landed on Steven Bronston, 96 West Seventy-fourth Street. He lives near the park, probably off Columbus. It's a lovely area and I mentally walk my way up the familiar streets in the Seventies until I get to Seventy-fourth. I can see the Baby Gap store, its winter windows filled with small outfits. The jewelry store across the street, the high school courtyard where the Sunday fair takes place every week. I picture Steven, a jogger living so close to the park, fit and muscular with curly blond hair. I bet he owns a dog, too. I think about calling, wonder what his voice would sound like. I could tell him I was an old classmate or that I was a friend of a co-worker who thought he might be too shy to ask me out, so instead she gave me his number. *Would you like to have coffee?* I'd ask. I could lie and say I live upstairs. He'd never really know.

With my parents away for the week in Montreal, I go into work, bags under my eyes, a fake smile on my face. I haven't slept in days because I'm having nightmares where I wake up in a panic, body drenched in sweat, hands shaking, mouth fighting for air. I'll be standing or sitting in a filled chapel, a different one each time, and like in the movie *Invasion of the Body Snatchers*, someone points and their mouth opens wide but all that comes out is an inaudible shriek. Everyone's heads turn and people join in the chorus of cries. They are deafening and I run, the procession of people chasing after me wildly like rabid dogs.

I greet a few people, chat with Lilly for a bit, check my desk, return messages, and sort through some mail before retiring to my father's office where I draw the blinds, dim the lights, turn off the ringer, and try to sleep on his couch. The office buzz calms me. I like the idea of being surrounded by activity. I sleep well here.

Hours later, I wake; the office is dark and everyone has gone home. It's well after midnight. I walk up and down the hallway, then break into a skip and start to sing like I longed to do as a child when my mother and I would visit. I jump into one of the chairs and roll around until I get bored. Then I snoop through people's desks. When I get to Shannon's, I stop. Her space is too neat, the mail piled too high. From the looks of it, she hasn't been in for days.

I sit in her chair, sink into the molded incline of her seat, and think how much bigger her body must be compared to mine.

There are no photos on her desk. No group shots at a park or restaurant celebrating someone's birthday. Nothing with her and a friend traveling to exotic ports of call or to foreign countries. There's just a black *Phantom of the Opera* mug which holds pens and pencils. A note taped to the blotter reads, *Out sick. Please leave a message or call Benita Thompson for help.*

While sifting though her "in" box I find several days worth of *The New York Times*. I turn to today's obits. The section is weak at best. Not many people have died since yesterday. Nevertheless, I skim the page to see if anyone sounds interesting. There's a service for a veterinarian, another for a chef, and one for a librarian. I retrieve yesterday's section from her box. Not much happens on a Tuesday. It seems to be the least exciting day to pay respects.

The one story I have been following is the recent murder of five women in the East Village area. *The New York Post* and news shows call him the Diner Killer. The last to be recovered was a forty-three-year-old photographer. The funerals have been closed to the public for obvious reasons and many haven't had a viewing because the bodies are still considered evidence. The families have had to wait weeks to bury their loved ones or they've held memorials for the spirit, not the body. This is the case with Annette Rowen.

The paper says friends and family will be holding a four-day remembrance for Annette at her cousin's home in SoHo. I've missed the first day, which was Sunday. Tomorrow, Thursday, and Friday are when the other evenings are taking place.

I love several-day sittings. I call them carry-overs. These are not so rare. People usually mourn for several days, offering friends and family a choice of options for the modern person with late meetings and crazy appointments to fit into their busy schedules. Last year I went to the home of Mr. and Mrs. Gardner, the parents of a high school teen who'd OD'ed on crystal meth. The vigil lasted all week. I went every day after work and sat with the same group from 6:30 to 9:30. They fed me dinner, read me his term papers, showed me his varsity jacket. By the end of the week, I was clearing plates and doing dishes. I'd practically moved in.

The paper says Annette is remembered by her parents, brother, and her partner, Karen. I clear my mind and prepare myself. I spend several hours researching her past work, reading articles that used her photographs, learning about certain techniques, and honing my camera skills.

I'd taken a few photography classes at Sarah Lawrence but my photos were either too blurry or overexposed, and I could never figure out the aperture versus film speed.

I want to wear something artsy and fashionable but my hand reaches for a conservative black turtleneck sweater and black wool pants. The obit doesn't read like it's a traditional party. It's in SoHo and sounds laid-back. I visualize a huge loft filled with other artsy people, all in different types of clothing to help express who they really are.

I have a very good feeling about this and rush around the apartment excitedly, like I'm going on a date. I wear some of my jewelry, put a few extra bracelets into small plastic bags in case I want to give them out as gifts. I could nonchalantly say I was delivering them off at one of the stores I sell to and these were extras. *Please, it would be my honor for you to have it.*

The subway drops me off several blocks from the loft and I pick up two bottles of wine at the liquor store. Since there's no service I feel as though I shouldn't come empty-handed.

The cousin, Patti, an environmental lawyer, lives in an industrial building and I ride in a creaky, rundown elevator where you have to close and open an oversized metal gate. As I travel upward, I can hear voices getting louder and excitement builds inside as I lurch to the eleventh floor. I lift the gate up and step out into the apartment, instantly becoming part of the action. Heads turn to see who has arrived.

The loft is huge and space is sectioned off by furniture, Pottery Barn and Crate & Barrel style, large and heavy. There are no walls aside from the four which hold the place up. People stand by the window, some in the kitchen area. Several women are seated in three long couches in the middle of the enormous space. Others are standing by the dining room table, filling their plates. As far as I can tell, there are no men.

As predicted, it's an ethnic, artsy mix. Far less traditional than I've been to in a while. Not one suit can be found. Many are in jeans, leather jackets, suede shirts, lots of sweaters and skirts, leopard this and tiger-print that. Vintage vests and long shawl things, pointed shoes and granola sandals, make this event feel like a book club in Woodstock rather than a memorial. My eyes glance around quickly, taking in the earthy women to see if I can pick out Patti or Karen.

I take a step forward, the gate snaps shut. I hear the creaky grind as the elevator reels back down.

An attractive, friendly woman with pixie-styled, dirty-blond hair greets me. Her apron reads *Don't be fooled. I'm not really domesticated.*

"Welcome. I'm Patti. Can I take your coat?"

"I'm Candice, here," I say, and hand over the bottles.

"Oh, thanks. We've been going through wine like water. I think everyone here is on a liquid diet today." She laughs. I do, too. And it is sealed. A business deal based on emotions.

"I'm so sorry to have heard about Annette."

"Thank you."

"What a sick thing for someone to do."

"Come in—let's introduce you to everyone. Have you met Karen yet?"

"No." I lower my voice a little, make my tone more intimate. "How's she holding up?"

"Okay, I guess. We're all still in shock."

I follow her into her bedroom, which is also sectioned-off by pieces of furniture. Two tall dressers and huge, double-sided mirrors, which hang from thick wire and are attached to the ceiling, help separate this area from the living room.

I hand her my blazer and wool raincoat, which she drops on the bed with the others. I'm suddenly very tired. I'd love to lie down right here with the coats.

I shake my head. "I still can't believe it. It's so surreal."

Patti leads me to the living room area where the majority of women reside. Several are perched comfortably on the couches; others sit on the floor, their backs leaning up against the furniture. They are gripping each other's hands, sitting close and stroking hair; heads are resting in laps. Some have their shoes off, some are smoking, everyone's hand holds a glass. Empty wine bottles are on a nearby coffee table.

In the far corner resides a projector and large screen. Next to it is a TV on mute, while a stereo, in another corner, is playing light jazz. The whole thing feels so comfortable and familiar I half expect Glenn Close and JoBeth Williams to come out from the kitchen, arms laden with dishes and pasta salad.

I have already picked Karen out before Patti formally introduces me. My hunch is she's the one sitting close to another woman, looking extra drawn.

"Everyone, this is Candice—Candice, everyone."

I get a 12-step hello. The woman I picked as Annette's partner stands.

"Hi. I'm Karen. Thank you for coming."

"I wouldn't have missed this for the world. I'm just sorry I wasn't here on Sunday. I was closing at the magazine and there was no way to leave, even on a weekend."

"Oh, is that how you knew her?"

"Yeah. A few years ago I worked on the editorial side when she was working in the photo department at *National Geographic*."

The woman on the end of the couch looks uncomfortable; the woman seated on the floor looks lonely; another, who is standing, seems angry. I label and break them down quickly, systematically collating them into the Seven Dwarfs and stop at Grumpy. She looks like Patti Smith and sounds like Stevie Nicks. She's talking with her hands, sitting on the couch Indian-style, glass of wine resting on the old LV trunk in front of her. She's dressed in black jeans and denim shirt with a baby-T underneath. Her dark hair is layered and wavy. She's animated and smart and talks very fast. She's totally self-absorbed as she criticizes someone in her office who she finds lacks common sense. She is selfish, angry, and unhappy, yet has the ability to be nurturing. I can tell all this instantly. She's perfect.

The thinking here is to find the most removed person and get them to love me. If I can win them over, make them care about me even though they don't want to, then I've accomplished the impossible. I've made them change. Up is down, left is right, and everything suddenly feels safe.

"I mean, give me a fucking break," she says loudly, as if on a debate team. "She's one of these people who goes to the movies to be entertained. What the hell is that? Film is a fucking experience. If you want to laugh, go to a goddamn comedy club."

"I hate people who can't handle depressing movies," says the woman behind me. I spin around. "It's like, excuse me for making you feel. I don't have any *Rugrats* movies in my home. Sorry."

If I'm going to impress her, I've got to work fast. "These are like the people who have no black or gay friends and live within a five-block radius from all of their conservative, numbing, Republican friends on the Upper East Side in co-ops, who are all unfathomably clueless as to how the real world actually works. Right?"

"Yeah," she says.

Our eyes lock. A showdown. I remember to follow the four Be's: be funny, sarcastically witty, smart, and helpful.

"Congratulations, you've just met my parents." My deadpan expression becomes a knowing smile. Everyone roars. I even get a few claps.

She lifts her glass in my direction—*touché.*

"Candice, let me break down the group a little. This is Joanna, Susan, Wes, and our soapbox mediator, Sloan. Over there is Lisa, Dylan, and Ann."

Sloan and I stand on opposite sides of Patti's elongated, Amish-looking dining room table, complete with wooden benches, as we fill our plates. Pizza boxes, a six-foot hero sandwich, and bowls of Greek salad are at the head and foot of the table. Plates, napkins, utensils, and wine and soda are in the middle.

One woman shimmies by and reaches for the open bottle. She pours the remaining contents into her glass. "I think between Sunday and today, I've finished this whole thing by myself."

A sharp pang of panic starts in my chest and I fear I've missed something. The world moved ever so slightly without my help or knowledge. Like the kid who transferred school midyear and has already missed the important bonding moments, the ones that cement friendships and create history, I, too, have been left behind. All the cliques have been formed.

I'm careful not to become Sloan's shadow and make a point of chatting with several other women. Wes and Joanna have been together for eight years, Patti is single and straight, Sue is Annette's ex, but she and Karen are very friendly, and on and on. Each woman has a story to tell. And I want to know them all.

Later, we sit through a showing of Annette's work.

Someone closes the drapes, another dims the lights, everyone gets comfortable.

By the fifth slide, Karen's voice has lulled me into a deep calm. The click of the projector, the changing of the slides, is hypnotic.

I'm sitting next to Sloan, who has her feet up on the LV trunk, and I've copied her position. We've scrunched together to make room for Dani, another of Annette's friends. We are sorority women in search of a theme song.

When a photo of Angkov Wat appears that I recognize from one of the magazines I've researched, I sit up, pull my feet off the trunk. I talk excitedly, one hand pointing to the screen. "That's the photo we used from the Cambodia article. We worked on it for months." I look to Karen. "This must be about three years old, right?"

"About that," she answers.

"I remember what a trauma that issue was. The magazine barely scraped by."

"Really?" she asks.

"Yeah," I answer quickly, "on a production level, that is."

Everyone is looking at me.

"Annette didn't mention any problems." There's a hint of anger in her voice.

"Sure. She was photo. Text is a whole other story. No pun intended." A few people laugh. "Photo is shipped first," I say, adding more authority to my voice. "I used to bitch about story deadlines each month. Finally, I threatened to go over to Annette's side if things didn't improve. Believe me, put a camera in my hands and you're looking at rolls and rolls of film with out-of-focus thumbs in each frame."

I'm silent for the rest of the show. I've exceeded my limit.

"See you in eleven hours," I joke, once we get out of the elevator. As usual, I'm one of the last to leave. Only Sloan, Karen, and two other friends of Patti's remain upstairs.

The eight of us hug each other good-bye. The embraces are honest and filled with emotion. I hate to leave but am reassured by the fact that I'll be back tomorrow, and the day after that.

It's cold and rainy outside. I can see my breath, a subtle hint that we're in for a long, brutal winter. Many came armed with trench coats and umbrellas; they break off into pairs, a new version of Noah's ark, and disperse into different directions.

At home I feel a little lonely, but in an okay way. It's been a very intense day and I'm glad to see the apartment. I shower, wash my hair, shave, and give myself a facial. Then I concentrate on making Sloan something from my jewelry stash. She mentioned she loves jewelry, but the artsy kind that I was wearing. I was sure to explain that I'd left the magazine to pursue my interests in jewelry design, but still freelance from time to time as an editor. Everyone seemed impressed with my work. I even took a few orders from some of the women, wrote down their addresses, made notes regarding what they wanted. I do more research online, trying to review every issue of the magazine that Annette and I would have worked on together. I call *National Geographic* and listen to the monotone operator rattle off the names of editors who work there now, just in case. I memorize the list as I fall asleep.

I wake up excited but anxious to go back to Patti's, to reconnect after the intense bonding experience we all shared.

These moments, if done correctly, are like first kisses, warm and unforgettable. Impossible to erase. I'll be there today to remind them of what occurred yesterday. To validate it, make them recall the incident.

I've put in a full day of work and its nearly 7:00 P.M. when I arrive. I say hi and kiss some of the women hello—the ones I became especially close with yesterday. I love being here. I feel instantly welcome. I look for Sloan and find her talking to Wes in the kitchen.

The first few minutes are awkward. I'm not sure what to say and don't want to come on too strong. The rules for "Follow the Leader" apply and I take a step back, waiting for her to receive me.

"Hey, Candice," she says.

It's a warm greeting. My insides relax as I reach for the wine.

Karen is dozing on the loveseat.

"She must be exhausted." I nudge Sloan. We stare at her for a second. "We should help clean up."

We remove glasses from the coffee table and stereo unit, pick up empty wine bottles from the floor, dirty ashtrays overflowing with cigarette buts. I steady myself a few times, not realizing how tipsy I actually am until I start to move around.

"I wonder if there's something we can do with Annette's photos?" I throw out to the group. "Maybe put together a show of her work to honor her memory?"

"Karen would love that," Wes answers, getting a foot massage from Joanna. "Among all of us here, we must have a million connections."

"What we saw last night was just a highlight. Annette was quite a shutterbug," Patti adds. A consensus starts to form as people give their ideas, make suggestions.

"We could do a charity event, set up a victim's fund," I offer before following Sloan into the kitchen with the glasses and ashtrays.

"Can you feel the synergy?" I joke as I stack empty take-out cartons.

Sloan looks at me, her head slightly tilted, her glass earring dancing back and forth. "It's a fabulous idea, but do you think it's too soon to honor her work?"

I stare at her face, look for who she is, how she feels about me.

"Candice," she's smiling, "is it too soon? What do you think?"

What do I think? That all of life is spent looking for the one person to make you whole, to give you what you've been missing your entire, pathetic life. Instead, I say, "I'm thinking of art galleries and media people I could call." I've disappointed her and myself.

Sloan pushes hair behind my ear. "You should get all this taken off. You'd look great with short hair."

"Really?" I reply.

"Yeah. My husband says shorter is sexier. It's just one more secret men keep from women."

I swallow hard. Sloan reminds me of everything I want. Of all I'm missing and that which is obtainable. *Will you love me?* I want to ask her. *Will you let me be part of your life even though you don't know me? Even though you just met me yesterday. Will you stay?*

"You know what we should do?" She's moved on to something else, her hands reach for the sponge. "Patti has an amazing roof. We had weekly barbecues here last summer."

She's cleaning the counter now. "We should go up, get some air."

She tosses the sponge into the sink, wipes her hands on the towel, then reaches for an open bottle of red and two glasses.

I follow her out onto the roof deck. We are tipsy and wobble up the stairs laughing, like sisters would. I almost want to say *Remember that time we got in trouble for coming home drunk from that party my last year of college? Mom was so mad.*

The roof door bangs open and I follow her to the edge. One step forward is all it takes. The cold air is slightly sobering. I see my breath. It reminds me of smoking; a cigarette would be great right now. I look out into the night. The neighboring buildings look like a checkerboard with the pattern of lights on and off.

"I wonder what everyone in that building is doing right this minute," I say.

"Half are having sex, the other half are wishing they were having sex."

We laugh, drink more wine.

"This is really nice," she says, reaching for my necklace. "Did you make this?"

I nod. "You want it?" I'm still laughing as I reach behind my neck to unhook the clasp. Sloan places a hand on my chest, holds the turquoise stone in place.

"No, I was just saying it was pretty." She keeps her hand there until the tears are deep in my throat, until I feel as if I could choke on them. I try to push them back down, almost strike a bargain with God. *Let me get through this without crying and I'll go back into therapy.* Her other hand comes up to my forehead and her fingers brush hair away from my face. I close my eyes, caught between giving in and fighting. *Don't cry. Don't cry*, I scream silently inside my head. *Don't. Don't. Don't.* I wonder if she can hear me, read my thoughts. They seem so visible. Sound so loud. I visualize them leaking out through my ears, tearing from my eyes.

"I miss her, too," she says. "She meant a lot to all of us."

"It's more than that." My voice cracks. Just tell her. Just say it. "These have been really intense days. And I feel lucky to have made new friends. I think that would please Annette."

She smiles a little, then takes a step back, picks up the wine bottle, and notices it's empty. "We're out of supplies."

Don't go.

"I'll get more," she adds, turning away. In the darkness I can hardly see her face.

Don't leave.

"You coming or do you want to stay out here for a few?"

"Can we get together sometime?"

She's already walking away. "Sure. When this is all over."

"Great." My voice is lost over the sound of evening, cars buzzing by, dog barking, a couple fighting on the street. I follow her down the stairs. She first, then me. We are not together anymore, our intimacy gone. Our intensity broken. It doesn't matter. She said yes and even if she doesn't mean it, or means it now at this moment but won't remember saying it tomorrow, it's what I needed to hear. It's something to hold on to.

Day three and I arrive early enough to seem supportive, but late enough not to look too eager. I've also come armed with a caramel cake from Greenberg's.

The smell of freshly baked cookies wafts into Patti's elevator as it brings me closer to the eleventh floor. I step out and instantly, something feels wrong. At first I think it's because only a few people are here—die-hard friends from her inner clan. But that's not it. The air is thick, the room cold.

I walk into the bedroom with the intention of dropping off my coat and accidentally find Karen and Patti. Their eyes are red. The conversation halts.

"Anything I can do?" I offer, placing my jacket with the others.

"No. We're okay."

"It's hard," Patti adds, "last day and all."

I walk out and catch Sloan entering the bathroom.

She's left the door open and I knock on the frame. "Hey."

Her face is temporarily hidden by the medicine cabinet door and she doesn't greet me until she slams it shut. A bottle of Tylenol is in her hand.

"I needed aspirin," she explains.

In her tipsy state she has trouble opening it. She laughs at first—it's very funny to her. A few seconds later, Sloan is banging the top part down on the sink.

"I can't believe Patti doesn't have Advil," she yells over the sound of pills shaking against plastic.

Giving up, she throws the bottle to the floor. I pick it up, twist the top off, and hand her two white capsules. I fill her empty wineglass with water, put that in her waiting palm, and close the bathroom door.

"Thanks." She starts to sway back and forth and steadies herself against the wall.

"You okay?"

She nods, swallows hard.

"Maybe we should stay in here for a bit," I suggest. The words are barely out of my mouth when Sloan slides to the floor.

We sit in the bathroom, each leaning up against a different wall.

"I've known Annette since I was fourteen. Sleepaway camp." She takes a deep breath.

I count silently in my head—5, 4, 3, 2—tears.

She lightly taps her head against the wall, eyes becoming glassy. "I've known her for twenty-eight years. I was there when she came out. I went to her twenty-first birthday. I met her first girlfriend. She introduced me to my husband."

I remain silent—that's my job right now.

"Her parents and brother were here the first week of her death—you've never seen people so distraught." She's crying harder now, not bothering to hide them. "They finally went back to Colorado." She grunts a laugh, shakes her head back and forth. "I was there when she broke up with her first major girlfriend, when she received a Guggenheim . . ." Her voice trails off. "What am I going to do without her?"

"I don't know." My voice sounds small. I glance at the tile, look for hair or dirt on the floor and in the cracks. "She had her whole life ahead of her. She was gaining respect and acknow-ledgment in her career." When I glance back at Sloan, she's staring at me. "What?" I ask.

"Nothing."

She sniffles and uses the back of her hand to wipe her face.

I reach over and pull toilet paper off the spool, hand it to her. I could sit here forever. "Seems like everyone's upset today," I add, trying to make her feel better. "I guess people are extra sensitive, it being the last day. Kind of like saying good-bye again."

"Karen's upset for different reasons."

"Oh?"

There's a long pause. I shift uncomfortably on the floor.

"Did you know Annette was planning on leaving her?" she asks, then blows her nose.

This is a trick question. If I say "yes," the boat sinks; if I say "no," I drown. Answering "yes" means Annette and I stayed in touch. But this is very personal information and my guess is she wouldn't have shared it. And would I have been the type of friend back then to be privy to such drama? If I say "no," I lose status. Think. Think. "Sort of."

She's stopped crying and eyes me suspiciously.

I've answered wrong.

"When did she tell you?"

"We spoke a month ago. I called about some freelance work, we got to talking. She sounded a little, I don't know, sad. Not her usual self."

Sloan nods. I continue.

"Anyway, she mentioned she and Karen were not connecting, that she was antsy. I recalled a conversation we had at the office a while back. There was this editor and Annette said if she wasn't with Karen, she'd ask this woman out. I mean, she didn't say she was dissolving the relationship, but I knew things weren't great back then, so when she told me about this a few weeks ago, it wasn't exactly a shock."

Sloan is motionless.

I play with the Tylenol bottle. Shake it back and forth. It sounds like jumping beans. I pretend to cucaracha, anything to get Sloan to smile.

There's a knock and we jump. Sloan's hand reaches for the door as Wes pushes in.

"Sorry, I wasn't sure anyone was in here." She looks from Sloan to me, then back to Sloan. "I could hold it in or pee off the roof if you guys need more time." She grimaces. "Okay, stand-up is not my strong suit. Everyone all right?"

We nod like puppets and file out.

Before Wes has a chance to close the door, Sloan whispers something to her.

I could go. I could pretend I need something from my coat pocket and just leave. I don't owe anyone a thing.

I take a few steps backward and wait for Sloan to say something—anything would be fine, and when she doesn't, I ask if she wants to get a drink.

She mumbles the word *Scotch* and all feels momentarily saved.

It's late. Hours have passed. We've had much to drink and I'm feeling really good. I wonder if Patti wants a roommate.

A few people are lounging in the living room, fewer mill

about by the food, drinking coffee and eating desserts. Everyone seems to have broken off into small clusters and are having intimate conversations. The more wine that gets opened, the more this feels like a party. Like I've known these women forever. Next week it will be my turn to host our weekly get-together.

I look for Sloan and find her in the kitchen by the sink, standing next to Joanna and Wes. They're whispering. Conspirators scraping plates, sponge-cleaning glasses. They stop talking when I walk in. My heart does a little a rhythmic dance of panic. I wonder if I've gone overboard with the slide show. Maybe Karen knows more about Annette's working relationships than I thought. Maybe it was the bathroom thing that did me in.

"I was coming to help," I say, holding up a few glasses and empty bottles.

"We've put a dent in the washing process, I think," Wes says, her hands sudsy. "The dishwasher should be finished in a half hour. I think we've done all we can."

She and I do a little soft-shoe as we swap spots. I put the glasses into the sink, the bottles into a brown paper bag on the floor.

The kitchen has always been a favorite spot of mine. The fluorescent lights, the calming effect of Formica, the clean, slick floor, the shiny marble top. But Patti's is California-style. There's no Formica, only wood. The fluorescent lights have been replaced with old metal cone-shaped lamps that hang from the ceiling. It's too open to feel intimate.

Sloan slides me a stack of plastic containers and I scoop out lo mein and beef fried rice from the white cardboard and transfer it into the Tupperware. The moo shu, garlic shrimp, and orange chicken, I keep in the aluminum tins they came in.

I finish my duties first and watch her slice the last of the fruit.

Her hands work carefully, precisely. Even as she scoops melon, there is thoughtful care. This is how she would comfort others.

In the past twenty-four hours I've seen her cry, laughed with her friends, been privy to intimate details about her life. I've witnessed so much in such a short time. I can't let go now.

"I think Patti's closing shop," Sloan finally says. "Looks like the girls are getting ready to leave."

I follow Sloan's gaze and see several women standing by the elevator, coats on, hugging Patti and Karen good-bye.

"Looks like it. I guess I'll get mine, too."

Sloan walks me to the elevator and pushes open the gate. I almost trip getting in as she leans close to my ear. For a moment I think she's going to give me a hug or whisper something warm and endearing. Her breath is hot against my skin and she takes a hand and wraps it around my shoulder. I remember the necklace in my pocket and am about to present it to her when she says, "I won't tell Patti or Karen, but I don't know who the fuck you think you're kidding."

I stop. My body shuts down, my mind races as a prickling feeling starts in my fingers. "What did I do?" The words scarcely come out. "Whatever it is, I'm sorry."

"I bet you are."

She releases her grip and pushes me into the elevator.

The gate bangs closed so loudly I think something in my head has burst.

The next morning I feel hung over. I showered when I got home but the smoke and smell of wine still clings to me. Faint memories of last night, a paper trail of humiliating moments. I've put my black turtleneck back in the plastic. Sealed in the smells, preserved them until it will be needed again. The black pants can be washed. I have the sweater—that's enough for now.

I sit on the floor of my kitchen and pour myself a Scotch and water, and unwrap the pack of Camel Lights. All morning long I feel as though I've been holding myself in, trying to understand why I feel so lousy.

Last night keeps flashing before me. I attempt to block it out. I blast music to interrupt the thoughts, to halt the feelings. I search the paper, looking for services, an addict waiting for her fix. I scan the paper so quickly the words blur and I can't read them. I force my eyes to focus but it's useless.

. . .

November spins out of control. The days are dark, the mornings not so bright. The air is cold and the trees are brown and dying. I hate my life. I haven't heard back from Sloan. I've left a message and e-mailed her twice, trying to explain the situation, but have gotten no response. Dean feels like a distant memory, too. A deep, sweet dream that happened long ago. Hard to tell the truth from the fantasy. Harder still to remain alone.

I go to funeral after funeral, sometimes two in one day. It doesn't matter who for. I just know I need to be around people.

On Friday I go to a thirty-two-year-old's wake who died of AIDS, and another for a social worker who was the victim of a hit-and-run. On Monday I attend Mass for Patrick McGuire, a baseball player for the Yankees in the 60's. Some of his memorabilia is on eBay and I ordered an old scorecard from David Raspen. He overnighted it so I could bring it with me to the funeral. It arrived yellowed and aged. There were notes about the game and about McGuire's performance in smeared pencil, making it hard to read. I walk right up to his daughter and give her the card while saying my father was a fan and though he is too ill to attend, asked if I would be his mouthpiece. She cries when I present it to her, cries harder when she shows her husband. The rest of the day, people congratulate me as if I've done something extraordinary, as if I've brought him back.

Tuesday afternoon finds me crashing Ming Lee's burial ceremony, a true Chinese cultural event. I learn that crying is not permitted. If tears are shed, the soul is left behind and cannot enter into another life. During the proceeding monks chant, ask the soul to be forgiven for any sins it may have committed, and paper money is burned so the soul has a plentiful, wealthy afterlife. I'm one of eight non-Asians and though I feel extremely out of place, I'm comforted by the strict rules of religion and tradition. The obit said Ming worked at the Asia Society, "Which I frequented often," I tell his wife, June. "He was a vat of information. I loved it when he'd explain the new artifacts the museum received." I bow my head and speak slowly so she can follow. So she can hear all of the accolades I pay her dead husband.

Ming's body is never seen by the mourners. Instead, it's wrapped in a yellow cloth, like a huge worm in a cocoon, and flowers are draped over the body. Then the deceased is placed in a casket and wheeled into a burning oven. The ashes are given to the widow three days later. Ming's cousin, Sue, explains all of this at her mother's home. She's not religious and couldn't care less if the body and soul are one or if the soul is free. Her eyebrow is pierced and her hair is buzz cut. She looks like a Buddha.

After I leave the Lee clan, I stop by Mr. Barber, who is having a reception for his wife, Judy. It is here where I make a terrible mistake. I confuse Judy's profile with a woman whose funeral I attended several days ago and give the wrong information.

"She was a truly vibrant gal," I say, mid-bite, fork full of creamy pasta. When Mrs. Miller asks how I know her, I say, "I worked with her at the restaurant."

"Restaurant? What are you talking about?" she asks.

My mind races as I try to retrieve facts about this woman. She was a chef? No, that was last week. A teacher, doctor, banker . . . This woman did something with food or flowers, table settings . . . parties. Yes. She planned parties. Children's parties. I'm tempted to excuse myself, find a bathroom, and review the obit I have carefully cut out and put in my pocket for emergencies like this one. I reach for it now and come up empty. Did I put it in my bag? Did I even bring it with me? I couldn't handle another scene like the one with Sloan. I take a deep breath. I've got to calm down. Got to pull myself together. "I mean, I worked at the restaurant where she organized many of her parties. I was one of the chefs. We often planned the menus together."

"Oh." The woman's face eases, forehead lines are erased, brows calm down and return to a more relaxed position. "I see. You're right, she was a most creative woman."

"She certainly was."

I'm skimming the paper on Saturday when I come across an obit for Natalie Brown Finer, a young woman in her late thirties who fell from her terrace high-rise on the Upper West Side last Thursday. A graduate of Vassar in art, she was married to her husband, Brandon Finer III, who she met at school. He is a VP at Merrill Lynch. She is survived by her twin sister Lena, her parents Keen and Milla Brown, and her husband.

Three hours later, I sign the guest book as Maya Hanker. On the table are several pictures of Natalie in conservative silver frames: one with her sister, one on her wedding day, and one graduating from Vassar. There is something terribly sad about Natalie. Even though she is smiling in each picture, something is missing from her eyes. Her face retains a suppressed look, as if she's holding back a scream.

The chapel is half full by the time I get there. I check my coat and try to obtain important clues from the snippets of dialogue spoken by the other women.

A line has already formed on the right and people are kneeling by her coffin, one by one. I watch them, a slow assembly line of drones as they wait patiently.

In an effort to meet more people and buy time, I double back and head for the bathroom, knowing I can gain more information from the bits of conversation. Afterward I detour and retrieve something from my coat pocket, a lipstick or hanky. Then I ask an attendant for some water.

Eventually, I get on line and wait behind lots of women in conservative suits, who clutch their husbands' arms with one hand, their Gucci bags in the other, and wait to see Natalie. It takes only eight seconds for the woman in front of me to look me up and down. I watch her eyes move from my feet to my chest, then to my face. Her lips are pressed together and she contorts them into a smile.

"Hi," I say.

"Hello," she retorts, her face unaffected.

"I'm Maya Hanker." I extend my hand. She shakes mine strongly, like a man.

"I'm Olivia—this is my husband, Greg."

"Hi."

We wait for a minute.

"So, does your husband work with Brandon?" she asks.

"No. I went to Vassar with Natalie."

"Oh," her voice climbs several octaves. "Me, too. Were you our year?"

"No, I'm two years younger."

Olivia frowns. "What dorm were you?" Her lips have gone back to a pressed position.

"The one on the hill." I look at my watch. Then glance around. "What a wonderful turnout. Natalie would be really pleased."

We move closer to the coffin.

"So you all went to Vassar," the husband reiterates.

I nod. "Natalie and I only had one class together but we talked shop whenever she came into the studio." I wait for them to say something and when they don't, I continue. "She was really talented. We were in different mediums—I make beads." My hand moves to my throat. I feel stone, cool and flat. "In fact, I made this."

Olivia seems impressed. Greg is not. He's bored and has yawned twice since we've started conversing.

"Have you seen Brandon yet?" I ask, feeling antsy. The two Valiums I popped this morning haven't taken effect yet. I found a dated bottle in my medicine cabinet and even though the prescription was a few years old, thought they still might be good.

"He was on the phone by the water closet," Greg says, contributing to the conversation. I picture the three of us on a game show, each rushing to raise our hands and reach for the buzzer. And he's finally answered a question.

Brandon is sitting in a chair directly outside of the men's room, just as Greg promised. I recognize him from the photo.

He's cradling the cell phone in his ear, hand on the small

gadget while patting his chest. He stands up, walks over to the console, and opens the drawer. I watch his frenetic state as he searches for what I guess is pen and paper while telling the voice on the other end to hold for just a moment. He can't possibly focus, he's just lost his wife. He finally reaches into his breast pocket and pulls out a pen, but no paper. I come up behind him and hand him a sheet from my purse.

I carry an array of obscure and helpful objects for such crises. Pen, paper, safety pins, package of tissues, quarters for meters, aspirin and Advil, matches, hairpins, mints, and gum. Someone is always in need. Girl Scout to the widowed, Florence Nightingale to the grieving.

Brandon smiles, mouths *thank you*. He smells of lemon-lime aftershave. I stand there a second, watch him lean over the table, struggling to hold the phone, the pen, and paper all at the same time. I bend toward him and steady the top of the white sheet without having to be asked, as if it's the most important task I've ever had. If I'm good at my job, I'm in. *Who's that?* I picture one of the guests asking Brandon later on while collecting his jacket from the coat rack or as they stand as a group outside, stealing a smoke. "Oh, she's the one that held the paper down for me as I took the plot information. I didn't have to ask her for help—she just did it, instinctively and all."

He clicks his cell closed. "Thanks for the assistance."

He's handsome with boyish charm and chiseled features. The quintessential WASP in a soft Kennedy way that must have made him the catch of the school. And yet, as I stare into his eyes, there is something missing. His pupils seem too dark and large, the white part too white.

"I'm so sorry. What a terrible thing to have happened."

"Thank you," he says, bestowing a hand. His grip is manly and strong, his skin firm and soft. It feels like we're closing a deal.

"I'm Maya. Your wife and I took art classes together at Vassar. Well, one class."

We hold the stare as my mind races. He was there, too, right?

His face suddenly brightens. His white eyes grow whiter. "Could I ask you for a favor?"

Yes. Tell me what you need and I'll give it to you.

"I was wondering if you'd say a few words on her behalf. I know it's last-minute, but her dear friends from school who are here—you might know some of them—can't seem to pull it together to say anything. I know Nat would appreciate it. There's no one else to represent that part of her life, and it was a rather important time for her." He looks away. "For us. That's how we met."

I nod. "I know. I remember her telling me about you. I was trying to coerce her into fixing me up with one of your friends."

He looks confused for a second. He's trying to remember if my name ever came up, if his late wife ever mentioned this. He smiles. "Matchmaking was never her forte. Besides, back then, you wouldn't have wanted to date any of my friends. You'd be spending your weekends at polo matches and fraternity parties, watching someone puke off a balcony."

If only, I think. I would have gladly done that. Been that.

"So, will you?" His voice is eager yet firm.

We've stopped shaking hands by this point. He's placed his on his hip, which meets his other. He looks like he's bracing himself for a blustery wind.

I've always wanted to deliver a eulogy, see if I could pull it off, give the performance of a lifetime. But something feels wrong. I don't know how Natalie died. There are too many whispers, too much is unsaid. Everyone is working overly hard to seem happy, in a sad way. There is excessive praising and generalizing. No one is speaking about her or her death. Instead, friends and relatives, business associates and club members, talk *of* her. Of her work. Of her charity functions. Natalie the person is lost.

There are hints, too. Short, breathy snippets of dialogue in the coatroom and bathroom where someone said she was pregnant. Another, her sister, mentioned she was unhappy and that she had broken plans with her earlier that week. Someone else mentioned she wasn't feeling well. I chatted with others, wives of Brandon's colleagues, and they said she was acting aloof and secretive. Distant.

Another woman comes up behind us, gives Brandon a peck on the cheek, then grabs him by both shoulders and brings him into her. "This. Is. Just. Awful." She sounds like Captain Kirk. "Please. Tell me. This isn't happening."

I want to clap and hand her an Oscar, ask her who did her makeup and which designer lent her the dress.

I clear my throat. She smiles and offers her hand. "We met in the hallway for a second. I'm Kelly. It's Sasha, right?"

"No, Maya," I correct her.

"Sorry, there are so many people here." She's holding Brandon's hand now.

"That's okay." Did I introduce myself as Sasha? I can't remember.

"I'm hoping Maya will say a few words about Nat from our Vassar days," Brandon adds, this time more emphatic.

"Oh, that would be wonderful."

"It would," he says, looking at me. "It really would."

He's used to getting his way and I'm not sure turning him down now would be ideal. I'm also not sure I can pull this off. I'm sweating and a little nauseous. There's too much saliva in my mouth. I need water. "I'm terribly flattered, but I haven't prepared . . ."

"That's fine. Nat wouldn't mind. She'd be thrilled to know

someone remembered her from back then. Especially someone she's been out of touch with for so long."

Kelly nods, puppet-like, puts a hand on mine. "It would be terribly gracious and we'd all appreciate it so."

I swallow a mouth full of drool. "Okay."

I steal Natalie's photo off the table, the one of her and Brandon on their wedding day. I slip into the bathroom stall and stare at her wedding picture, looking for clues to who she was. I read the newspaper blurb again, hoping something will come to me. I close my eyes and try to picture their high-rise on the Upper West Side. I see a huge marble foyer, chandelier, leather couches, modern furniture, glass table, pewter and silver items accentuating the stark, minimalistic look. I see her studio space, a room just for her art, a man's oxford shirt smattered with paint and oil, worn-in jeans, Keds sneakers. I see her with a paint brush in her mouth as she steps away to admire her work, towel in her hand, hair pulled back in a scrunched-up ponytail. I wonder if she went out for air. Perhaps the fumes from the paint made her dizzy. If she was pregnant it wouldn't be good for the baby; she'd be prone to nausea. Her neighbor thought she might be painting on the terrace. Maybe something caught her eye. Maybe she leaned over the railing to get a better look.

It was the neighbor who found the body on the sidewalk. Was there when the ambulance came. "The men didn't even try to resuscitate her," she told me during my first bathroom trip. "I watched them cover her body with a sheet. Blood leaked right through."

My hands are shaking and I can't catch my breath. My head is pounding so hard I sit down on the bathroom floor and rest my temple against the cool ceramic bowl. "I can't do this anymore," I say, as if hearing the sound of my own voice will make my statement final. More definitive.

Something is wrong.

Something is wrong with me. With how this woman died. With everything.

I have a desire to stick my finger down my throat and heave everything up from inside. I get up off the floor and bend over, finger already at the back of my mouth. My throat feels dry, my breath hot. My finger is just touching my tonsils and I'm in mid-gag when I stop. I have to stay. I owe it to Natalie. I owe it to this woman whose life seemed unnaturally short. For some unexplainable reason, I feel I'm the one person who understood her the best.

The door opens. I smell perfume, hear voices, the sound of heel against tile.

"I'm sure he'll move. How could he still live there and pass by the spot every day?"

"It's a beautiful apartment."

"Do they own?"

"Of course."

"Really. Lance and I have been looking in that area . . ."

"Three bedrooms," the voice sings.

I come out of the stall and realize I've left the photo on the floor. I panic. I can't go back and get it now. Maybe no one will notice, maybe I'll have a heart attack right here and no one will care.

As I wash my hands I glance up at the women, catch their reflection in the mirror. They are well dressed and perfect, like my mother's friends at my grandfather's funeral. I look like a ghost. Pale and gaunt. My makeup is smeared and my hair is frizzy and out of place. But it will be me holding court. Once again, I'll be speaking about someone I don't know. Nothing has changed since I was eleven. I close my eyes, resurrect my grand-father's funeral. The silver picture frame—much like Natalie's. The coffin. My mother and father acting as a unit. My mother's friends. Their perfectly coiffed hair, their perfect makeup. I think about Mrs. Resnick and her beautiful skin, about Beth and how lonely she looked. I switch to Annette and the funeral . . . some-one's hand is on my shoulder.

"Are you okay?" Concern is spread across her flawless skin, her beautiful green eyes look at me.

"You're Nat's art friend," says another.

I nod. "I guess public speaking makes me more nervous than I care to admit."

I splash cold water on my face. Someone hands me a towel, another is pushing a small seat in my direction.

"I'm fine," I insist. "Just needed to get my bearings."

Natalie's friends make room for me next to their husbands. The priest says several prayers, mutters a few things in Latin, douses the coffin with holy water. It all seems like a running gag until the priest utters my name. "Maya Hanker, Natalie's dear friend from Vassar, would like to say a few words." I actually look around the chapel to see who will rise and walk to the platform. Kelly nudges me and someone's husband gets up in order for me to slide out of the pew.

A huge statue of Christ is center stage. Colored beams of light from the sun streaming through the stained glass windows illuminate him from behind, making him appear as if he's rising up from the floorboards of the church. I look out and see rows and rows of saddened and serious faces staring back at me. My chest feels heavy, as if my heart is working too hard. Breath feels stuck in my throat and I wonder how I can possibly talk if it blocks my airways. This is payment. No, punishment. For all the funerals I've attended over the years, this is my apology. My penance.

"Natalie and I met years ago at Vassar." My voice sounds momentarily lost in the enormous room. I lean into the mike and speak up a bit. "We were both art majors and though we didn't take a class together until my second year, we'd see each other in the studio or at the coffee shop where I worked part-time. We'd talk about art, joke about our teacher, Mr. Phelps, who was always late and ended class half an hour early." My words are clear, my voice somewhat steady. I can hear a slight echo coming from the mammoth speakers above my head. I look out into the sea of bodies. It's odd to see them so attentive. Some dab a hanky to their eyes, others sit close to their spouses; the men have their arms resting on the edge of the pew or their hands wrapped around their wives' shoulders.

I've spent years fantasizing about a moment such as this. Now that it's here, I'm not sure how to enjoy it.

"One time we sketched outside on the lawn." Lawn is a safe bet. All schools have them. "She was a wonderful artist with an interesting and imaginative eye for detail. She was the type to see something and be able to extract a small bit of information or catch a glimpse of something unexpected. That day on the lawn, we talked about our families. About school ending and future plans, the things we wanted to do with our lives, the places we wanted to see our art shown, the goals we had." I skim the seats, each filled with a foreign face, an unfamiliar body. I try to picture my family, see if I can remember who sat where at my aunt's memorial a month ago. I mentally insert them into the picture, replacing them with the people who now occupy the seats.

I see my own funeral. See my mother next to my father; my cousins, Vicki, Robert, and David; and my uncle; a few people from my past—the shrinks in the corner, Dean off to the side. Karen and her lover and her cousin and Sloan and I'm dizzy and scared and I don't know what to say. I've lost my train of thought. I don't even know if I'm still talking and if I am, whether my words are making sense.

There's a wetness, too.

Small drops of water on my hands on the podium. I look up for a second, thinking there's a leak. The chapel ceiling is high and painted with gold. *Perfect*, I think, *water will come crashing down, baptizing me and forgiving me all of my sins, washing them all away, myself included.* My cheeks feel wet, too, and I realize the water is coming from me. I choke for a moment, but I can't stop the tears. I feel them running down my face, see them drop onto my fingers, which grip the stand. I don't know if I should wipe them away or if people can see them or what the hell is wrong with me. "She was a terrific person even though I didn't know her as well as many of you. And I regret not being closer with her back then and losing touch with her afterward." I can't catch my breath. They're going to have to carry me out. The pallbearers will have to come up and scrape me off the floor. ". . . And I hope we can remember what a wonderful person and passionate artist she was. I was proud to know her in school and honored to call her my friend."

There is such silence when I am done that I think I'm imagining it. That this is all a dream. Every eye is on me. Many people are crying now. I look to Brandon to see his expression. His mouth is open and his skin is paler than I remember. There are no tears but he's lost in thought. I see his and Natalie's parents sitting in the first few rows. My eyes jump to her sister, then to her three little girls who huddle close, talking in their own language made up of eye moments and special looks. They don't need more than that.

A pain starts in my chest. I can't look away.

The longer I stare, the more it hurts.

I don't move until the priest is suddenly standing next to me. He clears his throat, rests a sacred hand on my wet one.

I walk trance-like down several steps.

Natalie's mother and father stand to hug me. Her twin sister, one child on her lap, the other two seated next to her, thanks me profusely. Brandon smiles weakly, mouths the words *thank you*, then looks away.

I walk to the back of the chapel, aware that everyone is staring. Some people stick their hands out to touch mine while uttering, *That was lovely*, or *You spoke so well*. Others simply bend their heads forward, a solemn nod of praise.

I hit the last pew, think about sitting down in the empty space but remember my dream. It's now where people would turn around and point, their voices pitched high enough for dogs to hear, loud enough to wake the dead. It would be the priest who yells *God will never forgive you*. I wait for a moment. Stand contemplating what to do, still expecting to see hands shoot up and fingers point, mouths drop open while screams come pouring out. I almost prepare myself for this, but nothing happens. The priest introduces the next speaker, a friend from Nantucket. I watch Cynthia make her way to the pulpit, notes gripped in her hand.

I retrieve my coat from the young girl and interrupt her reading of *Marie Claire*. I'm halfway through the main doors when I remember the sign-in book.

I only have to turn back one page to find it.

Maya Hanker is printed neatly on the sixth line. I pick up the yellow lacquered fountain pen, cross it out, and write in my real name instead.

Nina Perlman stares back at me.

I hardly ever write my name except for checks and the occasional letter. Seeing it in the book amongst the others is odd. My strokes are bold and my name looks a little thicker than the rest. If my mother were here she'd smile, proud to see it standing out from the others.

I feel as though I've unleashed a small piece of myself. Left it here for Brandon to take home. In return, I slip the pen into my pocket, a final memento, find my way out of the chapel, and walk down Madison Avenue. Sunlight bounces off my back like the Jesus in the chapel. I engulf the moment as I finger the pen.

READING GROUP GUIDE

THE JOY OF FUNERALS

1. Which story did you find most intriguing and why?

2. Which character did you connect with most and why?

3. Did you feel Strauss was successful at interweaving the stories?

4. In each of the stories, what do you feel Strauss's characters are looking for, and do any of them achieve their goals?

5. At the end of "Swimming Without Annette," do you think Karen has murdered an innocent man or her lover's killer? Why?

6. At the end of "Still Life," do you feel Natalie jumps or falls? Why?

7. How do you feel about Nina's funeral-attending habit?

8. Why do you think Strauss's characters are so lonely?

9. Do you feel funerals are a celebration of someone's life or a mourning of their loss? Explain.

10. What role do dreams play in the book?

11. How does the family change as Daddy deteriorates?

12. How have the funerals you have attended been similar or different from those described in the book?

For more reading group suggestions visit
www.stmartins.com.

Get a
Griffin 🦁 St. Martin's Griffin